Loving Lucy

A *Murder on Skis* Mystery

Also by Phil Bayly:

Murder on Skis

Loving Lucy

A *Murder on Skis* Mystery

Phil Bayly

SHIRES✺PRESS

4869 Main Street
Manchester Center, VT 05255
www.northshire.com

Loving Lucy

A *Murder on Skis* Mystery

©2020 by **Phil Bayly**

WWW.MURDERONSKIS.COM

ISBN: 978-1-60571-521-6

Cover Design: Debbi Wraga & Carolyn Bayly
Msanca & Roger Thornhill / Dreamstime.com
Author Photo: Carolyn Bayly

NORTHSHIRE
BOOKSTORE

Building Community, One Book at a Time
A family-owned, independent bookstore in
Manchester Ctr., VT since 1976 and Saratoga Springs, NY since 2013.
We are committed to excellence in bookselling.
The Northshire Bookstore's mission is to serve as a resource for
information, ideas, and entertainment while honoring the needs
of customers, staff, and community.

Printed in the United States of America

This novel was finished during the coronavirus pandemic. It is dedicated to Marcelle Muniak, her family, and all those who lost loved ones to the virus.

"It is good to love many things, for therein lies the true strength, and whosoever loves much performs much, and can accomplish much, and what is done in love is done well."
—Vincent Van Gogh

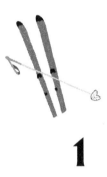

1

She was on her hands and knees in the dirt, shaking uncontrollably. Her eyes were watering as strings of spit hung from her open mouth.

It was night, and this wasn't the first time she'd vomited in the bed of arborvitae hedges. They offered her a sense of secrecy on the edge of the carefully manicured lawn.

There were tiny flakes of snow falling on the ground around her. Normally, the first flakes of the season would be cause for celebration in her household. But what was normal any longer?

The little girl couldn't hear the voices inside her home, and neither could the neighbors. Not through the thick brick walls of the century-old mansion.

"God," the woman yelled. "You always take her side!"

"Well," the man yelled back, "someone has to!"

"That little bitch is going to learn ..." the woman growled.

"She's a little girl," the man interrupted.

"And she has you wrapped around her little pigtails," the woman spewed.

"What did she do?" he asked in a quieter voice. This fight exhausted him. He couldn't count the number of times they'd had it.

The woman threw the contents of her drink in his face. And then she laughed. She was laughing at the humiliating sight of red wine dripping down his hair and onto his expensive dress shirt.

He harnessed his anger: "What set you off this time?"

"Not this time," she hissed. She had a menacing smile on her face. "It's the last time. I told her so, too. I've called County Family Services. They're coming to pick her up. I told them they can have her back!"

"What in heaven's name!" the man erupted. "This is her home! You're her mother! We're her parents! You can't just throw a child out when you get tired of her!"

His shout was now almost a plea. The first time they had this argument was only a couple of years after Lucy moved in with them.

The adoption went smoothly, at first. But slowly, state Senator John Buford's wife had begun to resent the child. It wasn't easy to bring a nine-year-old into their house. She'd had a rough start to her life, and she brought emotional baggage into her new home.

It also seemed that the closer Senator Buford and the girl became, the more volatile his wife, Fiona, became. John and

Fiona tried to work it out, as a couple, but the rift only grew wider.

Over the five years, it had become John's job to protect his daughter from Fiona. She was cruel to the child. There was the cold silence, the degrading remarks and the isolation she forced on the girl.

Fiona seemed to sabotage Lucy's attempts to forge friendships with other children her age. Fiona's promises to drive Lucy to birthday parties, or a friend's sleepover, would be broken at the last moment.

The child wasn't allowed to bring friends home with her and she wasn't allowed to go to the homes of friends. Gradually, the invitations from other little girls stopped. Efforts to include Lucy disappeared. It was too much trouble. Fiona made sure of that.

"Did you really call them?" John asked his wife. He pulled a paper towel across his wet face and then dabbed his shirt to absorb the wine.

"I sure did," Fiona answered with a great deal of satisfaction. "She's outta here!" Fiona chuckled.

"Why do you torture her?" John pleaded. "What unknown evil has she unleashed on you? Why do you hate her so?"

Fiona laughed in the senator's face. It was a sinister laugh. "Call them back," he demanded. "Tell them it was a mistake."

"Oh, it was a mistake, alright," Fiona snarled. "And I'm the only one with the guts to fix it."

But her sneer was replaced by a look of shock. She'd not anticipated the speed her husband moved with, or the strength of his hands.

He was staring at her, their faces only inches apart. Flecks of his spit landed on her eyelashes. He was staring at her, but there was no sign of recognition in his eyes.

He would have no memory of the actual moment he grabbed Fiona's throat. He never questioned that he'd killed his wife, but he had no recall of it. And to his own surprise, no remorse.

He remembered thinking, as Fiona was dying in his hands, it had become his duty to protect Lucy. She was defenseless, and the forest was full of predators.

Lucy knew he would protect her, and she loved him even more because of it. He was the Daddy she had always dreamed of. She would always feel safe in his arms.

"Honey, I called Aunt Beverly. You're going to go to her house and stay the night, OK?" Senator Buford explained to his daughter as they sat on the front steps of their home. "I have to go back to the capitol for a meeting and your mommy doesn't feel well. She's lying down."

The 14-year-old had cleaned herself up, as she always did. She'd pulled on a hoodie to hide the stains. She didn't want her daddy to be upset. There was no dirt on her knees, no vomit to be seen on the front of her blouse. That would be her secret. It always was.

Lucy was comfortable at Aunt Beverly's house. John's sister also lived in Albany, New York. That's who John would call when he had to get his daughter away from the terror that his wife could become.

Senator Buford gave his daughter a hug before she departed with Aunt Beverly. Maybe the hug was a little longer than they usually exchanged. He kissed the top of her head and whispered, "I love you." Lucy treasured the hugs and kisses. He was the perfect daddy.

After Beverly drove away with Lucy and an overnight bag in her car, Buford opened the hallway closet. Fiona's body had been secreted away in there. The senator left the closet door open, now that there was no danger of Lucy stumbling across the corpse.

He didn't mind making it easy for the police to find. In fact, Buford would make the anonymous call to police alerting them to a problem at his home. But that would have to wait until he packed a small practical bag. Perhaps the call would even wait a day, allowing him to arrange matters.

What would he need, he thought to himself, for a life on the run? He didn't know how long he'd take before he turned himself in, but he needed time to think.

Would he just plead guilty? Would he argue that he was defending his daughter? Would he make up a story about an intruder? He needed time to think.

He packed a bag containing blue jeans and work shirts, not the attire a powerful New York state senator would usually be seen in.

He knew he couldn't take his own car. It had N.Y. Senate license plates on it. He needed to disappear into the night. He needed to vanish for a while.

Now, the Buford home was quiet. Buford wondered if was it an eerie quiet or finally a peaceful quiet? The body of his wife, Fiona, was protruding from a hallway closet. Some of her own expensive coats and wraps hung inches over her head. There was no sound of shouting, no sound of a child crying. Finally, Buford thought, there was peace in his house. And he was on the run.

2

JC Snow was sitting on a bench in a Denver cemetery. He could see the peaks of the Front Range turning white. It was almost Thanksgiving.

He was wrapped in a wool coat that reached down to his knees. There was a two-piece suit underneath. It was the uniform that television reporters wore.

JC thought of himself as a blue jeans and tee shirt guy. But as the temperature dropped, he was glad to be wrapped in his thick wool outer shell. He loved the sight and smell of winter's approach. But he saw no need to shiver for the privilege.

The first of Colorado's ski areas had opened for the season. He could see them in his mind as he faced the Front Range. He couldn't really see them, but he knew exactly where they were and could imagine exactly what they looked like at that moment.

"Really?" he blurted as he caught another annoying typo he'd punched into his script on the phone's tiny keyboard. No matter how proficient he became at this, he thought his fingers were never going to fit on those microscopic keys.

In a couple of hours, the reporter would inform viewers on television that someone was stealing anything that was or wasn't cemented down at cemeteries along Colorado's Front Range.

That included brass flower vases bolted to monuments and statuettes chiseled off gravestones. The thief had struck graveyards from Fort Collins to Denver to Pueblo.

The crimes were being committed inside large burial grounds covering dozens of acres. Who would witness the transgression? Dead men tell no tales.

Most of the artwork was from an era when cemeteries and headstones were more decorative than they are now. Some of those sculptures were creations of artists who went on to great fame.

The relics would resurface in antique stores. Where did the antiquities come from? The store owners could ask, but they wouldn't. They suspected, so they didn't.

The most unique pieces would bring thousands of dollars to their store. The stolen contraband would add a powerful presence to the gullible buyer's living room or foyer.

JC would tell his viewers on television that the thief had almost devised the perfect crime. Anyone is allowed into a cemetery. A mourner during the day could be a thief by night.

The story was being told on television news because of confirmation coming from a single South Platte Cemetery board member. He'd broken from his colleagues on the board.

Most cemetery overseers believed silence was golden when it came to thefts from their grounds. It would only encourage more crime, they thought. And, they feared that no one would place their loved ones to eternal rest in a park where crime was epidemic.

The original source of JC's story disagreed. He'd had enough. Silence had accomplished nothing. The police had to be informed. And when approached by a television reporter, the cemetery board member agreed that the public should be asked to help catch the thief.

JC sat in the sun. It more than compensated for the cold, late-autumn air. He was reviewing his script when a text popped up on the phone's screen. It was from the newsroom's executive producer. It read, "Check the schedule, I've got you working a dayshift on Thanksgiving. Sry."

The notification didn't come as a surprise. JC was a new hire. Newsrooms didn't close for the holidays, and new hires were at the back of the line when it came to getting holidays off.

He was working for his second television station in Denver. He'd been fired from his last place of employment. That seemed odd to many viewers, and they hadn't been told the inside story.

JC's contract hadn't been renewed almost immediately after reporting about a series of murders at a ski resort in Montana. His own life had been placed in danger. His station won an award for his coverage.

But JC had ruffled feathers in the television station's ownership group. One of their members was treated like a suspect in Montana. He was a suspect. It wasn't the first time a journalist had been fired for the wrong reasons. It was a subjective business.

It hadn't taken long to find a new job, once JC put himself back on the market. He'd had offers to choose from, because he had an army of followers among television viewers.

Before meeting his photographer and their live truck at the cemetery, the reporter had started his day at the District Two police station. Denver Detective Steve Trujillo had taken the initial phone call about the cemetery thefts. It was Trujillo's case now.

"Lucky," JC thought to himself. The cemetery board member had dialed a number for the Denver Police Department and he'd been connected to perhaps the one cop who would give a crap.

A lot of police investigators, burdened with bigger problems like solving murders and high-volume drug sales, would have dismissed a complaint about some missing trinkets at a cemetery.

It wasn't that they didn't care at all, but an arrest for vandalizing a cemetery might result only in a few months in county jail. It wasn't the crime of the century. But Trujillo was interested.

JC drove to District Two's headquarters on the edge of a large industrial area. He was escorted up to the detective's office. He was seated in an open room filled with a mix of repurposed desks. Some were new and some were old. Some were metal and some were wood. It was a relatively new building, but JC thought it had the same interior decorator as every police station in the past one hundred years.

The décor made a statement: We're not here to be pretty. We're here to catch the scumbags and make them regret their chosen path.

The room holding the detectives had overhead lighting, battle-ready blue carpet, white walls, and nothing that particularly matched. The detectives sat at cubicles.

There were some office doors lining the walls, but Trujillo's desk was in the open "pen" with most of the other detectives. The room seemed overcrowded, even if it wasn't. It was full of movement and a lot of big guys.

The reporter pushed past the other desks and the bodies leaning on them. His expensive coat and TV haircut singled him out from the others. The law officers eyed him suspiciously.

JC spotted Trujillo speaking with another man. Probably a cop, JC thought, despite the man's casual dress. He was wearing blue jeans and a denim shirt. Maybe he was undercover?

He nearly collided with JC as he was heading for the exit. "Sorry, man," he said with a warm smile.

"No problem," JC responded as the man continued moving on.

"Ah, Mr. Snow," was Detective Trujillo's greeting as he rose behind his desk and shook the reporter's hand.

"Funny, isn't it?" Trujillo said as he sat back down. "Modern-day grave robbers. Only, they've found something more valuable than selling bodies to the local medical schools."

The journalist had crossed paths with the detective before, at crime scenes. JC recalled thinking that Trujillo was smart. And it was in the law officer's wheelhouse to refer to a historic wave of grave robberies in Europe two centuries ago.

At that time, it was the actual bodies that the ghouls were after. They'd sell the cadavers to medical schools to be used as learning tools, to develop skills like dissecting and anatomy.

Trujillo was bigger, physically, than JC. The law officer was probably six foot two. He was stocky and had big hands. He had thick dark hair and dark skin.

JC guessed that he was in his fifties. And he dressed like he seemed to care about his appearance. Neat more than snappy.

There was a computer at his desk, along with a phone, a lamp, a couple of pictures of his family, and too much paperwork for his liking.

JC also thought Trujillo was civil. Smart and civil. The reporter couldn't say that about every cop, nor could Trujillo say that about every reporter.

"How much is this stuff they're stealing here worth?" JC asked the detective.

"Some of it is sold for scrap," the detective answered in a dismissive manner. "They get as little as ten to a hundred dollars for those plaques commemorating someone's military service."

"But here's the interesting thing," the detective said in a more animated fashion. "Some of these cemetery thefts, the guy walks right by the small stuff. He goes for the pieces that can be resold to antique dealers and art galleries. That stuff is worth thousands of dollars. So, he does his homework."

The detective opened a drawer and pulled out a file full of newspaper clippings. He slipped on some reading glasses.

"Look at this." He kept some clippings in front of him to read from and pushed others across the desk toward JC, "In Texas, someone cleaned out a graveyard of its brass urns and sundials. They pulled the cast-iron fences right out of the ground! That stuff was estimated to be worth sixty-five thousand dollars!"

"Are you working with the other towns in Colorado?" JC asked.

"Oh yeah," responded Trujillo as he pulled off his glasses. "An eighty-year-old hand-carved angel disappeared in the mountains, worth four-thousand dollars to replace. A three-hundred-pound marble statue walked away in the San Juans. That's valued at twenty-five-hundred bucks."

"So, you think there's more than one thief?" JC asked.

"I do. I think there are probably dozens of small-time perps stealing the little crap. They sell it to the local scrap yard, probably to go get high," the detective said. "But I also think there's a guy, or maybe a ring of guys, who are stealing the big stuff. They're the ones I'm interested in."

Detective Trujillo rearranged a file on top of his desk. Then he looked over both shoulders, like he was going to say something to JC that he might not want anyone else to hear.

"Do you know why I let you come up here?" Trujillo asked in a lowered voice. He looked the reporter in the eyes.

"You remember that fatal shooting over by City Park?" the law officer asked. "The guy robbed at gunpoint and killed in his apartment?"

JC nodded, remembering the murder the previous spring. He said, "Everyone thought he was a law-abiding citizen. No reason to be targeted like that. Executed, really."

"Right," said the Detective. "That's what we were told, that he was straight-laced. So, on the noon news, you go live from the scene showing video of our guys pulling a safe out of the apartment that morning."

"Yep, I remember," JC acknowledged.

Trujillo said, "You reported that we found a gun and cocaine in that safe." Trujillo started to laugh. "But we'd come back here by then, and there was a problem. Our guys couldn't get the safe open."

Trujillo continued to laugh. "And all my colleagues are watching the TV while you tell the audience what was found in a safe that hadn't even been opened!"

The detective, still smiling and chuckling, continued, "And we had been told by everybody in that neighborhood that the victim was a good guy, worked three jobs and didn't get involved in drugs or crime."

"You hadn't opened the safe yet?" JC asked. He hadn't known that.

"Nope," the law officer answered as his grin grew. "And my fellow officers were getting quite a laugh at your expense." JC was getting concerned about where this story was going.

"Anyway," the cop continues, "the phone rings. It's one of the forensic guys in the basement working on the safe. He says, 'We just opened it. You'll never believe this. There's a gun and a bunch of cocaine!'"

Trujillo laughed at the story again before saying, "It was just like you'd said. That's when I knew you were smart. You'd done a better job investigating that poor guy's murder than we had. No one here was laughing then. They got back to work. They were trying to catch up with you!"

The detective and the reporter looked at each other with respect.

"So," JC asked, "How many officers can I report are working on this case?"

"One," Detective Trujillo responded as a smile returned to his face, "and you're looking at him."

"What about that guy?" JC pointed his thumb over his shoulder. It was the direction taken by the man in blue jeans and denim shirt when leaving.

"Him?" Trujillo answered with a chuckle. "He's not a cop."

"I saw you shake hands. It looked like you were on the same team," JC explained.

That drew another little laugh from the detective. He thought for a moment, about what he should and shouldn't say to a reporter. Then he said in a low voice, though still smiling, "He's a snitch."

3

"No body snatcher, not even a zombie?"
"Stealing the cemetery relics? Nope," JC told
the assignment editor, who was mocking disappointment. "I
know. Bummer, right?" They both smiled a bit.

Gallows humor was common in newsrooms. It was
necessary, and journalists offered few apologies. Their days
could be toxic. They saw death and they saw lives ruined.
Journalists needed a tonic for what they witnessed, before
they brought it home with them. Tasteless jokes were better
than drinking.

JC was still pulling off his wool coat and hanging it on the
side of his cubicle. He had thick dark hair and a mustache.

Mustaches had never really fallen out of fashion in the Rocky Mountains.

Even covered by a suit coat, it was apparent that JC's frame carried a lot of muscle. He was still athletic. He was a ski racer in college and still raced, when he could, on weekends.

He wasn't a 32 waist anymore, not even close. "I could be, if I didn't drink," he'd say. His face revealed that there was no chance of that happening.

The reporter had just walked into the newsroom the morning after his live report on the cemetery burglaries. The story was well-received by his co-workers, mostly.

"Thumbsucker," complained a grizzled news photographer named Milt Lemon. Milt was of the belief that TV news should only be viewed via a "live truck" if the reporter was standing in front of a burning building or a gunshot victim who was still bleeding. If the fire was out or the victim stopped bleeding, Milt felt "going live" was just phony window dressing, a thumbsucker.

He wasn't alone in that thinking, but he was in the minority. JC was OK with doing "thumbsuckers." He was willing to acknowledge that a half-hour news program took a whole day of planning. A lot of people had to do their job right in order for the anchors and reporters to make it look effortless.

So, unless a better story came along, it was decided at ten in the morning that JC's story would be reported "live" from a cemetery where a crime had been committed. There were three other live trucks available for that newscast. Any of them could be sent to breaking news, be it a fire, a car crash or a shooting.

The producers liked JC's story. They also liked that the reporter arrived at work almost every morning with good fresh story ideas. Some reporters showed up with nothing, just waiting to be hand-fed their assignment for the day. JC got the feeling that some of those journalists had "checked out," already thinking about what they were going to eat for supper that night or what they were going to watch on television.

JC had no objection to Milt's viewpoint. "I just think you're giving the term thumbsucker a bad name," he told the photographer.

The reporter mostly liked Milt. That was not a common position in the newsroom. First of all, Milt tended to refer to reporters as "Human microphone stands." So, some of those human mic stands begged the assignment editor not to pair them with Milt. JC figured that he must have a higher tolerance level.

He also recognized that the sometimes grumpy, occasionally offensive photographer always worked hard on an assignment and produced positive results.

JC looked at the newsroom as a place of work, not a cocktail party where you got to choose your dinner companions. Milt and JC agreed to disagree on the value of thumbsucking.

The assignment editor, Rocky, followed JC to his desk. Rocky Bauman was middle-aged and balding. He was an experienced news junkie. He had neither a wife nor children.

No one on the news staff disagreed that Bauman took his work home with him. They all pictured him eating alone with his work spread out in front of him. They were only divided on whether he actually took it to bed with him.

"You working on anything?" Rocky asked JC.

"Nothing that can't wait," JC told him.

The smile on Rocky's face assured JC that he had provided the right answer. Rocky said, "I want you to go talk to a woman who says her husband has been missing for a week."

"Are we sure he didn't find a new flavor of the month?" JC asked.

"No, we're not," Rocky responded. "But she sounds nice, like she's not nuts."

JC and Milt drove up to Loveland, near the mouth of the Big Thompson Canyon. Rocky was right, she was nice. Lisa Miller was polite, articulate, pretty.

Her husband's name was Scott. He worked for a storage locker company. He earned enough money, she told JC, to buy them this modest home in Loveland.

It had a view of the Front Range and a small garden in the back. The garden had thick evergreen bushes. In the middle, there was a sculpture of a soldier. JC thought it was probably a Civil War soldier. The piece looked like granite. JC could admire it all from the sunroom where he sat with Lisa, while she told her story.

"Scott said he was going out to do a day of errands, and he promised to bring home Mexican food for dinner," Lisa told JC. "He never came back." She began to cry. "It was a week ago."

"No one saw him?" JC inquired. "He didn't call?"

"No," she answered. She said he didn't have any enemies, he wasn't in trouble and he didn't gamble.

"Did police find his car?"

"Yes, up the canyon," she said. "It's funny, not ha-ha funny, but odd," she said.

"What," JC asked.

"Scott's father died in the Big Thompson flood. It's just odd that Scott's car was found in the same canyon, only a few miles from where his dad died."

JC was familiar with the history of the Big Thompson flood. It was in 1976. Nearly 150 people died. Small communities along the river were wiped away, buildings and all.

Some bodies were carried twenty miles downriver. Some bodies were never found. A forty-foot wall of water crashed down the canyon after a freakishly powerful rainstorm stalled over the canyon.

"Scott's mom eventually remarried. But Scott wasn't crazy about the guy," Lisa said. "His mom died about five years ago."

The reporter was writing notes as Milt shot the interview. "If you don't mind me asking, does he have another source of income?" JC inquired. "That antique sculpture of the soldier, impressive."

Lisa laughed a bit. "Oh, he brought that home. He found that in a storage locker that had been abandoned. His employer told him he could keep it."

Lisa reached for a framed photograph of her husband and seemed to be reflecting. JC didn't say anything.

"Scott took care of storage lockers at four sites," Lisa Miller continued. "He hosed them down and got them ready for the next customer. He fixed broken lights and doors. He's a real handyman. But the soldier statue? It's unreal, what people walk away from. Sometimes, he'd clean up stuff and sell it. But we liked that one, so we kept it."

Milt shot video of some still photographs of Scott Miller, provided by Lisa. The one in the frame was her favorite.

"Maybe he hit his head," she said. "Maybe he's out there and he doesn't know who he is." She was holding out hope that she'd see her husband alive again.

JC knew the odds of that happening were small. Scott Miller's body was probably off a hiking path or over a cliff in Big Thompson Canyon, near his car. Most likely, it was suicide or an accident.

The bodies of some missing persons are never found in Colorado. That's despite massive search efforts, especially for hikers. There are a lot of places to hide a body in a state as large as Colorado. There are areas so rugged or desolate that human eyes don't often peer at that exact spot.

Hunters, JC supposed, would probably find Scott Miller's body. That might be a year or more from now. The reporter had covered all too many of these stories to have much hope of Scott Miller's safe return.

Driving back to the TV station, JC and Milt stopped for lunch at a Mexican restaurant downtown. The day was still warm enough in Denver to eat outside on the sidewalk patio.

A brilliant sun was shining. Most passersby were wearing sunglasses and had left their jackets at home or at the office. Some wore tee shirts and others wore a fiberfill or fleece vest.

A Denver Post had been discarded at their table by the previous occupant. JC was thumbing through it when his eyes stopped on the picture of a familiar face.

He couldn't quite remember where he'd seen the man, but the black-and-white photo accompanied coverage of a murder trial underway in a Denver courtroom. The article described the man in the photo, probably in his late twenties or early thirties, as the star witness for the prosecution.

The defense attorney argued that the witness couldn't be believed. The defense asserted that the prosecution witness would say anything, because he'd had several run-ins with the law. "He's been arrested a dozen times!" the defense lawyer was quoted saying. "His testimony is leverage for the next time he's apprehended."

The newspaper said the man's name was Troy Davis. He was described as a small-time offender who shared a jail cell with the murder defendant. It was there, Davis told the court, that the defendant admitted to the murder.

JC looked at the black-and-white photo again. It was taken yesterday. The man had a full head of hair and was wearing a denim shirt and blue jeans. JC remembered bumping into him in the police station. Troy Davis was Detective Trujillo's snitch.

4

"Who's this guy?" JC asked as he looked up at his assignment editor, Rocky Bauman. He was holding a photograph and hovering over JC's desk. The reporter had just returned from lunch and was preparing his story about the missing Scott Miller.

"Probably someone you're never going to see," Rocky answered as he waved the photograph in the air. "But keep an eye out for him." Rocky lowered the photo in front of JC's face. The man in the picture was handsome, with salt-and-pepper hair and wearing a tie and jacket.

"Look for him, because?" JC inquired.

"Do you remember this guy?" Rocky asked as he handed JC the photo. "From a few years ago. Well, four years ago, to be exact."

JC studied the photo. He had an institutional memory. He just needed to find the context. "Jeez," he began recollecting. "Is this the guy from New York? Killed his wife and took off? Still missing … a state senator?"

"Very good," Rocky smiled. "I just got off the phone with New York State Police. They figured Senator John Buford had probably committed suicide. There have been zero sightings."

"Where does a guy that well-known go to hide?" Rocky asked. "But they never found a body. And now, there's been an unconfirmed sighting in Colorado."

"Of Buford?" JC asked.

"Yes," replied Rocky. "At a ski area. Someone from the same town in New York, and says she always voted for him. She swears she saw him here."

"Unconfirmed?" JC repeated.

"Very unconfirmed," the assignment editor acknowledged. "But a cop that I called here in Denver told me that he got a call from cops in New York. They're not blowing off the sighting. I called Albany and the state police confirmed that they're taking it seriously. They're not flying a SWAT team out here or anything. They just want police to be on the lookout for him."

"Wow," was all JC could say as he stared at the picture. "Great story."

Then the reporter thought he heard opportunity knocking. "So," JC looked up at the assignment editor, "do you need me to go up to ski country, undercover, and spend all winter looking for the senator?"

The reporter looked playfully pensive, "You'll need to buy me a season pass, because I'll need to ski every day so that I don't look suspicious. And you can probably subcontract me a condo."

"Yeah, that's exactly what we want you to do," Rocky answered with sarcasm. "But, it would be too much for us to ask of you." He paused to witness the disappointment, both the fun part and the real part.

"But we do want you to keep an eye out," said Rocky, getting back to business. "We know you'll be up there. How many times do you ski a year?"

"Forty to fifty," JC answered. "It would be more, but this job-thing keeps getting in the way."

"Yeah, sorry about that," Rocky smiled, "We just want you to know about this. Let's send you up to Snow Hat to do a live shot on Monday. They just opened for the season, right? You can tell our audience what we've learned up to this point."

JC nodded.

"And this winter," the assignment editor added, "ask around when you're skiing. See if anyone knows anything. Keep that picture of Buford, I've got more. It'll be looking for a needle in a haystack, but you're right, it's a good story."

"Cool," JC affirmed. "I'll be up there on Saturday. I'll start asking questions."

"You have a race?" the assignment editor asked.

"Yep," JC told him.

"You going to win?" Rocky was trying to be inspiring.

"Maybe," JC responded.

"I thought that you guys always believe you are going to win," Rocky said.

"Yeah," JC said. "But when there are thirty or forty guys who also think they are going to win, and everyone of smaller aspirations thinks they have a shot at second or third, there are bound to be some broken dreams."

"Well, good luck," Rocky told him as he walked back toward his desk.

"Give that undercover-skier thing some more thought," JC told the departing assignment editor, raising his voice to cover the distance. "It's a sacrifice I'm willing to make. I'm a giver."

"Um hmm," Rocky replied as he turned his attention to the next matter on his checklist. JC liked Rocky. He was a descendent of Russian- Germans who came to Northern Colorado to farm sugar beets over a century ago. Russian-Germans had once been the state's largest ethnic group.

JC liked Rocky because he had a plan. Most assignment editors rarely had plans that extended past the next thirty minutes. Rocky was already planning for Monday. Mondays were a habitually slow start to the news week. Plans could always be changed, but you had to have a plan. JC believed that Rocky always had a plan.

JC's day was wrapping up. His interview with Lisa Miller was edited and ready for the show. He watched his story at his desk in the newsroom.

Lisa Miller was good TV. She would come across to viewers at home as pretty and likeable. Believable. She delivered a little laugh at the right moment and cried at the right time. Honestly, it made JC a little suspicious.

He knew that all people are not created equal inside a television set. The screen can enhance facial features, but it can also inflate someone's face like a balloon.

Pixels can add personality or twist it. He thought about Richard Nixon sweating away the presidency in a televised debate with John F. Kennedy.

It is noted that television can put ten pounds on anyone standing in front of a camera. JC had been playing tennis with a friend a few months ago, with not a television camera in sight. JC pulled his shirt off in the summer sun. And his friend remarked across the net, "I thought you only gained ten pounds when you were on TV!" Funny guy, JC thought.

But Lisa Miller had the look. She was almost flirting with the audience, coy and getting away with it. JC couldn't put a finger on what she was up to. He thought she was lying, but he wasn't sure what she was lying about.

He grabbed his fleece vest and headed out the door. There was still daylight. He thought he'd make the short drive to a strip of antique stores on South Broadway. He knew of a few that would be open for another hour.

He was no stranger to antique stores in the old section of town called Bonnie Brae. But the neighborhood was quickly changing. He wondered how much longer the old stores would survive.

He passed new buildings that were going up, only blocks from Antique Row. There were apartments on the upper floors and trendy retail shops on the ground floor. The stores were geared toward millennials with money.

"Rents have been going up since the pot shops opened," complained one antique store owner. JC had seen multiple storefronts selling either legalized marijuana or CBD.

He found a parking spot on the street for his SUV, a red 2012 FJ Cruiser. A man walked out of an antique store, stared at the car and said, "They don't make those anymore, do they?"

JC responded, "And they don't make them any better." The used FJ Cruiser was a recent acquisition. JC couldn't understand why the manufacturer had discontinued making the 4x4. It was a handsome brute of a car.

He looked in the store windows of assorted antique stores near Arkansas Avenue. One had vintage ski posters from Europe for sale. He was disappointed that it was closed for the day.

He found a store that was still open and walked in. He'd never been in this shop before. "Am I too late?" he asked the man behind the counter.

"No," the store owner said. "I'm starting to close up, but it will take me fifteen minutes. Let me know if I can show you anything."

The store was called The Faded Fence. It was full of aged barbed wire and Western décor. There were the usual tables, chairs, hutches and lamps. And there was a pair of stone gargoyles gaping at each other, their faces faded by the outdoor elements.

JC spotted a weathered sculpture of a column. On top of it was a pair of hands holding an open book. The journalist figured the book to be a bible. The stone was worn and pitted, but it looked like there was scripture written on the pages of the book.

"Wow," JC said in a raised voice, so the store owner could hear him. "Where did you get this?"

The shop owner stopped what he was doing and walked over. He put his hands on his hips, "Yeah, that just came in."

"Nice," JC picked up the price tag. It read "$2,000." JC loitered by the sculpture. He wasn't sure what he was looking for. He doubted that he'd find anything stamped "Property of the municipal cemetery."

"You're the guy on TV, aren't you?" the shop owner said to JC.

JC nodded and introduced himself. "Eric Crabtree," the man responded.

The store owner scratched at his day-old growth of beard. He was thinking. Then he said, "Yeah, listen, I know what you're thinking, but I don't know where it came from. The guy who got it for me, he supplies me with a lot of stuff. He's got a business. He's got to be legit, right? Otherwise, he'd get arrested, right?"

"You saw my story last night?" JC asked. "About the cemetery thefts?"

"I did," the businessman replied. "I usually have your news on here. I think you guys are great. I really don't buy stuff that I know is stolen, honest. I don't buy from just anyone who walks off the sidewalk."

The man was nervous. JC had no reason to think he was lying, and he had no reason to think he was telling the truth. "So, this guy is a regular seller? He provides you with stuff like this regularly?"

"Yeah, he does."

"Does he have a name?" JC asked.

Crabtree's mouth formed a half smile. "He's all over the news right now, with the trial going on."

JC drew a blank. "Sorry, I'm not following you."

"The big murder trial. It's on your TV station. One of your other reporters is covering it. He's the star witness for the prosecution."

JC was struggling to find the name he was looking for. "Davis? Troy Davis?"

"Right!" the store owner replied. His spirits brightened with the thought his information would put himself in a better light. "Troy Davis! He's been selling me items for the last two or three years. He's got a demolition company. They take down old homes and stuff. He forages through the rubble and he brings me anything he thinks has some value."

"Really," JC replied. "So, he just finds this stuff sitting around. In the rubble?"

"Yeah."

"Yeah," thought JC. The newspaper had called Troy Davis a small-time offender. A burglar, he would guess.

JC was turning all of this over in his head. He knew Detective Trujillo was using a snitch to convict a murderer. And Trujillo was looking for a guy who was stealing relics from the cemeteries.

The question JC was asking himself, was whether the detective knew Troy Davis might be the same guy.

5

The drive west into the Rocky Mountains from Denver had changed. In a few hours, less attention could be paid to exploring the beauty of the surroundings, because more time was required keeping an eye on the cars in front of you, in back of you, and on both sides of you.

The Denver megalopolis had grown north and south, but it had also grown west. JC thought that a get-away in the mountains could no longer be described as getting away from … well, anything.

It was true even approaching the once-isolated Colorado ski resorts. New roads had been built to accommodate the new houses, new condominiums and rentals. Ski areas were now surrounded by ski villages. They were full of restaurants, stores, real estate offices and more living units. Those seeking paradise would still find the mountain escape they hoped for, but much of what they were escaping from was also waiting for them at their paradise.

JC wouldn't have difficulty finding a good parking spot close to the ski lodge. It was still early in the morning and the lifts wouldn't open at the Snow Hat Ski Resort for another two hours.

The sun wasn't even up. He always liked arriving early on race days, especially if he got there in time to watch sunrise. One or two other racers, usually the same ones, enjoyed the same practice. They got used to drinking coffee together, talking quietly and watching the day begin.

In a couple of hours, the ski lodge began to fill up. Other racers crowded together at the same metal tables, laminated on top to look like wood grain.

The friendly competitors exchanged jokes and encouragement. They told stories about their families, the drive that morning or the past work week.

The conversation held half of their attention. The other half was already focused on the risky job ahead. Being the fastest down a hill of ice was fun, but scary fun. It was dangerous.

Those who entered the race at Snow Hat were grown-ups who had grown-up jobs. They might have raced in high school or college. Some might even have survived at the development level of the national team for a couple of years. They were good racers, just not good enough to be famous for it.

JC pulled a worn elastic speed suit from his backpack. Until last year, it had belonged to his best friend, Al Pine. Pine was dead now. The other racers saw the garment and were reverent as they nodded knowingly. They muttered, "Cool suit."

Al had been a friend to many of them. He was a ski racer too, until he was murdered in Montana. The same monster had tried to take JC's life. Instead, JC took his.

The skin-tight fabric of Al's suit had a pattern of spots resembling a black and white dairy cow. Al wore it to add some levity to the tense moments before a race. JC wore it because he missed his best friend.

"Moooo," was the odd sound of encouragement as JC pushed toward the start gate at the top of the race course. He looked like a lumpy Holstein.

Some of the lumps belonged to two knee braces and a set of pads on his shoulders. Ski racing had rewarded JC with a number of medals and trophies, but it had also honored him with four knee surgeries and two operations on his left shoulder. He thought that he'd gotten the better of the deal. He loved ski racing.

He pushed through the timing wand at the start and began cranking big GS turns. He loved race- courses that began fast.

This was the first race of the new season, after a summer of mountain biking and weight training to stay in shape. Summer was fun, he thought, but it was a long seven months without ski racing. He'd missed the adrenaline.

The joy of JC's flight ended abruptly at forty-five miles an hour. He was about halfway down the run called Mel's GTO. He caught an edge and headed off the course.

But it was a new season and snow at the edge of the trail was not intended to be skied on. It had the texture of concrete with frozen snowcat tracks. The broken chunks of ice and snow scattered across the top were like jagged marbles. "Death cookies" is what JC and the other racers called them.

His head slammed into the frozen snow with a terrible force.

When gatekeepers along the course first reached him, he was facedown and motionless. When he regained his wits, he was in the arms of a man wearing a red jacket.

"Mr. Snow," came the voice from the ski patrol member who cradled him in his arms. "Do you know what state you're in or which ski area you're at?"

"No clue," responded JC slowly, still trying to work through the cobwebs.

The injured racer scanned a small crowd looking on with concerned expressions. "I've got to get to the finish line," JC told the man in the red jacket with a white cross. He said it with urgency. "I think they'll give me a rerun." Some in the small crowd chuckled.

"All in good time," the ski patrol member answered as he restrained JC from crawling away. "I think we'd better get you checked out first."

"I'm OK," JC told the ski patroller. "I can ski down."

The ski patroller just shook his head. "Mr. Snow," he said in a nurturing manner, "I'm going to tell you five numbers. A few minutes from now, I'll ask you to recite them back to me, in the same order, alright?"

JC wasn't up for the fight. "Dandy." He was taken down to the ski patrol hut in a sled. The sled bounced from time to time. Each time, JC grimaced. His ribs felt like blades probing some of his most useful organs.

Upon the sled's arrival at the hut, the ski patroller said to JC, "Mr. Snow, can you tell me what numbers I told you on the hill? Can you tell them to me in order?"

JC had no idea. He couldn't even fake it. Still groggy, he asked the ski patroller, "Is this a multiple-choice test?"

"I'm afraid not," was the response. Then JC was ushered into the back of an awaiting ambulance.

It was parked. It wasn't going anywhere at the moment. JC found himself sitting upright with a blanket over his shoulders.

The ski patrol member asked, "Are you staying here at Snow Hat?"

"Am I dead?" JC asked.

"No," was the response.

"Then, probably not," JC told him. A moment later, he thought that might have sounded rude. Snow Hat was a nice resort, but he wanted to go home.

"No offense," JC told him.

"None taken," was the response.

The EMT checking JC's ribs got a chuckle out of that. He was arriving at the conclusion that JC was probably tough enough to release, as long as he promised to go to a doctor when he got back to Denver.

"I just want to be sure that your ribs are OK," the EMT said. "I think they're broken, but I need more time for an X-ray to confirm that. If you promise to see a doctor, I'll let you go. But you've got to see a doctor. They have to check for any internal bleeding."

"Broken ribs? That isn't so bad," JC said, though it hurt to speak, and he grimaced.

"And there's no doubt you have a concussion," the EMT told him. "But they have doctors at the hospital to make that official, too."

"Are official concussions worse than unofficial ones?" JC asked through clenched teeth. Official or unofficial, his ribs were really starting to hurt.

JC promised he'd report to the hospital upon arrival in Denver. He turned down an ambulance ride and estimated he'd saved at least fifteen-hundred dollars in the deductible for his health insurance.

Sitting in the ambulance, allowing time to clear his head, JC thought about his dad. When Doctor Snow met Shara, while she and JC were still in college, his father told her, "We have four children. Every child is remarkable and different in their own way. JC is the one who likes to hurt himself."

JC thought back to his first severe injury, to a knee while playing high school football. Then came his first surgery, to his shoulder. The damage had lingered since football, but surgery became unavoidable after a few seasons of playing college rugby.

JC couldn't remember a time that he argued with his dad. Dad was always right. No point in arguing this time, either. Dad's youngest son liked taking risks with his body.

The EMT was on the phone with the hospital in Frisco, comparing notes with a doctor there. JC remained huddled under a blanket. His mind wandered to the subject of Shara.

He'd fallen in love in Montana. Right now, Shara was about a ten-hour drive from Denver. It was only about two hours if he flew, but that could become an expensive habit. Besides, long drives in the Rockies were part of the culture.

He didn't like to think about it. His distance from Shara wasn't something he felt good about and there wasn't a clear path to improving the situation. They both knew where most long-distance relationships ended. He didn't like to think about it.

When JC was finally released from his captors at the ski patrol hut, he collected his skis and bag and carried them to his car. He blessed the good fortune of grabbing the closest parking spot that morning.

Lugging his gear caused a pain akin to someone taking shots at his ribs with an axe. When he reached his car, he was sore and short on breath, and he was groggy enough to forget that driving home was a stupid idea.

It hurt to squeeze his broken body into the car seat. He'd refused opioids and taken some Advil to deaden the pain.

It occurred to him that the drive home wouldn't require the slightest sense of direction. He'd just follow the cars in front of him.

Interstate 70, with steep canyon walls on each side, went only two ways. It went east and west. He chose east. He set the car's GPS to tell him when his exit at Larimer Square was approaching.

He was grateful that it wasn't like the old days on I-70, before the Eisenhower Tunnel opened. Then, the trip home over Loveland Pass would guarantee at least one traffic jam, and at least one Texan with bald tires who would slide sideways and come to rest blocking both lanes.

JC looked for a car that he could follow, likely also heading for Denver. He tucked in behind one with a University of Denver Hockey sticker in the back window. Then, his groggy gray matter unwisely thought of things other than driving.

He thought about using Sunday to heal on the couch while he watched football. He'd taped today's Colorado State game. He could watch that in the morning and then he could watch the Denver Broncos. It actually sounded like a fun day.

He could try putting ice on his ribs. Sometimes, he thought, that worked better than drugs. These weren't his first broken ribs, and this wasn't his first concussion. Doctors couldn't put either of them in a cast. He thought he'd skip the hospital. He knew the drill.

As he steered the car east toward Denver, JC thought about the events before and after the crash. He couldn't remember the actual crash. The EMT told him that he might never gain recall of those few minutes.

JC found himself scanning his memory for what he could remember, like the faces of the small group of skiers and snowboarders crowded around him.

Many of the faces had stayed to watch as the ski patrol checked out JC's injuries, and as he was carefully loaded into a sled. JC scanned the faces.

"Whoa!" he said out loud. It actually hurt his ribs when he blurted the words. He clenched his teeth. But for a lucid moment, he believed he had total recall. "I may be crazy," he said out loud, "but I think one of them was John Buford."

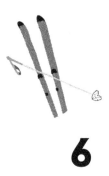

6

"**D**o you know how much of our tax dollars are wasted on these guardrails?" Milt Lemon was driving west on I-70 toward the Snow Hat Ski Resort. JC was in the passenger seat.

Milt was ranting about the guardrails alongside nearly every road in the United States. "We ought to be doing a story about that! How much money are we blowing on these things?"

JC was looking over notes pertaining to the day's story. Ranting was what Milt Lemon did a lot during their drives to stories. JC had become accustomed to it.

"You know what we could do instead of paying for billions of miles of guardrails?" Milt squawked. "Not drive off the road!"

They were passing through Summit County, famous for ski areas like Keystone, Breckenridge and Copper Mountain. Vail, Beaver Creek and Snow Hat were just beyond them.

JC felt much better than he had Sunday. He slept through most of the two football games. And he had a hard time following the action when he was awake. Concussions really screwed up watching football.

But he felt well enough Sunday night to look over old news accounts of state Senator John Buford. The television station's assignment editor, Rocky, had asked JC to travel to Snow Hat on Monday and break the Buford story.

He would report that someone thought they saw Buford at the ski resort, however fragile that sighting might be.

Sitting on the couch of his apartment above Larimer Square, finding a sitting position that didn't make his ribs roar their disapproval, JC had peered over articles describing Buford as a powerful presence in Albany. The city is New York's state capital.

Buford was chair of the Senate Finance Committee, controlling the spending bills. He was included in negotiations with the governor and the state Assembly. It was a position from which Buford could reasonably expect to launch a bid to become the next powerful Senate majority leader.

He was popular with voters in the Capital Region. He'd grown up in Albany, raised by middle-class parents. His impressive home, acquired after some time in the Senate, was only a brisk walk from the state Capitol. He often made that walk, rather than drive to work in the morning. All the way, he'd say hello to constituents he'd pass on the sidewalk.

JC read that Buford's last election offered no real opposition. The opposing party didn't want to see him removed, even if they couldn't admit it publicly. Buford's influence brought hundreds of millions of state allocations to the area. He was on the rise, and the Capital Region would rise with him.

The newspaper clippings described the discovery of Fiona Buford's body in the home she shared with Senator Buford and their adopted daughter. It was shocking to the public.

Buford had a clean reputation up to that moment. Albany was a town that thrived on political drama. In absence of facts, innuendo would do.

But the senator from Albany had never been accused of being unfaithful to his wife or taking a bribe. He was considered a straight shooter. He was regularly seen being a dad at Lucy's school pageants and games.

He also showed up, being a politician, at Little League baseball games in his senate district, and fundraisers for volunteer fire departments and tributes to war veterans.

Fiona's murder, and the senator's apparent guilt, owned the headlines in Albany for months. Any new development or rumor merited front-page news. Newspapers named it "The story of the year."

Attempts by the local news media to track his movements on the night of the murder proved unrewarding. A witness said he saw Buford at the bus station, downtown. But the sobriety of the witness was not convincing. Neither was his story.

There were a couple of stolen cars that night in Albany. But would Senator John Buford steal a car? Did he even know how to steal a car?

He wasn't seen at the airport and he wasn't seen at the train station. He had vanished. That's why suicide became a popular conclusion to police.

On the other hand, John Buford had forged a career of making friends and allies. If he found the right friend, one that could keep his mouth shut, that's all it would take to get him out of town.

There was another nagging question in the Albany news media: Why did he do it? What was Buford's motive for killing his wife? Repeated questions by reporters to police came back with the same answer: "We're looking into it."

There was less written about Lucy Buford, the adopted daughter who had now lost two sets of parents in her young lifetime. She had gone to live with Buford's sister, Beverly, and her husband, Stanford Pruyn.

The child's privacy was largely respected by the local news media. She was only fourteen when she tragically lost her adopted mother. Lucy wasn't to blame for the murder, and newsrooms allowed her to grow up in relative normalcy.

The only departure from that unspoken policy was one attempt by a downstate tabloid. That was one of the differences between Upstate and Downstate New York.

The search for her famous adopted father became a cold case. Stories in the newspapers and on television would revive the mystery each year on the anniversary of the murder. Otherwise, suicide seemed the likely end to the gripping tale.

All that was needed, and expected, was the discovery of Senator Buford's body. For four years, every time human remains were discovered, conjecture began about whether it was the senator's remains.

But every time, the body that surfaced in woods outside Coeymans or near Lake Desolation, or tangled in brush along the river in Valatie, turned out to be someone else.

JC had brought more clippings with him in the car. He was scribbling notes into his long, narrow reporter's notebook as Milt Lemon drove.

Remembering to pause from time to time and take in the magnificent landscape, JC determined that he needed to start working the phone. He was fortunate. The people he wanted to talk to were in the East, where the time zone was already two hours ahead of Colorado.

He reached a New York State Police investigator named Rick Hotaling.

"It's a Dutch name," the investigator told JC, unsolicited. "There's lots of Hotalings around here."

They discussed the four-year search for John Buford. "I don't have four years of results to show for it, though," said Hotaling. "I've never seen anyone so thoroughly disappear as Senator Buford."

"Do you think he's alive?" asked JC.

"Not so sure about that," the law officer acknowledged. "He's pretty well-known. I guess he could have gotten out of the country."

"But you had a sighting in Colorado recently?"

"Yeah, that's what she says. It was at the, let's see ..." JC could hear him flipping through paperwork. Then Hotaling returned, "It was at the Snow Hat ski area."

"Is it someone who knew the senator? Is it a good ID?"

The investigator quickly responded, "No, it was a voter. She'd voted for him and she lived in Albany, so she saw him from time to time at community events and on TV."

"Do you believe her?

The police officer exhaled into the phone, as though he was letting air out of a balloon. "I don't think she's lying, but I'm not sure she isn't mistaken."

"Why would he be in Colorado?" JC asked.

"That's the thing. It's possible. He liked to go skiing with his daughter," Investigator Hotaling told the reporter. "It was usually just the two of them. Mrs. Buford had lost interest in skiing, or something, so the senator and his daughter would go. They went a lot. They'd do weekends at ski areas in Vermont, New York, Massachusetts, New Hampshire, Maine. They'd travel quite a ways."

"Had they skied in Colorado together?"

"Yeah, they had," Hotaling replied. "Snow Hat seemed to be their favorite. That's what the daughter, uh, Lucy, had said. That's why, when this woman said she saw him there, it kind of caught my attention. It's possible, you know?"

"There's something that I can't find in the news clippings I've been looking over," JC disclosed to the investigator. "A motive. Do you know why he would kill his wife?"

"Honestly," the trooper responded, "I'm not sure. We haven't been able to talk to him, and Mrs. Buford certainly isn't talking. We have some theories, but none we're willing to share."

Hotaling ran down the possibilities they'd explored and dismissed. "There was no girlfriend, as far as we can tell, and there was no money trouble. We hear stories about arguments between the couple, but what couple doesn't argue sometimes? We're convinced that he killed her, but the truth is, we're not certain of the motive."

"Do you keep tabs on the daughter," JC asked, "to see if Buford tries to contact her?"

"Not much," answered the BCI investigator. "We kept an eye on the house for a while. You can't tap her phone, and it's been four years. We still keep an eye on things. We talk to her once in a while, and we talk to Beverly, Buford's sister. It only takes one clue, one confirmed sighting. But right now, we're no closer to finding him than we were four years ago. That's if he's alive, and that's still an if."

There were still about twenty minutes before Milt and JC were to arrive at the ski resort. JC had another 518 phone number he wanted to try. He hoped his cell phone would hold a signal in the mountains.

"Oh my God, they did everything together," Beverly Pruyn told JC over the phone. "I've never seen a father and daughter who were closer. My husband has a great relationship with our other daughter, our birth daughter, but it isn't close to what John and Lucy had. It's very sad."

"The murder's sad?" JC explored.

"Yes," Mrs. Pruyn responded. "Of course it is. But I was thinking about the two of them being separated. Listen, Stan and I have tried to raise Lucy as though she's our own daughter. She's been in our house since the night of the murder. We love her, and she's a happy child. But she's never gotten over losing her father. She loves John, to this day. Her heart is still broken, just because she misses him."

"Does she blame him, at all, for Fiona's death?"

"That's a tricky question," Beverly answered. "Lucy knows murder is wrong. But that woman was a witch to Lucy. She terrified the poor child. I used to get along with Fiona, especially in the early years, but she was horrible to that child. You should hear some of the stories."

"Is Lucy glad that her dad killed Fiona?"

Beverly Pruyn paused on the other end of the phone. "She doesn't really talk about it. But I think she believes John did it to protect her. He was her knight in shining armor, and this is what knights in shining armor do, isn't it? They slay the dragon. That's a terrible thing for me to say, but it's the best way to explain to you how Lucy feels."

"Wow," JC said softly. He considered the possibility that John Buford killed his wife to protect his daughter. Was it some twisted act of kindness rather than hate?

"Do you think Lucy knows where her father is?" JC asked. "Do you think they're communicating?"

"I don't think so," Beverly told him. "We keep a close eye on things around here. I can't say I'd object, if there was a way for the two of them to be in contact with each other, legally. But the police still keep an eye on us. They say they don't, but they do. We've got to keep Lucy out of trouble. That's what John would want us to do."

"The knight in shining armor," JC said.

"You know," Beverly then added, "they used to have a thing. Lucy had told John that he was her knight in shining armor. And after that, when he was out of town on business or something, he'd text her a 'good night.' Only, he'd just type 'knight,' like 'good knight.' Isn't that sweet?"

"They loved each other," JC said in an almost reverent tone.

"They loved each other," she whispered back.

7

The Snow Hat Ski Resort was named after the mountain it sprawled across. Mountain men named the thirteen-thousand-foot peak two centuries ago.

As winter approached each year, and snow gathered at the mountaintop, those living in the valley would say that the peak was putting on its snow hat.

JC's live shot was set up in the Snow Hat Ski Resort's village. He was outside of The Spilled Cup, a quaint coffee house where skiers and snowboarders liked to collapse after a day on the mountain.

The ski resort had provided a spokesperson. She told the camera that they had no clue whether John Buford had been there. The Colorado Bureau of Investigation had circulated an old photograph of Buford among merchants, but it hadn't triggered any memories.

"This sounds inappropriate," the spokesperson had confided before the camera was rolling, "but if you were a fugitive, wouldn't you want to hide here?" She was smiling brightly at JC.

When the interview was over, JC thanked her for the resort's cooperation. Her response was candid, "Honestly, it's self-serving. While we answer your questions about a horrible murder elsewhere, the picture over our shoulder is showing TV viewers how great our snow is. We're talking, but they're not listening. They're thinking, 'Let's go skiing up there!'"

The snow at Snow Hat was clearly satisfying the skiers and boarders who were already there. JC did a few "man-on-the-street" interviews, asking if they'd seen the face in the black-and-white picture.

The M-O-S responses were similar. One couple, a skier and a snowboarder, told JC, "He murdered someone? Whoa. But, it's great skiing. If he is here, I just hope he doesn't beat us to first tracks."

The man and woman laughed and exchanged a high five. They turned for the mountain, saying over their shoulder, "Take care, dude."

JC's eyes scanned the village, the windows of the condos and the crowds carrying their ski gear down the pedestrian path. They had helmets on their heads and goggles over their eyes. JC shook his head, "He could be hiding in plain sight."

The reporter finished writing, and Milt edited their story for that night's broadcast. It was ready for air and there was still an hour before the TV station's satellite truck was due to arrive.

"I can't do it," JC said to Milt, who had been expecting the news. They had an agreement whenever they had a story to cover at a ski area. At least, it was their goal. If they could finish in time, they'd take a couple of ski runs. It was a little reward for their hard work.

"I probably would have stopped you if you tried," Milt told him. Milt was JC's designated skiing photographer. It wasn't easy to ski and shoot broadcast quality images at the same time. Milt could. As a result, JC kept Milt equipped in good ski gear, normally JC's hand-me-downs with plenty of rip left in them.

"How about some coffee instead?" JC offered. Milt said with a grin, "Sure, you pussy."

They sat next to a large window at the coffee shop called The Spilled Cup. There were townies there, waiting for their work shifts, and skiers taking a break.

In the back of the shop there were soft, aging chairs and sofas, and the walls were lined with books. It was dimly lit and there was a small bar that was open in the evenings. But the front of the coffee house was busy in the day, with small wooden tables and chairs and plenty of windows that the sun was shining through.

The reporter and photographer had been working non-stop since they'd arrived at Snow Hat. Milt caught JC grimacing as he searched for a comfortable position in his seat.

"You know," Milt told JC, "we've still got time. We can re-edit the end of our story so they can run it without your 'live' presence. Then, we could head home now and you could get into bed where you belong. Skip the thumbsucker."

"I really don't want to do that," JC groaned. "We're already edited. I've still got two hours to clear my head so I don't sound stupid."

"Oh, if you just sound stupid," Milt said with a grin, "the audience won't notice a thing."

JC smiled and they drank their coffee in silence, watching skiers and snowboarders walk past the window. Some were approaching the chairlifts in anticipation of an exciting afternoon on the snow. Others were walking toward the parking lot. They were done, helmets askew or hair disheveled, jackets half-zipped and looks of exhaustion on their faces.

"Can I tell you something?" JC asked as he looked toward Milt. "I know you're a grumpy old bastard and you'll tell me it's my concussion talking."

Milt Lemon was older than JC. He had gray hair and a gray goatee. He was overweight and not particularly good-looking. But he never fell behind at a news scene, lugging his camera and light kit and whatever. Milt delivered the goods.

JC felt Milt was smart but preferred to think that everyone else was dumb. It lent flavor to Milt's sense of humor. JC thought Milt had a pretty good sense of humor, though quirky and sometimes crude.

"Oh, geez," Milt erupted, "you're not attracted to me, are you? This always happens to me!"

JC laughed, making his ribs ache. "You could do worse."

Milt continued, "It's these long car trips. None of you can help yourselves."

JC was still smiling, "Are you done, jackass?"

Milt fell silent. He'd thoroughly enjoyed himself and now he was done. His eyes, which always had dark circles around them, turned to JC.

"My crash on Saturday," JC began, "I was out cold. And when I came to, I was being cuddled by a ski patrol guy."

Milt interrupted, "Did he take liberties with you? Is that what you're trying to tell me?" He smiled.

JC rolled his eyes, raising his hand asking Milt to control himself. "There was a small crowd of skiers and snowboarders standing there. Some were seeing if they could lend a hand and some were probably hoping to see a dead guy."

JC paused. He was deciding if he really wanted to share what was probably a figment of his damaged head's imagination. "In the crowd, I think I saw John Buford."

Milt stared at JC without changing his expression. He nodded his head a little, letting JC know that he took him seriously. Then he said, "It's the concussion."

A short time later, JC was able to endure the live shot, introducing his television audience to the story of Senator John Buford.

For most members of the audience, it was the first time they'd heard of John Buford, or at least the first time they remembered hearing his name. Buford's infamy unfolded on the East Coast. Four years ago, it probably received attention for one day in Denver's news. It was another tale about the crazy East Coast making viewers glad they lived in Colorado.

JC did not mention to viewers that he might have seen Buford in a crowd of faces only two days ago. A fresh concussion made him a lousy witness.

He was short on breath after the live shot, because of his ribs. He hadn't told his employer about his ski-racing crash or the resulting discomfort. He felt that was part of the pact. He was free to play hard on the weekend, but he'd better show up for work on Monday.

The reporter knew from experience he could save himself a lot of discomfort during his live shot if he kept his intro and his outro short. Between that, the rest of the story was already recorded digitally. While viewers were watching that, he'd have time to cough, cry and otherwise compose himself.

"You alright?" the producer in the control room asked JC. The voice was coming from Denver through the IFB JC wore in his ear. The producer had watched the reporter wince while the audience at home was watching the story on video.

"Never better," the reporter lied. He looked at Milt as he put the microphone down, "Please, take me home."

8

"What am I going to do with you?"

"Gee, I usually have to give a girl fifty dollars before she'll ask me that," JC replied.

"Fine, see where getting smutty gets you, when I'm ten hours away," responded Shara.

That was a painful reminder that JC didn't need. His girlfriend lived in Montana. He fell in love with her when they were both in college at Colorado State University. He'd lost her and found her again.

But Shara Adams owned a bar and restaurant at the Grizzly Mountain Ski Resort in Montana. "Let me come down and take care of you," she begged. "Once ski season really starts going up here, you won't see me for four or five months, unless you come up here."

He had called Shara after returning from Snow Hat. He'd already crawled into bed, exhausted.

She had answered the phone eagerly, "How did the race go?" He told her about his racing mishap. He attempted to make it sound like a much smaller incident than it was. But Shara wasn't fooled. She had been on the same college ski team as JC. She knew how injuries happened and how severe they could be.

"Let me think about you coming down here," JC told her. "My brain is draped in fog. I'm just sitting in bed. I'd be a bore."

"Since when were you a bore in bed?" she teased. "And who cares about your brain. That's not your strong suit, anyway." JC smiled. It only made him miss her more.

"Maybe you could come up and see me," she suggested.

"What? People try to kill me when I come up there," he joked.

"Just one man," Shara answered. "And technically, he was trying to kill me. You stuck your nose where it didn't belong."

JC had saved Shara's life last winter, when she stumbled across a serial killer that JC had been tracking. It nearly cost both of them their lives. Instead, they fell in love.

"How's Jumper?" JC inquired about Shara's black lab.

"He misses you, too," Shara sounded pouty.

"Listen, let me think about you coming down," JC told her. "I'm already back at work. You wouldn't see much of me. Sorry, I really do miss you."

He hung up the phone, reluctantly. "I must make a command decision," JC announced to himself. "I'm moving from the bed to the kitchen to the couch." He tried to bounce onto his feet, but it caused his head to pound. "New plan: I'm going to slowly move from the bed to the kitchen to the couch," he amended.

He knew that there was another flaw in his plan. He couldn't cook. He'd do it to avoid starving, but even with a functional cerebrum, his attention span in a kitchen was crippled.

He had a history of self-inflicted food poisoning. He'd nearly burned a hotel down when he tried to heat a breakfast sandwich. "I guess I hit 'one hour' on the microwave when I meant to hit 'one minute,'" he told an alarmed hotel employee who was investigating the smoke.

JC's cooking capabilities could fill a three-item menu. He could cook a mean omelet, he could steam an artichoke, and he could make a dip using small shrimp, mayonnaise and cream cheese.

If an anthropologist searched for a single common thread between JC's dating history, he would find a small bowl of dip with little shrimp, mayo and cream cheese.

Now, given a hammer and nails or anything involving an engine, JC was quite competent.

It all had to do with his attention span, and JC acknowledged that in the kitchen, his couldn't span the distance between the refrigerator and the oven.

He wasn't about to starve. His freezer always had instant dinners with healthy ingredients. His refrigerator had some fruit, juice, milk, wine and his favorite beer: Belhaven Black, a Scottish stout.

His kitchen pantry had cashews, coffee, some kind of cooking oil, salt, pepper, popcorn, tee shirts, gym shorts and shoes at the bottom. There was still room on the lower shelf, so he was thinking about moving some sweaters there.

He reached into the freezer and pulled out an instant meal of Indian food in a cardboard tray. It required heating in a microwave, but he decided to risk it.

While the Mattar Paneer heated, he filled up a glass of water and popped more ibuprofen.

Armed with a fork and napkin, he now shuffled to the coach. He pushed aside a bent photo of John Buford. "Was it real or imagined?" he asked himself.

His mind, though compromised, drifted back to what he thought he'd seen two days before, as a small gathering of skiers watched him being loaded into a sled by the ski patrol.

Had he seen Buford? Considering his condition, JC was beginning to doubt himself. The man he saw had a ski helmet on. JC's identification was based on a face without hair or ears, and he was comparing it to a black-and-white photo taken four years ago. JC had never set eyes on the real John Buford.

JC called Milt and asked him to keep their conversation about seeing Buford between them.

"In fact," JC added, "keep the whole thing about the accident between us, for now. K?" Milt agreed and hung up the phone, saying that he had to get back to looking through some video he'd shot last summer.

"Don't let it fall into the hands of any children," JC told him. Milt just laughed

JC, and anyone else who knew Milt Lemon, thought he was an odd man. But he was somehow lovably odd, like an ugly dog who loved everyone.

After a hitch in the Army, Milt had found employment as a police officer on a small force east of Denver. He didn't last long. He was in the squad room one day, showing fellow officers his quick-draw pistol tricks. The gun fired. So was Milt. He'd shot a coffee pot.

His resume, including the short police career minus the coffee pot murder, got him a job as a photographer in a television newsroom in Grand Junction. It turned out that he was good at it. He eventually landed a job in Denver.

Milt was a peculiar legend among those who knew him, especially at TV stations. He was a good man to have on a story in a tight spot. And his lovable ugly-dog persona delivered strange successes.

Some were stranger than others. When sent on assignment alone, maybe to get a shot of sunbathers for the weather department, he'd occasionally approach women and innocently say, "Show me your tits." And as many women as not would smile into the camera and comply.

Both men and women in the newsroom shook their head in disbelief when Milt would slip into an edit bay and say, "Hey, look at this." But they'd look. Milt was usual about bringing home the unusual.

His love life was a disaster. To the shock of anyone who knew Milt, he started showing up at dinners, or stopping by for a beer after work, with the same beautiful woman.

"I want to introduce you to my girlfriend, Sandy," Milt said the first time he brought her to socialize with his brethren from the newsroom. All in attendance were waiting for the punchline to the joke. How had Milt the Mess lured this lovely woman?

"What is wrong with her?" a friend whispered into JC's ear.

"Nothing," JC responded quietly. "I met her at cocktails once. She's smart and kind of fun."

"Is he paying her?" the colleague murmured.

"I don't think so," JC said. "Milt doesn't make that much money."

She wasn't showing yet, but she was pregnant, Sandy confided in JC when she had to tell her story to someone.

She said that she'd met Milt in a bar. He was boyish with a twisted type of charm. She said that she was naïve. She still lived at home with her over-protective parents. She was very religious. She'd been a "rule follower" her entire life. That night, she decided to break the rules.

"That's all it took," she told JC, "one night." She said that her faith would not allow her to end the pregnancy. Not if she wanted an afterlife. She said that she was going to marry Milt so her baby would have a father.

The months wore on and Sandy's bump became obvious. She continued to live in her parent's house. She continued to confide in JC when they found themselves together.

She told him that she cried every night. She swore JC to secrecy. Nothing was to be said to Milt. The marriage would happen. JC hoped things would work out, that Milt and Sandy could find love.

JC watched the remaining months in horror. Milt thought that he had finally done something right. He was going to have a beautiful wife and a beautiful baby. He was in love.

But JC looked at Sandy when Milt was all smiles, maybe telling an anecdote he found amusing. Sandy's eyes revealed that she had come to find Milt revolting.

They were married in the chapel at the hospital. Hours later, Sandy delivered a perfect beautiful little girl, Jayne. Twenty-four hours later, Sandy filed for divorce.

Milt never saw it coming. He was destroyed. But Baby Jayne had a father and a last name. And Sandy was assured of an afterlife. JC never set eyes on her again.

9

"For being broken, you are doing an annoying amount of thinking," JC told his brain.

He'd called the newsroom first thing in the morning. He told them he needed time to work on the cemetery story. He wanted to sleep, but his mind was beginning to wander.

Now he was thinking about Troy Davis, the supposed demo-man who found relics worth thousands of dollars in the rubble of buildings he tore down. JC fired up his computer. He went to a listing of professionals licensed by the state. If Davis really did own a demolition business, his name would be on some document, some license.

It wasn't, and it did not come as a surprise to JC. He'd already left a message on voice mail, Monday, with Colorado's

Department of Revenue. JC now found a message left on his phone. It told him that the state had no record of a business owned by Troy Davis. In fact, they had no recent record telling them that Troy Davis even existed. He sure wasn't paying taxes.

JC telephoned Eric Crabtree, the owner of The Faded Fence antique store. "Are you going to be around in a half hour?" JC asked.

"Uh, yeah," Crabtree answered. "Sure. What's this about?"

"Troy Davis," JC replied.

It didn't take long to get to the antique store on South Broadway. It wasn't that far from his apartment in Larimer Square.

The store's door was locked when he arrived. He peered into the window and the lights were off. He looked at the time on his cell phone. It had been a half hour exactly. The store hours posted on the door informed shoppers he'd be open until six. Where was Crabtree?

JC found a back entrance to the store, but it was also locked. JC returned to the front of the store, getting a bit aggravated. "Where the hell is he?"

JC called the number he had for Eric Crabtree. He could hear the phone ringing inside the shop. It was a landline.

After waiting a half hour in front of the darkened business, JC walked back to his SUV. He didn't want to return to the couch and he didn't want to let go of the story.

He drove north and pulled into a driveway leading him past tall cast-iron gates. He drove past an old chapel with flying buttresses and a distinctly French look. Odd, JC thought, because the French never had a great deal of influence in Colorado.

His eyes scanned a landscape designed over a century ago to be a sprawling park. It was where loved ones would come spend the afternoon visiting the dearly departed. It was a place for the living to relax, surrounded by those taking an eternal rest.

South Platte Cemetery was rich in shade trees and fountains and gravel paths winding though the rolling knolls. Some of the paths were for walking along the South Platte River. There were a few miles of paths for carriages. This was how great cemeteries were designed in that day.

There were aging mausoleums buried beneath ivy. The ivy was now brown and dry, hibernating until next spring.

There were monuments bearing the names of families who were famous for founding Denver. There were old soldiers and cannons and flags. A flock of geese grazed nearby.

JC stopped his car in sight of a couple of employees. They were standing near a small backhoe as JC approached.

They'd both been leaning on a gravestone sculpted to look like a tall tree trunk. They were staring at the backhoe when they saw JC coming. They quickly removed their weight from the marker, as though they'd been told not to defile the monuments in that manner.

"Is the ground still soft enough to dig?" JC asked. He was trying to let them know that they weren't in trouble. He didn't care what he caught them leaning against.

"We're going to find out," said one of the cemetery workers. Both the men started snickering. An unexpected sense of humor, JC thought, for men who worked amongst thousands of people who didn't want to be there.

He showed the two men a black-and-white photograph. He asked them if they had ever seen the man in the picture before.

"I don't know," said one of the jovial employees. "Ask around." He waved at the graves in close proximity. The two graveside gagsters were giggling again.

JC acknowledged their humor and quoted the old standup gag, "Gonna be here all night?"

"Hell no," one of the workers retorted. "It's scary here at night." The two men were now in stitches.

They composed themselves and one of the men, with thinning blond hair and wearing a thick dirty jacket, stepped forward. JC handed him the photograph. The man held it in a hand covered with a filthy glove with his fingertips exposed. "Where'd this come from?" he asked.

"From a newspaper," JC told him.

The two workers looked at each other. One scratched his neck. The other said to his colleague, "Isn't that the feller ..." and the man scratching his neck nodded.

"We seen this guy," the man with fingerless gloves told JC. "We seen him going for a jog through here."

"Going for a run?" JC asked.

Both laborers nodded their heads. The man with fingerless gloves became the spokesperson. The other looked on silently. "We see him a bunch. He's in good shape. I've spoke to him before. He says he likes to jog in here because it's peaceful and there's no traffic. It is nice here, for that."

"You're sure this is the guy?" JC repeated.

"We're sure," the spokesperson said as he nodded. "But we haven't seen him in a couple of weeks."

JC looked over the landscape of the cemetery as he digested this news. He knew that he hit his head hard, but the significance of this discovery wasn't lost on him. Then, he searched the pocket of his jacket for another photo and pulled it out.

"You ever seen him?" JC asked the men.

The two workers looked at each other, and then the one with dirty gloves told JC, "Yep. Not as much, but we seen him."

"The two of 'em," the other one, silent up to now, corrected.

JC's eyes widened, "The two of them? You've seen them together?"

"Yep, the one guy, the first one you showed us, he's here a lot," the first one said.

"But the other guy, he's with him sometimes," said the one who more recently had found his voice. "But we haven't seen neither of them in a couple of weeks."

JC looked at the photos again. One was of Troy Davis. The other was a picture of Scott Miller.

10

"You going to report it to your viewers?" Detective Trujillo's face had a serious look. There was a pair of empty shoes on the pavement next to them. They looked like a woman's walking shoes. The shoestrings were still tied.

JC sort of shrugged. "Even if I'm right about the significance of it, I can't report it unless you confirm it, or if you arrest him for a crime." JC paused, waiting for a response from the detective that didn't come.

The wind was picking up. The cold was getting bitter. Both men tightened whatever was fastening their jackets.

"Because If I'm wrong," JC continued, "I'll get sued. I've got to have proof or you have to arrest him. So, I'm not going to report it today, anyway."

JC had to search for Denver Police Detective Steve Trujillo before he found him. District Two Headquarters had told the reporter that the detective was out on a call, an auto-ped.

He found Trujillo at the corner of East 35th Avenue and Colorado Boulevard. A car had hit and killed a pedestrian trying to cross the intersection.

JC had found Trujillo at the spot where the body had been found. Her shoes had been thrown off her feet by the impact with the car.

It was near a golf course. A police accident reconstruction team was piecing together events. They'd closed busy Colorado Boulevard. Traffic was a mess. Trujillo was just wrapping up his responsibilities and said he had time to talk.

"Pretty girl. It's a shame," Trujillo said. He told JC that the victim had been rushed to a nearby hospital, but she was dead on arrival. "Hit-and-run," he told the reporter. "We don't know who she is yet."

JC searched the scene with his eyes and saw that a photographer from his newsroom was already there, spraying down the scene. Police would release what they wanted to release to the news media, shortly. JC stayed focused on Troy Davis.

He informed Trujillo that he had two eyewitnesses who placed Troy Davis in the cemetery going for a run, "Multiple times, mind you. It sounds to me like your snitch was casing the scene before he committed the crime. I think Davis is the guy stealing from cemeteries, at least the expensive stuff."

"Off the record?" Trujillo's eyes were starting to water in the cold wind. But he looked at JC for confirmation that they were about to talk of something that the journalist wouldn't report, yet.

"Sure," JC told him. "Off the record, if that's the only way I can get you to tell me."

"It is, and I think you're right." Trujillo said. He shuffled his feet and looked at the asphalt before continuing. "We're on his trail for these cemetery thefts. He's going to be arrested soon. We're off the record, right? You can't report what I'm about to tell you." Again, the detective looked at JC to see he agreed with the terms. JC reluctantly nodded.

"Here's my problem," Trujillo disclosed. "Right now, I've got a jury considering the verdict for a guy who is guilty of murder. Believe me, he did it. And Davis is the star witness."

JC nodded, aware of what the police department would consider an inconvenience. Trujillo leaned in. "If a member of that jury watches television tonight and sees that the prosecution's best witness is the guy who's robbing all the cemeteries, this murder trial could be lost."

"I thought judges told their juries not to watch news on television while they're on jury duty," JC offered.

"That's exactly what the judge tells the jury," Trujillo confirmed. "They're not sequestered, so the judge just asks them to forego watching the news on TV or reading it in the newspaper."

"So, what's the rub?" JC asked.

"Jurors lie," the detective told him. "Not about the case they're hearing. They take that sacred oath really seriously. But we know for a fact that some jurors just can't resist the temptation to see if their picture is in the news, or to watch coverage about the big story they're in the middle of."

"Could your snitch be lying about that jailhouse confession?" JC asked the detective. "So you guys don't look into what he's doing when he's pretending to be an angel in court?"

"It's happened before," Trujillo admitted, "but I don't think so. Davis has always been a small-time punk. That's why we don't lose any sleep at night, using him as a snitch."

"Well, don't you have to share this with the defense?" JC remembered a law in some states to that effect.

"We haven't arrested him yet," Trujillo smiled. "And when we do arrest him, it will be pretty clear that we didn't make a deal with him. What he thinks he's going to get in return for his testimony is his problem. We're going to arrest him."

"Well, I've got more news," JC looked at Trujillo.

The law officer's face got very serious and he surveyed the scene on the street before turning his eyes toward his police vehicle. With a motion of his hand, he told the reporter to climb into the passenger seat. "It's freezing out here."

Trujillo climbed behind the steering wheel, started the car and turned on the heat. He turned in his seat slightly and gave JC a signal that the journalist had his full attention.

"Davis and Scott Miller have been seen together, more than once," JC said.

"The guy missing up in Larimer County?" the detective asked.

"Yep," JC responded. "What are the odds?"

"Jeepers, you want to work for us?" Trujillo sort of smiled, allowing JC to see that he was impressed with the reporter's efforts. "Who told you that?"

"The same cemetery employees who watched Davis go for a run on the carriage paths," JC disclosed.

The detective reached inside his jacket and pulled out a small notebook. He wrote something on a piece of paper. "A co-conspirator would make it easier for us," he mumbled. Trujillo rubbed his eyes, "That jury had better hurry up."

JC had a visit to make when he left the police department. And he wasn't going to call ahead.

He parked his car on South Broadway a half block from The Faded Fence antique store. He wanted his visit to be a surprise, though he wasn't planning on making it a pleasant one.

"Are you screwing with me?" Those were the first words out of JC's mouth when Eric Crabtree laid eyes on him in his store. JC was visibly agitated, and he thought for a moment that Crabtree considered running in the other direction.

"You said you were going to be here this morning," JC spat. "You blew me off and let me stand around, like an idiot, wasting my time until it was clear that you had blown me off!" The volume of JC's voice was making his own recovering head hurt.

The store owner looked worried. Frightened was a better word. "Look," he said to JC, his voice shaking a little, "I'm sorry. I had to. He said he could kill me!"

JC glared at Crabtree. That was not the answer he'd expected. "What?"

"Well," Crabtree retreated behind a glass display case, out of JC's reach. "He said, precisely, he'd cut my balls off and stuff them in my mouth." JC could see that Crabtree was both scared and sickened. The store owner pleaded, "How would you like that?"

"It's an acquired taste," JC told him without mercy. "Who are we talking about?"

"Davis," the businessman uttered haltingly, "Troy Davis."

"The guy who's bringing you all the artifacts that he is NOT finding in buildings he's NOT demolishing?"

"Look," Crabtree begged. "I'm sorry for lying to you and I'm sorry that I closed the store when I said that I would meet you. He's a scary guy. I'm not up to this."

That was evident. Eric Crabtree may or may not be a lover, but he definitely was no fighter.

"So, you knew this stuff was stolen?" JC accused.

Crabtree rubbed his forehead. He couldn't make eye contact with his accuser. To JC, it was a confession.

The reporter pulled a picture out from his jacket pocket. "You ever see this guy?"

Crabtree looked at the photo of Scott Miller, "No."

JC gave him a disbelieving look. "No, honest," the store owner implored, "I'd tell you if I had. Look, I told the police everything I know." JC shook his head in disgust and headed for the door.

He stopped short of the exit when something caught his eye. "What is this?"

"That just came in," Crabtree told him in a defeated voice. He was sorry that the angry journalist had delayed his departure.

"Who brought it here?" JC asked. "Davis?"

"No," the shopkeeper whined. "I've never seen her before. She said it belonged to her grandmother. She just died."

JC gave Crabtree a look of impatience. "Don't lie to me. The woman: blonde, pretty, 40-ish?" Crabtree nodded his head in the affirmative.

"You got her name?" JC asked.

"No, cash," Crabtree apologized.

"Figures," dismissed JC, as he looked at the granite Civil War soldier.

Sitting in his 4x4, JC thumbed through the options offered by the search engine on his phone. He'd typed "Stolen War Monument."

In response, his eyes were drawn to the third slug from the top. It was a headline from a newspaper on the Western Slope. It read, "Statue Stolen From Soldiers Monument in Town Square."

JC punched an address into his phone's GPS. He had to make another stop. He knew the location, but his focus was diminishing. This would be his last stop, surrendering the remainder of the day to the stamina-depleting effects of a concussion.

He drove north on I-25, turning off at the Loveland exit. He headed for a neighborhood near the mouth of Big Thompson Canyon. He parked his car on a worn street with no sidewalks and knocked on the door of Scott and Lisa Miller's home. There was no answer. He wasn't going to get his questions answered.

Then, he looked over both shoulders and walked to the side of the home. A gate offered a view into Lisa Miller's garden. In the middle of the evergreen bushes, there was a bare spot, where the granite soldier used to stand.

For the entire drive back to Denver, JC thought about the connection between Troy Davis and Scott Miller. It would appear that they were partners in crime, including the cemetery thefts.

It was a lucrative business. It would explain how Scott and Lisa Miller could afford a home near Big Thompson Canyon on the salary of a handyman at four storage locker sites.

JC picked up some tacos on the way home. Using the last of his energy to climb the stairs to his third-floor apartment, he swallowed some ibuprofen and stretched his legs out on a coffee table. He turned on the television. The news was on.

He recognized the drill. A somewhat breathless reporter explained to the audience that she had just run from the courtroom. The jury had reached a verdict in the big murder trial. JC could see other news crews behind her, dashing out the front door of the courthouse to report to their respective organizations.

The reporter on TV brushed hair away from her face and glanced at the notes she'd written on her phone. She reported that the jury had found the defendant guilty. The wind blew her hair back into her face. She brushed it away.

She explained to her audience that the crucial piece of evidence in the trial had been testimony from a small-time thief who was a witness for the prosecution. He'd told the jury that the defendant had confessed to the killing when they shared a jail cell. "It seems," the reporter said, "the jury believed him."

"They're not the first ones to make that mistake," JC said to himself.

11

"**D**ammit!" His kneecap throbbed as it dropped to the hard rock surface beneath his feet.

It wasn't the first time Troy Davis had stumbled under the weight he was bearing. He grabbed at a crack in the rock wall to help pull him uphill. "Have you been sneaking a meal?" he asked his silent partner. The dead man didn't respond.

Davis was frustrated and exhausted. He was strong and he didn't know it would be this difficult.

His old man would have told him, "Keep working," except when he was drunk. And he was drunk a lot. "Nothing works like hard work," Davis remembered that old bastard saying. He must have gotten that off a calendar, he was not that clever.

"This is the thanks I get," Davis grumbled. He climbed the hill with Scott Miller wrapped in a blanket and secured to his back. Davis' work boots slipped on small pebbles underfoot.

It was dark. No one was going to see him from the road below, but it wasn't easy to see where he was going.

Over the knoll, he could use his light to find the cleft of rock. Miller's body had rested, for just over a week, on a grassy outcrop. It was close to the road but unseen from Highway 34. Now it was time for a proper burial, Davis thought.

Finally carrying his payload over the knoll, Davis unbuckled the belts he'd used to secure his cargo and dropped it onto the rocky soil. He placed his light on its own perch and aimed it at a slim cavern he'd picked out. "Alright, Scotty," Davis panted as he paused to catch his breath, "let's see if we can't make your new house a home."

Davis' pickup truck was parked off the road below, but no one would think twice about it. Even if it was possible to see his light, this was what mountain life was about. Folks do what they want, when they want. Rules are for city folk. Mountain folk do what needs to be done.

When Troy was honest with himself, he'd admit that it was his own fault. He'd left the body, intending to come back to dispose of it sooner.

But where? He wasn't comfortable spending so much time with the pesky police. They always asked where he'd be. They'd pinned their hopes on his testimony in that murder trial. He smiled at that. They'd owe him for that, he thought.

Troy knew that it was only a matter of time before hikers or hunters found the corpse. He thought about just leaving it there on the ledge. But he began to worry that he had left evidence at the spot. He'd disposed of the gun. But maybe he'd overlooked something that could be traced back to him. It was better to hide the body.

He had combed over that rocky hillside. Finally, He had found a fitting burial site for his friend. But now that it was time to execute his plan, Davis was irritable. It was dark and the work was hard.

"This is the thanks I get," he barked as he patrolled the ground for rocks. He wanted them no bigger than a watermelon and no smaller than a grapefruit. "I went out of my way to make that a special day for you," he grumbled.

"Did I get your favorite meal? How many people even give a damn that lobster is your favorite meal?" Davis was starting to shout at his dead friend now. "We came to your favorite spot. You got to spend the day with your dad! I didn't have to do any of this! I did it because I care!"

Davis was only making himself angrier. "And you made more money than you knew what to do with! Could you have bought that house with the money you make? Or get a nice piece of ass like Lisa?"

"I did that for you," Davis yelled, as he dragged the corpse into the hole in the rock. Davis' shoulders would not allow him any further into the rocky gap, so he sat down and used his feet to push Miller's stiff body into the cleft.

He'd met Scott Miller when Davis was renting a storage locker to hide some of his ill-gotten gains. He couldn't budge a big sculpture. Adrenaline must have allowed him to get it into the back of his truck, when he liberated it from a cemetery.

But he asked Miller if he'd lend a hand when trying to move it into the storage locker. Miller was happy to accommodate him. They had a conversation and seemed to have good chemistry.

Davis asked Scott if he wanted to make some extra money. It was only going to be a temporary thing. Scott was a straight arrow, and he had a new wife. Troy asked Scott just to help him on a job or two. But two jobs became three, and then four. Scott liked the money, and then he became accustomed to it.

"We were as thick as thieves," Troy laughed as he began to place rocks at the opening of the hole in the rock.

"It was fun," Davis chatted, as though Scott Miller were standing next to him instead of peering with lifeless eyes from a dark chasm.

"You took to it nicely," Davis told his partner. "Seeing you rock that soldier loose. You nearly destroyed it!" Davis was laughing now, remembering the good times.

"You wanted that thing for your wife in the worst way." He laughed some more.

The rocks were piled. The cavity was closed. Troy had gotten the idea from the Ute Indians. He'd read that they used to place the bodies of their dead in clefts and caves. He remembered that the women would chant outside the resting place.

He tried to come up with something. "Oh, Great Warrior in the sky," he chanted, "please accept my brother into your kingdom of the afterlife." That wasn't so bad, Davis thought.

Troy sat down to catch his breath. He started thinking about his new line of work. He needed a new plan. Trujillo had been asking about him at antique stores.

The new plan would be hatched, for the first time, tomorrow night. "No room for you, though, Scotty. This will be a one-man job."

It was cold, now that the sun was down. Steam was rising off the sweat on Troy's skin. He looked up at the dark sky and the bright stars. He loved this canyon. Scott had taught him to love it, Troy thought.

"The problem was," Troy told his friend who was now meeting the Great Warrior, "you would have turned on me. Don't try to deny it. Once the cops picked you up, you'd have spilled your guts.

"I don't argue that you wouldn't try to hold out for a while. You'd try to be loyal to me," Davis said to his companion. "But the thought of leaving that beautiful wife for prison? You would have rolled over on me, pal. I know it. I don't even blame you. I just couldn't let you do it."

"I will never go to prison again," Davis snarled. "I'll die first."

They were only about a quarter mile from where Scott's dad used to have a little cabin. It was washed away in the flood. So was Scott's dad. It was a special place.

That's why Troy had brought his friend here. They ate lobster on the bank of the river that day. The lobster was on sale for five dollars a pound.

Troy thought, "It was a nicer picnic than I bring for my women." The two friends spent the afternoon drinking beer, sitting in the autumn sun and jumping into the very cold water of the Big Thompson River. They shivered when they climbed out of the water and laughed at themselves. They laughed at stories from their capers.

They built a little campfire and warmed up. It was a great day. "This is perfect," Scott had told Troy as he stared into the flames, unknowing. Davis was glad he'd provided such a special day for his friend.

He stood behind him and pulled a handgun out of a folded sweatshirt he'd brought from the truck. Scott continued to stare at the fire as he said, "Really, thanks for everything, man."

The sound of the gunshot, to the back of Miller's head, echoed off the canyon walls. No one within earshot would think twice. Up here, folks do what they want, when they want. Mountain folk do what needs to be done.

12

Police were dragging their feet with precision. After they got a conviction in the big murder trial, they quietly issued an arrest warrant for their star witness, Troy Davis. It was the Wednesday night before Thanksgiving.

The police brass had their news conference Tuesday night, crowing about the big trial, before reporters would begin to ask about their snitch.

Now that the murder trial was over, police could do the right thing and go after Davis. But by issuing the arrest warrant on the night before Thanksgiving, police hoped it would go unnoticed by newsrooms working with a skeletal staff.

There would be no press release from police about the arrest warrant, though the paperwork would be in the public file. But most journalists would be taking a four-day weekend and court offices would be closed until Monday.

Police were prepared to charge Davis with the cemetery thefts, maybe two hundred thousand dollars' worth. "At least they can't say we cut him a deal," one prosecutor said. "We're going after him."

The trouble was, police couldn't find him. They searched for Scott Miller, too. They couldn't find him either. Detective Trujillo figured they'd taken off together, despite Lisa Miller's denials.

Efforts by police headquarters to bury the "arrest warrant story" for a few days didn't entirely work. JC broke the story on television Wednesday night, saying police were looking for Davis.

JC showed viewers an old mugshot of Troy Davis. The story also reported that police had a "BOLO" for Scott Miller as a "person of interest." JC told his audience that BOLO was police slang for "Be On the Look Out."

He also told his audience that it was unclear if Miller was involved in the burial-ground burglaries, but he'd been seen with Troy Davis.

Lisa Miller had phoned JC after the broadcast, saying Scott had nothing to do with Davis' criminal activity.

JC had no proof to the contrary, just a hunch. Lisa admitted to the reporter that she'd met Troy, in Scott's company. However, she said she never liked Davis. She didn't trust him. She'd told Scott to stay away from him.

Davis was presently four hours away from the corpse of Scott Miller. Davis had driven west all night. He rented a room in Glenwood Springs.

In a matter of hours, he would drive past the steam rising from the hot geothermal water. He would turn south at Grand Junction and continue to his destination on Route 50.

There's a lot of open land along Colorado Route 50. Anyone traveling between Grand Junction and Montrose might see wild antelope. There was plenty of room for fly fishing and hunting, too. Scenes from classic Western films like "True Grit" and "How the West Was Won" were shot there.

The towns along Route 50 are small, but they are proud. Their high school football rivalries can be fierce. They also like to display their pride in small, interesting museums.

That's what caught Troy Davis' eye. Cemeteries had proven to be a good living, but Trujillo was on his trail.

Troy believed Trujillo was about to run into a wall, a dead end. What proof did the detective have that Troy had stolen anything? He certainly didn't have a good witness, only a jumpy antiques store owner who would shut his trap when faced with confessing to fencing stolen goods.

Crabtree would probably blame a bad memory, Troy thought. He did all the deals in cash. Crabtree would say that he can't be sure who he bought that stuff from. Everybody looks alike. Still, Troy needed a new angle.

A small museum, dedicated to the old days on the Western Slope, was reaping the benefits of a big effort. The collection on display for tourists and town folk included old gold and silver fishing trophies. There were also antique belt buckles given to some famous rodeo riders. Troy surmised that some of those were gold, too. There were even antique trophies from county fairs and horse races.

Troy didn't like to brag, but he was more worldly than people realized. He'd been to Europe. That's when he realized what a bonanza there could be selling authentic Old West collectables from the United States. And once he found his way around the global market, he could even sell in Asia.

This would be a test. He'd steal enough from that little museum to be considered a solid pay day, but not enough to merit too much attention. He had a buyer and he had a plan to get the materials out of the country. He'd use small airports without the money for more than barely adequate abilities to snoop around in the boxes he shipped.

These small museums, Troy thought, are a treasure. The staff really does work hard to bring some big-city culture to their tiny towns. But they don't have the money to pay for big-city security systems.

Troy had visited a handful of these museums. He saw the impressive artifacts they had, and the less-than-impressive methods they employed to protect their valuables. "I love culture," he said, laughing to himself.

The museum in this particular town was protected by a burglar alarm. It would make a lot of noise and he assumed it was connected to the police department. It was a shame to wake up the officer on duty overnight, especially early Thanksgiving morning. But Troy estimated it would take said officer five minutes to get to the scene of the crime, let alone summon backup.

That would be a very lucrative five minutes, and he didn't need all five.

Troy wouldn't employ anything particularly sophisticated. He'd mimic an old-fashioned "smash-and-grab" like the liquor-store burglaries he'd hatched when he was a kid.

He'd cave in a window and give himself three minutes. He knew where the most valuable items were. He'd cased the building. It was a small museum, so there wasn't a lot of ground to cover.

He would be careful not to drive away using the same path as the police car responding to the scene. He would be out of town without anyone laying eyes on him.

The police officer, by the way, probably would assume the alarm was a mistake, seeing that no real crime ever occurred in their little community. Police might take seven minutes to get there. But Troy only needed three, and he would be gone.

Now, he was sitting in his bed in Glenwood Springs, going over his plan. He'd paid cash for a room, under the radar and with no credit check.

Glenwood Springs was a crossroads to Utah, Aspen and Denver. A lot of truck drivers stopped there to rest. Tourists came to soak in the hot springs or passed through to go skiing. Troy wouldn't stand out in the crowd.

Rocky approached JC at his desk and told the reporter, "The news director wants to speak with you." JC mocked fear, grabbed his tie and rose it above his head as though he was being executed by hanging.

"No, nothing like that," Rocky told him as he snickered. "Actually, I think you'll like it."

JC entered the office of the news director, Pat Perilla. He was a little overweight so his name left him susceptible to nicknames like "Fat Gorilla," but JC liked him.

He thought Pat had probably endured those nicknames growing up. He most certainly did in the newsroom. Kids can be counted on to be cruel. Some journalists just can't pass up a good piece of wordplay.

"Our audience loves the story about Senator Buford," the news director told JC.

"Great story," his reporter answered. Rocky sat in the chair next to him.

"Would you accomplish anything by flying to Albany?" the news director asked.

JC listed the certain accomplishments from such an assignment. "I'd get to stay in a great hotel room and eat a lot of food while billing it to the company," JC jested.

"Seriously," Perilla said.

"Let's see," JC thought out loud and more seriously. "I could interview Buford's sister, I'd love to do that. And Lucy Buford is now eighteen, I think. She's an adult. I could try to talk to her. I think the state police would talk. They'd like to get people out here looking for Buford. Plus, you have the great setting. The state capitol where Buford was a big deal is a stunning backdrop. And since legislators in New York never get voted out of office, we could find lots of his old colleagues to talk to."

"That sounds like we'd get our money's worth," the news director decided. "How about leaving early Monday? You can do live shots that evening. Rocky, can you book the flights, set up whatever JC needs?"

The assignment editor said that he could. JC said he'd provide Rocky with the names and information he needed.

"OK, we'll set up live shots with our local network affiliate," the news director said, adjourning the meeting. "Two days on the ground enough time?"

"Yeah," answered JC. "It should be if Rocky and I can get everything set up. Thanks, Rocky."

JC walked back to his desk in the newsroom. Tomorrow was Thanksgiving. Most offices would be closed Friday, too. He'd be working, but most newsmakers wouldn't be. That meant JC would either be reporting on a tragic house fire or be sent to a church providing Thanksgiving dinner for the homeless. He was rooting for the church dinner. This was a lousy time of year to see your home go up in flames.

He sat at his desk, trying to tie up some loose ends. There were new emails, but nothing of particular interest.

There was an invitation to speak to school children about his exciting life as a journalist. He gave the teacher a quick call and said he'd try to work out a day convenient to both of them.

He'd also received a phone call from upstairs. The general manager's office wanted him to sign the legal form sent from corporate. It had been sitting on his desk for an undue amount of time. He signed and walked it upstairs.

Friday morning, a new email appeared on JC's laptop. It was from a TV anchor he knew in Grand Junction. They'd raced together at a ski area on the Grand Mesa called Powderhorn. The journalist's name was Peter Post.

The email was brief. He said, "Knowing your interest in history, I thought you'd like to know that a museum on the Western Slope was robbed yesterday morning. A lot of old trophies and collectables," the email said. "I was surprised when the sheriff told us how much it was worth, like $60K."

13

"Hey, I'm getting on a plane."

"Oh! You're coming to see me?"

JC was at the airport in Denver, getting ready to fly. He tried to hear Shara's voice over the noise.

There were TV sets blaring a national news broadcast and there were conversations going on in the seats on both sides of him.

There was a mix of static and English coming from the airport's public-address system. Funny, he thought, you can always understand what those speakers are saying except when you're trying to.

"Mmm, I'm flying to Albany."

"You realize," Shara asked JC, "that's further away from me, right?"

"Yeah, sorry," he replied. "Wanna join me?"

"I can't. We're getting set up for the start of ski season, this weekend. How are you feeling?"

"A lot better," he told her. "My ribs aren't so sore. And my head isn't so foggy. I wouldn't trust myself operating heavy equipment, but I can remember what you look like naked." He smiled into the phone.

"Well, that's all you're going to get. Take care of yourself. I'm sorry you're not coming to see me."

"Sorry, Babe." He pressed the red button on his phone, disconnecting. He wondered how long he could stay away from Montana before his relationship was disconnected.

He read over notes and conversed with Milt, his news photographer, during the flight. He had a book to read, a murder mystery by a Scottish author he liked. JC thought that was probably his favorite thing about flying, a chance to read without interruptions.

He had worked on Thanksgiving Day, as scheduled. It was a light news day, as holidays usually are. There were no fires or gun violence to report. So, JC visited the home of a man having his 100th birthday.

The man was quite bright and had great stories to tell. The best one was about the day he went sailing with the most famous scientist in the world, Albert Einstein. The old gentleman was living in Princeton, New Jersey, just after World War ll. He was selling a sailboat and had placed an ad in the newspaper.

"There was a knocking at the door of my home," the man told JC. "I opened it and standing there was Albert Einstein!

"'I understand that you're selling a sailboat,' Mr. Einstein said with a German accent.

"'Yes,' I told him.

"'Well, let's go!'

"'Where?' I asked him.

"'Sailing,' said Einstein. 'I can't buy a boat without learning if it floats.' So, I spent the afternoon sailing with Albert Einstein," the man told JC.

JC didn't have any family in Denver, so because he worked on Thanksgiving, someone else got to spend the day with their family. JC was more than fine with that.

Milt nudged JC awake, book lying on his lap, as the intercom told them, "Please put your trays up and return your seat to its upright position. In just a few minutes, we'll be landing in Albany, the state capital of New York. Currently, it's thirty-seven degrees in Albany."

JC looked out the plane's window. There was an intersection of two rivers below. That would be the Hudson and Mohawk Rivers, he remembered. There was a lot more water than he saw out the window when the plane took off from Denver.

There were a number of towers, closely configured and jutting above the rest of the city skyline. It was part of the state capitol complex.

JC told Milt that it was strange to be coming "home" to Albany. He grew up just forty-five minutes north of the airport. However, both of his parents had passed away and his siblings had also left the area. JC hoped to touch base with some high school friends.

Walking out of the airport terminal to pick up their rental car, JC noted that thirty-seven degrees in Albany did not feel like thirty-seven degrees in Denver. The humidity in the Capital Region made everything feel colder.

Albany is one of the oldest cities in the country. Franklin and Teddy Roosevelt were both governors there before ascending to the White House.

Albany was presently attracting tourists who wanted to see the colonial home where Alexander Hamilton courted his wife, Elizabeth Schuyler.

Their passion was reignited, two hundred and forty years after their marriage, by the musical about them on Broadway.

The East Coast time zone worked in JC and Milt's favor. There was still time to get work done and broadcast live back to Denver that night. Because of that difference in the time zone, they wouldn't broadcast until 7 p.m. in Albany. They had plenty of time.

Once inside their rental car, JC turned to Milt and said, "It's Monday, legislators at the Capitol don't return from their home districts until mid-day. We can go there and get our beauty shots out of the way and shoot a standup. But on the way, let's roll the dice."

"OK," agreed Milt.

JC guided Milt, who was driving, to a tree-lined boulevard occupied on both sides by big homes. They pulled up in front of a brick, three-story house. It had a large yard on the side and a good stretch of lawn between the house and the street. JC guessed the home was built just after the Civil War.

There was still a stone "carriage step" on the driveway-side of the porch. The garage in back looked as though it used to be a carriage house.

There was a dusting of snow on the grass. In the front yard, the property line on each side of the house was lined by arborvitae hedges.

JC knocked on the door. Milt had left his camera equipment in the car. It was going to take some convincing to get the homeowner to allow Milt to shoot video inside the house. First, JC knew they had to win the homeowner's confidence.

A man in his fifties opened the door. "Hello," he said, in an exploring tone of voice.

"Hi, Mr. Ryan, I feel lucky that we caught you at home. I'm sorry we didn't phone ahead, we just got off a plane," JC explained.

The man had a wary look on his eyes. He wore glasses and his hair was graying. But he was fit and seemed to have a natural smile.

JC introduced themselves and described the story that brought them to town. "Oh, I remember," Terry Ryan said, in a tone disclosing that he'd never forget what happened in the structure's prior life.

"This house sat empty for three years, I only bought it a year ago," Ryan told them. "Not many people are comfortable with the thought that their home was the scene of a notorious murder."

"But you're OK with it?" JC asked. "Not afraid of ghosts?"

"No," Ryan snickered a little. "It helped drop the price. If there were ghosts, I'd shake their hand for helping me save a good deal of money."

Ryan allowed JC and Milt to enter the house. He gave them a tour, including a "Here it is," when they entered the living room where Fiona Buford met her fate, and the closet where she was discovered.

JC and Milt were led into the basement. Concrete floor, stone walls and an old boiler.

In the work room, there were skis screwed into the overhead beams and the thick wooden posts holding up the ceiling.

"Yeah," Ryan smiled. "They were already here. Senator Buford put them there. I'm told he was a big skier. They're kind of neat, so I left them there."

JC perused the collection of old skis mounted on the beams. There were old Kastles, some Head 360s, Rossignol Stratos and Olin Mark 1s. "Quite a collection," JC remarked.

"There were more in the boiler room, just leaning against the wall," the current occupant informed JC. "I took some and made an Adirondack chair out of them. It's out in the yard."

"You could open a museum down here," JC joked. Ryan nodded in agreement. The reporter asked if Milt could bring his camera in and shoot some news footage."

The homeowner expressed reluctance, which JC preferred to think of as indecision. "You could stand right next to me. If there's something you don't want to show, we won't shoot it," JC assured him.

"This is going to be shown in Denver?" Ryan inquired.

"Yep, that's our plan," JC told him.

"I suppose that would be OK," the property owner concluded. "Folks here would probably never see it, right? It might look like I'm seeking attention, which I'm not."

"I can never make a promise like that," JC told him, "but this is being shot for our TV station in Denver. Our network affiliate in Albany could see that we're doing a story and want to run it one night, or they may not. Either way, you'll be standing with us when we shoot it. We're not going to do anything like the tabloid shows. No shaky zoom into the closet as scary music is being played in the background."

Terry Ryan gave his permission. "Did you know him?" JC asked as Milt was retrieving his equipment and setting up.

"Buford?" asked Ryan. "No. I knew who he was, of course, but we'd never met."

Ryan's hospitality reminded JC that most people in the Capital Region are nice, polite, and unafraid. The majority of the world's population believes all of New York State is hidden beneath skyscrapers. They think all New York residents walk the sidewalks nervous to make eye contact with each other.

But Upstate New York, JC would tell them, wasn't unlike Colorado. The mountains aren't as tall, because they are older and eroding.

The Adirondacks and Catskills are great places to enjoy the outdoors. The trees are thick and green. There is water everywhere. Colorado would like to borrow some of that water, he thought.

When JC and Milt finished their work, they departed the former home of Senator John Buford. They headed toward the Hudson River for the state Capitol building.

Milt had time to shoot footage of the impressive landmark. JC thought that it was the prettiest Capitol in the country. It was almost 150 years old, decorated with carvings of buffalo, wildcats, birds and the faces of people who lived in Albany in the 1870s.

JC had learned, on a field trip to the Capitol when he was in school, that the Italian and Irish craftsmen who carved faces into the stonework had run out of famous New Yorkers to portray.

Then, they carved the faces of their family members into the stone. And some clever craftsmen would meet girls and bring them to the Capitol to pose for the carvings. Their faces would be immortal.

"You could have knocked me over with a feather," one state legislator told JC as the camera was running. "John? I never would have thought he could do something like that. The police say they're convinced that he did it, so I guess he did it."

Another state lawmaker told Milt's camera, "We've had no shortage of scandals involving state legislators over the years, but Buford being accused of murder probably tops them all. Crazy."

After more interviews displaying similar shock at Senator Buford's crime, many of the goals JC and Milt had established for the day had been achieved.

JC stood in front of the east side of the state Capitol in Albany and went "live," reporting back to his evening news audience in Denver. He stood next to a huge monument of General Philip Sheridan, a Civil War hero who grew up in Albany.

People in Albany were still fascinated by the Buford story. People in Colorado, still becoming acquainted with it, were eager to hear more. JC was able to show them video of the scene of the crime. And they heard from fellow senators who were as shocked as anyone.

The trip to New York was a good investment for JC's TV station. News content was harder to find as the holidays approached. This story was a beaut.

Tomorrow, JC hoped to find even better material than he'd collected today. But tonight, he had dinner plans with old friends from high school.

Milt had a sister in the Albany area, so he made plans to spend the evening with her. The team would meet again for breakfast at their hotel, The Renaissance, across from the Capitol.

The Albany area saw the arrival of its first European settlers in the 1600s. Old murals of the city's four-century history are painted on the ceiling above the lobby of The Renaissance Hotel.

JC was picked up at the hotel by an old high school friend named Davey Kay. They had played football together.

Davey pointed the car east for Massachusetts' Berkshire Mountains and a seventy-five-year-old ski resort called Jiminy Peak.

"Does Jiminy still have the big college ski race each year?" JC asked.

"Oh yeah," Davey confirmed. "The Williams College Winter Carnival."

"You still teaching at Jiminy with Stride?" JC inquired.

"Yep," Davey said. "I'll be there tomorrow."

Stride is a program that teaches children with disabilities and wounded war vets how to ski and snowboard.

In a restaurant at a slopeside inn at Jiminy Peak, JC and Davey Kay met with other high school friends. They routinely took this day off to ski together.

The group had just come off the mountain. They were still wearing nylon bib overalls and heavy sweaters. Their faces were flushed from exertion. Their hair had been pasted to their skulls by their helmets.

The old high school classmates ate dinner and drank toasts to each other and their memories.

They recalled embarrassing stories about each other and embellished the worst of it at the expense of a selected victim sitting at the table.

"Are you going skiing with us tomorrow, dude?" one of JC's friends asked.

"I've got work to do," JC answered. "I didn't fly here to give your wife a day off. It's her fault she married you, not mine." JC and the rest laughed.

"How about the day after?" Davey persisted. "It'll be dust and crust. Do you remember how to ski it, or do you just cruise on that Colorado carpet now?"

JC grinned, recollecting the East's sometimes intimidating blend of ice covered by a fresh layer of snow. But modern grooming now made it fast and cut to carve.

Pressure continued on JC to ski before departing.

"Come on man, we'll find some hooters in booters," said an unmarried colleague who thought that would add to the offer.

"No wonder you're single," JC responded. "Does anything come out of that mouth of yours that actually works with women?" Everyone laughed.

The begging didn't stop. As old friends could do, they began to heap on guilt.

"Maybe we're confusing him for someone else," one of his other companions said. "I thought I was invited to dinner to see someone who really used to know how to ski. Maybe I was thinking of another guy." JC rolled his eyes.

"OK, OK. Tell you what," JC offered. "If Milt and I get what we want tomorrow, we're supposed to be done and fly back to Denver. If I can, I'll delay my flight by a day. I'll tell the news director that I've got to see a sick friend."

JC scanned the faces of his old buddies and said, "You truly are as sick a bunch as I've seen in a long time. Anyway, if I can get away with it, I'll stay another day and we'll go skiing."

Dinner was over. Davey drove JC back to his hotel where they had one more drink in the bar at The Renaissance and then called it a night. Tomorrow would determine if the reporter really got what he came for.

14

"I used to work in your business," the man told JC and Milt as they sat at their table having breakfast.

The man, sitting at the table next to the pair, had started up a conversation and turned out to be another state legislator. He said that he knew John Buford, too. "I thought he'd be our next Senate leader. You never know, do you?"

"Tell me this," JC asked the senator. "If Senator Buford had to get out of town, fast ... If he told someone it had to remain a secret, could he find someone to do it?"

The balding politician pursed his lips. "Without a doubt. Mind you, the senator would be asking someone who didn't know that John had just killed his wife, unless John told him."

Then the senator sort of shook his head and said, "There were so many people in this town that would punch their next-door neighbor if they thought it meant Buford would owe them a favor. That's the kind of influence John had."

The senator surveyed the room. "Look at this restaurant. It's full, and three quarters of them are lobbyists or people coming to the Capitol to get something they want. John could have asked anyone in this room to quietly get him out of town. They'd be fighting each other to win the privilege."

"Would you say that on camera?" JC asked the senator. Milt looked on with interest.

The senator waved his hand at JC. "No, some voters wouldn't like me talking this way. It's all true, and you can use it. Just don't use my name, OK?"

JC expected that answer. He'd paraphrase the senator's insights during the live shot that night.

"So, you said you were in our business," JC noted, to end the conversation in a friendly way. "You were a journalist?"

The senator laughed and pulled his seat a few inches closer to JC and Milt. Now he could do what politicians love to do, make new friends and tell stories about themselves. "Not exactly," he said with a smile.

"I worked for a big cable TV franchise, when cable first came to my town. They served a big area and had a big warehouse full of movies on video." The senator paused to let his audience envision this.

"So, I worked in the warehouse. It had smooth concrete floors. I was given a pair of roller skates and told by my boss, 'Learn how to use these.' It was my job, when a customer called to order a movie, for me to roller skate as fast as I could through the warehouse, find the movie and then roller skate back to a guy at a desk. He would take the video from me and slap it into a tape player. That's how you got to see the movie in your own home!" The senator was laughing now. So were JC and Milt.

"Really?" JC asked.

"Hand to God," the senator answered.

JC and Milt paid for their meal and headed for a neighborhood called the Pine Hills in Albany. Beverly Pruyn opened the door of the house and invited them in.

"It's pronounced 'pry-n,' like 'pine,' right?" Milt asked. "We don't have that name out in Colorado."

"It's Dutch," she responded. "It's not unusual around here, but of course, the Dutch didn't get out to the Rocky Mountains. The explorer, Henry Hudson, looked for a river that might take him there, but he didn't find it."

JC was familiar with the name, having grown up nearby, but Milt was born and raised in Colorado.

"It was quite a distinguished name here," Mrs. Pruyn told Milt. "My husband is a distant relative, but the riches were spent long ago. We didn't get any of that," she smiled.

They sat in the living room. There was lots of polished dark wood, the molding around the entryways, the built-in bookshelves and display cases with glass doors. JC guessed that the wallpaper was new but patterned after something old. The house, he supposed, was built in the late 1800s.

Milt set up his tripod and camera and placed a lapel microphone on the woman's blouse.

JC explained that he'd ask her some of the questions that she had already answered over the phone when he'd called from Denver. "This time, we'll have them on camera," he explained. "And then I'll ask you some new questions."

Beverly Pruyn began to look nervous. JC saw that and tried to assure her. "Beverly, you're not guilty of anything.

We're not going to accuse you of anything. If there's ever a question I ask and you don't know that answer, it's OK to tell me that you don't know that answer." She looked a little relieved.

"I don't allow criminals that luxury," JC smiled at her, "and I don't let politicians get off that easy. But you're not asking voters to trust you and you didn't commit a crime. K?"

She smiled. As the interview unfolded, JC thought it demonstrated that Beverly Pruyn loved Lucy Buford and worked hard to allow the child a normal upbringing.

"It was difficult sometimes, in the beginning," Beverly said. "Lucy's taste in music grew dark. Her grades began to drop. She was a smart girl, but her schoolwork no longer reflected that.

"She stopped playing sports, too," Mrs. Pruyn continued. "She quit the basketball and lacrosse teams at high school, when she used to love to do that."

Beverly then described how life improved for Lucy. Over time, she grew more comfortable in the Pruyn household. She was no stranger to them, and her spirits eventually rebounded. She started playing sports again and her grades rose.

"Except," Beverly paused, "except that she really missed her father. She'd be going along fine, and then something would happen to remind her of her father, like skiing. Especially skiing."

"When you were growing up," JC asked Beverly, "what sort of brother was John?"

"Oh," Beverly smiled, "he was my older brother, in every way. He made sure I was OK, you know? If someone was giving me trouble at school, John would pull them aside. The trouble ended."

"Would John fight them? Give them a good licking?"

"You know," Beverly answered, "I don't remember ever hearing that John fought anyone. He could have, he was a good athlete and strong. But I think he had a way with people. They respected him. But yes, I think he convinced people that being mean to me would bring consequences."

JC asked, "Did Lucy ever express that she missed her mother?"

Beverly Pruyn looked at JC and said nothing. JC believed that she was thinking about what she should say. Then, her eyes dropped to look at her hands that were folded in her lap. "No," she said, "never."

JC thought something else was on Mrs. Pruyn's mind. He was getting the feeling that this interview meant more to her than just a courtesy extended to the journalists.

She knew what they wanted. JC could sense that, and this interview was Beverly's way of determining whether they'd get what they were looking for.

Mrs. Pruyn looked up from her hands and asked, "Would you like to speak with Lucy?"

JC was surprised. Milt was staring at him with big eyes. It was what they were hoping for. JC had been looking for a diplomatic moment to submit his request. Lucy had just turned eighteen. He knew she had the legal authority to make a decision for herself, but the Pruyn's were still going to protect her. There would be no going around them.

"She'd like to," Beverly told JC. Mrs. Pruyn informed JC that she and Lucy had already had the conversation. When Lucy was informed by Beverly and Stan Pruyn that the news crew would be coming to their house, Lucy told her parents that she wanted to speak on camera.

JC now understood that his day at the Pruyn house, so far, had been an audition. Beverly Pruyn would decide if JC and Lucy both got what they desired.

"Lucy?" Mrs. Pruyn called without getting out of her chair. And through the doorway of the living room walked an eighteen-year-old woman with a shy smile on her face.

Lucy Buford took small steps into the room. JC rose from his chair and extended his hand. The teenager accepted it, with a slightly wider smile, and said, "How do you do?"

Mrs. Pruyn stood, to give Lucy her chair. Milt quickly freed her lapel microphone and reached for another chair. He walked it over for Beverly Pruyn to sit, not far from her nervous niece.

JC waved Lucy over to the chair in front of the camera. She had a pretty face, but it also reflected sadness. She had brown, shoulder-length hair that was pulled back. She wore a dress that reflected the fashion sense of high school girls of the day.

Milt fastened the microphone on her blouse. JC studied Lucy's pale complexion. He wasn't sure that she was wearing any makeup at all.

He made a little small talk before the camera was rolling. He said, "I understand you've skied out in my neck of the woods. Snow Hat?"

"Yes!" the eighteen-year-old said back to him, her eyes brightening. "I have been there with my father three or four times. I love it there."

JC also disclosed to her that he had gone to high school not far from Albany. They spoke of high school rivalries. That kind of thing doesn't change in fifteen or twenty years.

"Are you ready?" JC asked Lucy.

Lucy nodded her head and gave him a nervous little smile.

JC's interview began with the basics, like what Lucy remembered about the night she last saw her father. The reporter asked the young woman if she had seen her father since that night. Lucy said that she had not.

JC asked, "Do you miss your father?"

"Desperately," Lucy responded.

"Do you wish you could see him?" JC asked.

"More than anything in the world," she said.

"Do you know where he is?" Lucy was asked.

"No," she said quietly.

"Have you ever spoken with him, since that night?"

"No."

JC paused and asked, "Do you miss your mother?"

"Not really," Lucy said as she broke her eye contact. "I mean, that sounds terrible, but you weren't there. I mean, she was nice at first, but then she changed. I became very unhappy."

"Did your father, John Buford, protect you?" JC asked.

Lucy nodded her head to indicate that he had, "Yes," she said. JC thought that she looked like she was having a memory, perhaps of a happy time with her father. She was smiling.

"Do you question," JC asked, "whether your father took your mother's life?"

Lucy looked at him silently and blinked her eyes. He could tell that she was considering the possibilities of her answer.

"I don't know," she finally said.

"You didn't see anything?" JC asked.

"No, I was outside," Lucy told him.

"Can you think of a reason your father would want to kill your mother?" JC asked.

Beverly Pruyn rose slightly from her seat. "I don't think ..." Mrs. Pruyn began to interject.

But Lucy interrupted her, "It's alright, Mom." JC noted who Lucy wanted to call mom.

The young woman remained silent, forming her thoughts in her mind before they passed her lips. She's smart, JC thought.

"He protected me," Lucy finally said of her father. "He would do anything for me. I truly believe that. He would sacrifice his own life, if he thought he could keep me safe."

Her face showed that she was describing someone she loved, unconditionally. Her eyes, JC thought, were pleading with him to believe her, to help her.

He caught himself, just before uttering the assurance that he wanted to utter: "I do believe you."

The interview wrapped up. JC and Milt had what they'd flown nearly two thousand miles for.

"It's the first time I've ever done that," a relieved Lucy told JC as Milt unclipped her microphone.

"You've never done a television interview before?" JC asked.

"No," Lucy said as she looked at Beverly. Mrs. Pruyn was also shaking her head to indicate "no."

"We never thought it was in her best interests," Mrs. Pruyn told JC. "Why did she need to be part of the sideshow? She hadn't done anything wrong."

Then, Mrs. Pruyn looked at Lucy. "I'm sorry dear, were we wrong?"

"No," Lucy jumped to her defense. "I wasn't ready for that. Now, I'm ready."

Milt was wrapping up his gear and JC made more small talk. "Any plans to come back to Snow Hat?"

"Yes!" Lucy became animated. "I'm going out there with some friends. We'll be there for a week in early January." She smiled and bounced a little with anticipation.

"I've already skied there once this year," JC shared with her. He did not share details of the crash ending his day. "You'll be glad to get back there, I'd imagine."

"I'll be in heaven," she smiled at him.

15

"What do you want?" she asked.

"I want to rid the world of death," JC responded.

"So, how's that going?" she asked.

"I'm off to a slow start," he confessed.

Shara was lying naked across JC's bare chest. She'd picked him up at the airport, when his flight from Albany landed in Denver. It was a surprise. His heart raced when he spotted her red hair and beautiful athletic build. She was waiting for him on the other side of the security gate.

"The weather warmed up," she told him. "The mountain isn't opening for skiers for another week. Kit's there to receive shipments."

JC knew Kit, the head bartender at Shara's restaurant in Montana. The delay in the arrival of the season's first skiers to Grizzly Mountain meant that Shara could make a quick visit to see JC in Denver.

"Thanks for coming," JC whispered as he kissed her again. She traced the lines of his healing ribs. Her fingers found one that stuck out more than the others, "You have to take better care of yourself."

"I like to learn from my own lumps," he said with a smirk.

"Then you must be very smart," she whispered, and kissed him.

They laid together in silence for a while, happy just to be in each other's arms. Then she said, "And now you're after another dangerous man?"

"Technically, police are after another dangerous man," JC told her. "I just get to watch."

"Since when," she asked, "did you just watch?" The expression on his face awarded her that point.

"Well," he rationalized, "If I die young, I'll look fabulous in all the statues they'll erect of me." JC smiled. He thought that was funny. Shara didn't.

"And I don't think he'd hurt me," JC said as he stroked her hair. "I'm friends with his daughter."

JC explained to Shara that he didn't think Buford was a danger to anyone on the street.

"He killed his wife!" Shara exclaimed. "That doesn't make him a nice man."

JC couldn't refute that. "He killed his wife, but I don't think he'd kill anyone else. I honestly think he killed his wife to protect his daughter. Twisted, huh? But Lucy believes that, too."

The journalist told Shara some of the stories Beverly Pruyn had shared with him, off the record. Fiona Buford's treatment of Lucy was inhuman. "It's the kind of stuff that you hear after a kid takes her own life."

"What if you found him, and he knew you were going to turn him over to the police? Maybe he'd worry that would hurt his daughter, too," Shara asked.

"Oh, well yeah," JC conceded. "He might kill me then."

Shara just looked at him with concern in her eyes. "And what about the other guy?"

"Davis?" JC thought about Troy Davis. "He hasn't been accused of killing anyone. He's just a thief."

Before flying home from Albany, JC and Milt had received blessings from their news director to delay their return by a day. After scoring the first interview with Lucy Buford, JC thought that he could have asked for a Ferrari and his boss would have at least leased him one. Instead, Milt got to extend his visit with his sister and JC got to go skiing with his old pals.

He visited his favorite ski shop in Glens Falls and rented some high-performance equipment. Then he traveled the few remaining miles to West Mountain. It was the hill they'd all grown up on. The runs were longer now, and the snow was groomed to perfection. His ribs were still sore, but he thought he'd survive.

"Just don't fall," he told himself. Of course, he was taking advice from a slightly damaged brain, so how much could that be trusted?

They tested a new race hill that was fast and demanding. West Mountain had always been a training ground for ski racers. They had high school state champions and even a few who made the national racing team.

JC told Shara that day of skiing among friends was the only time he really felt like he was home. "It's strange. I grew up in my hometown, moved away but I still made regular trips back to see Mom and Dad. It was still home."

"Now, Mom and Dad have died and my brothers and my sister have moved away. Is it home anymore?"

"Is it?" Shara asked.

"I was just there," he told her, "but most of the time, I felt 'home alone.' What's going to bring me back from now on, funerals when my friends start dying?"

"Wow," Shara said as she lifted her head. "That's a depressing thought."

"It is," he admitted. "OK, I'll stop having those." They had the rest of the evening together. Good restaurants were only at the bottom of his stairs in Larimer Square. Restaurants, bars and shops stayed open late. JC and Shara had each other for the next three days. It was a good life.

The next day, and sixty miles away, childhood was still being thoroughly enjoyed by two brothers. They had the day off from middle school because of some teachers meeting or something. After breakfast, the day was all theirs.

They liked climbing the rocks in the steep canyon near their home. They envisioned treasure that must have been buried there by gold miners. They had also been told that the Utes used to bury their dead in the rocks.

The boys played in the natural setting near their house. The games began as soon as they ran out the back door.

They took risks that would terrify adults. The children dared each other to climb higher up a rock face or jump from a taller cliff into a mountain lake. Every tree had its own ladder of limbs to the top. Sometimes it just took a few falls for the path to become apparent.

They didn't have cable television and their mother couldn't afford the latest video games. There was nothing to do if they just sat on the couch like some other kids. The ground wasn't even level enough to ride a bike.

But out their back door, their imagination saw sticks that could become spears or rifles. In their mind, there were crumbled forts and ancient ruins to explore and there were monsters to track.

The children tracked their share of bear and mountain lions, at least they thought so. Those tracks could have belonged to the neighbor's dog.

What would they do if they actually came upon a bear? Their uncle told them, "You don't have to outrun a bear, you only have to outrun your brother."

By the time they were due home for dinner, their mother was impatiently waiting by the back door. They scrambled past her and obediently marched to the sink to wash their hands. They were stealing glances at each other.

"What are you two hatching?" she asked, smiling to herself.

"Nothing," one said as the children exchanged a grin.

The three of them sat down to dinner in the kitchen nook. "What smells?" the mother asked. "What have you been getting into?" The children tried to suppress their laughter.

"What did you two do today?" their mother asked. It was a routine fulfilled each evening at the dinner table. The question was usually followed by tales of a fight at school and pleas to be allowed to go to a new movie that weekend.

She had learned that the boys rarely shared the information their school had asked them to share with parents. She had to rely on neighbors to learn of the parent-teacher meetings or the public hearings about school taxes.

"Well," one boy offered, "we found a human body." Both boys diverted their eyes from their mother. They wondered how the news would be received.

"You did not," the mother responded sternly.

"Did too!" both boys exclaimed.

"Stop it," the mother told them with a serious face. "You did not. And that's a morbid thing to say. Eat your dinner."

"I knew you wouldn't believe us!" one boy objected, and he reached into his pocket for something. He held the cell phone she'd given them, in case there was an emergency and they needed to reach her.

It was a used phone a friend had given her. It was outdated, but it could place a simple phone call and gave her a sense that she was still tethered to her children. The phone had a camera. She didn't know how to work it. But the boys did.

"I knew you wouldn't believe us!" Her older boy, by a year, was holding the phone's screen toward her.

She gasped and put her hand to her mouth, "Put that down!" she ordered as she dropped her fork.

The boy did as he was told. He sensed that he had gone too far. There was going to be a price to pay. But the screen still held the image that had frightened her so. The picture of a human head.

16

The two boys perched on a rock as they watched police officers and men in white hazmat suits come and go from the back of a van with a large badge on the side. A rope had been strung along a path up the mountain, to make it easier to climb in the wrong shoes.

"Any ID?" one man in a windbreaker asked another man in a windbreaker.

"Nope," the second windbreaker answered. "He's been here a week, maybe two."

A 4x4 pickup truck pulled to the side of the road below the crime scene. A county death investigator, working for the county coroner, had arrived. He marched up the steep path and met with Larimer County sheriff's investigators.

"Two boys, aged 11 and 12, found him. That's them over there," said one sheriff's investigator, pointing in the direction of the two brothers sitting on the rock.

"Do we know who he is?" the death investigator asked.

"Not for sure. We have someone coming who's investigating a case," the other sheriff's investigator told him.

"Well, let me take a look," the death investigator told them.

An SUV pulled up behind the death investigator's pickup and an ambulance. JC and Milt climbed out. They approached the yellow police tape and were stopped. They were informed by a uniformed sheriff's deputy that they had to stay behind the tape, and no, they wouldn't be allowed up to the scene.

The journalists had expected that greeting. It was routine at a crime scene. "I wish it were more like the TV shows, where we got to duck under the tape and stand with the cops next to the body," JC told Milt.

The TV photographer crossed Route 34 and took some wide shots of the scene and the police presence. JC shared a greeting with a newspaper reporter from Loveland. "You know whose body it is?" JC asked the print journalist. They'd worked stories in Larimer County before. JC thought he could be trusted.

"I don't have any idea," the newspaper reporter told him as he snapped some still pictures of the event.

"Where are we?" JC asked. "Near Drake?"

"Yeah," the print reporter answered. JC estimated the reporter's age, thinking he could have covered the Big Thompson flood as a young reporter.

JC asked, "Big Thompson flood?"

The aging newspaperman lowered his camera and looked at JC. "Yeah, this is Drake, what's left of it. This road was gone. The Purdy monument is just up there." He pointed up the canyon.

JC wasn't alive when the Big Thompson flood hit. But he'd visited the monument to Hugh Purdy.

State Patrol Sgt. Purdy was a hero. He lost his own life trying to warn residents and campers in the canyon that a wall of water was coming. Some heeded his warning and climbed to higher ground. Others ignored him and were swept to their deaths.

"I've never seen it rain that hard in my life," the print journalist said, remembering the night of the flood. He turned his head to the sound of another car, "Hey, who's that?"

JC turned his head in the direction the newspaper reporter was looking. A man in a sport jacket and khakis was climbing out of a car, parked behind JC's news vehicle. "That may be the man who can identify the body," JC said.

"Hi JC," Detective Steve Trujillo said. "Not now." And he walked by the two reporters.

"Did you happen to get a shot of him?" JC shouted to Milt as Trujillo disappeared behind the tape and around a corner.

"Yep," Milt said as he crossed the road to JC. He lowered his voice and said, "Detective Trujillo, Denver. Right?" JC nodded his head with a smile on his face. Milt had captured the "money shot."

The journalists waited at the bottom of the hill next to Route 34, occasionally asking if a spokesperson for the investigation could come down to speak with them. "They'll talk to you before they leave," the uniformed deputy told them.

Another print reporter showed up, from nearby Fort Collins, and a KLOV radio reporter from Loveland.

JC was growing impatient. The longer they waited, the more JC thought Trujillo was up at the scene for a reason. Why would he hang around if the body didn't belong to one of his cases.

JC had two potential victims in mind: Troy Davis and Scott Miller. Both had fallen off the radar screen. Trujillo had an arrest warrant out for Davis. Miller had been seen with Davis before he went missing.

Above and out of sight from the reporters, the death investigator was supervising as the dead man's body was loaded into a bag. The man from the coroner's office instructed the deputies to load the body into the bag facedown, as they had found him by the cleft in the rock.

Rolling the body over would destroy any evidence on his back. He was found lying face-down and that's how he would be delivered to the medical examiner in Fort Collins.

It was a lesson learned in the OJ Simpson murder prosecution. The throat of Simpson's ex-wife was slashed. She was found facedown on the floor. There were also blood drops observed on her back.

Famous forensic pathologist Michael Baden later noted that those blood drops had to belong to the killer, probably cutting his own hand with the knife.

It couldn't have been the victim's blood because she wouldn't have bled onto her back. But when Nicole Simpson's body was flipped over and placed in a body bag, that blood evidence was destroyed, unusable in the trial of Mr. Simpson. It was a lesson learned the hard way by the law enforcement community.

There was another problem. The two boys had walked across the scene. But police were able to identify the footprints of eleven- and twelve-year-old boys. Still, police would ask mom for the shoes the children were wearing when they found the body. The shoes would be taken back to the lab.

The death investigator accompanied the body bag down the hill to his truck. Milt was shooting video as the investigator declined a request by JC for a quick interview. The 4x4 pickup and the ambulance turned around in the road and headed for the morgue.

A patrol car left the scene as JC and the other reporters waited along the highway. Then, Detective Trujillo came down the path, holding the rope as his shoes slipped on the loose stone. "I can't say anything, JC," the detective told him as the other reporters listened in. "This isn't my jurisdiction. Maybe the sheriff will have something for you later."

Trujillo pulled away in his car. JC knew that something was in the works, and he was trying to come up with his own next move.

As a reporter, he had been burned more than once waiting for a news conference that wasn't going to happen. If police believed that saying something would compromise their investigation, then they'd remain silent. They weren't concerned about ruining a journalist's day.

Milt Lemon looked at JC, waiting for a directive. JC looked back and said, "Let's get out of here."

"What if they come down and make a statement?" Milt asked.

"They're not going to. They would have by now. The sheriff isn't even here. The undersheriff isn't going to upstage his boss," JC told his photographer. "We've got to figure out who they found up there, and I may know a way. But we've got to leave now."

Milt stowed his camera in the trunk of the car and climbed behind the wheel. JC was in the passenger seat and said, "I'll give you directions."

They drove to the mouth of the canyon into Loveland. JC directed Milt to turn onto a worn street with no sidewalks.

Outside of Lisa Miller's house, there was a patrol car and an unmarked police unit. It was the vehicle Trujillo had driven up the canyon to the crime scene.

Trujillo and the deputy were walking out the front door of the Miller home as Milt and JC were climbing out of their car. Milt was quickly grabbing his camera to capture the law officer's presence for TV.

"I can't say anything, JC," Detective Trujillo shouted across the distance between the two men. "And this deputy is remaining here, so you don't bother Mrs. Miller."

JC looked at the front door. The blonde woman closing the door was holding a tissue to her face. She was crying.

JC looked at the deputy, who returned a look indicating he was serious. No one was going near that door. JC was not happy about it. There was not going to be a chance to even ask the widow for an interview, right now. But any doubt had been removed. There was only one reason the Denver detective had visited that house.

"It's Miller," JC told Milt as they sat in the car. "They found Scott Miller's body. And Troy Davis has something to do with it."

17

It was starting to snow outside. Detective Steve Trujillo knew they'd be erecting some plastic tents at the crime scene in the canyon, to protect evidence from the weather. They'd gotten a decent look at the ground, but then it got dark outside.

The days were getting shorter. That didn't do anyone any good, he thought. They'd want to take another look at the spot the body was found, when the sun rose again. The snow was going to cover some things up.

Trujillo and an investigator from the Larimer County Sheriff's Office walked into the morgue in Fort Collins. Trujillo introduced himself to the coroner, who was also the medical examiner. Trujillo, outside of his jurisdiction, explained his interest in the body.

Trujillo wasn't a stranger to dead things, even before he became a cop. He grew up on a large farm east of Denver. His father was a hired foreman there.

As a child, Steve and his siblings would try to adopt a calf or a lamb. But their father would warn them, "You can like them, but don't love them. They don't belong to you, and they were born to become food."

And Steve Trujillo grew up witnessing the cycle of life. Animals were there to be cared for and enjoyed, and then came a time for their harvest.

He came to understand the natural relationship between life and death. There was a place for both.

Detective Trujillo was the first in his family to graduate from college. But his dad was smart, too, Trujillo thought. That's how he rose from being a field hand to being a foreman.

Trujillo's grandfather, Wilfredo, immigrated from Mexico as a teenager. He got one job and he never gave it up. He worked in a hotel in Denver.

He worked hard, doing anything they asked of him. And because money was so hard to come by, Willy pinched his pennies.

He earned enough to move his wife and small children to a little farm on the outskirts of Denver. He'd toil at his hotel job all day and then come home to his farm and tend his small vegetable fields and feed his few animals.

So Detective Trujillo knew the cycle of life, as well as the value of it.

"It's clearly a homicide," the coroner told the lawmen. "One shot, close range, to the back of the head."

"Any struggle?" the sheriff's investigator asked.

"I don't think so. I'm not sure he saw it coming," the ME responded. "He has scrapes on the back of his hand, but I think it's post-mortem. Maybe he was scraped as he was carried up to the spot where his body was found. You told me that you don't think he was killed where his body was located?"

"We don't think so," the deputy said.

"There were also lesions to his face," the coroner declared as he looked down at his patient. "But, again, it was after his death. Long after. They are probably from someone dragging the body out of the gap in the rock. You say two children found the body?"

The sheriff's investigator sort of laughed and said, "Yeah, tough kids. They say they didn't think it was real, so they grabbed his feet and pulled him out. They took a picture and showed it to their mom. She near fainted." They all shared a laugh at the bravado of the boys.

"How long has he been dead?" Trujillo asked.

"Two weeks, three? I'll know more, but that's the best I can do right now," the ME responded.

Detective Trujillo looked around the room. It had white walls, four steel tables. There was a camera over the table. It was to spare family members like Lisa Miller the trauma of identifying a body.

The blow could now be softened. The camera could send an image of the victim's face to a TV screen in the family room. The ID could be confirmed there.

Trujillo was thinking about what was missing. There had to be a clue in this room that would give him something to work with. He asked, "He have anything to eat?"

"Yes," the medical examiner replied. "He went out in style. He was still digesting a lobster dinner."

"Like a last supper," Trujillo said.

"Like death row," the sheriff's investigator added.

That, Trujillo thought, might work.

JC reported that night on the discovery of Scott Miller's body. The audience learned that Miller's death was being investigated as a homicide.

Law officers still weren't disclosing details, JC reported, but the presence of a Denver police investigator outside his jurisdiction couldn't be ignored. The reporter also told the audience that Miller had been seen in the company of Troy Davis, who was already the subject of an active warrant with his name on it.

JC couldn't come right out and say that Davis killed Miller, but that's what he was thinking. He remembered Lisa Miller telling him that she didn't like Davis. She said that she'd told Scott to stay away from him.

Trujillo wasn't watching JC's newscast, broadcast live from the mouth of Big Thompson Canyon. The detective was going to be working late.

JC was back at his Larimer Square apartment, sharing an intimate dinner with Shara. They watched snowflakes falling outside. The food came from a French bistro down the street.

"Do I remember you being this romantic?" Shara asked.

"It's easy to set high standards when you won't see each other again for half a year," he said.

He knew he'd made a mistake as soon as the words came out of his mouth. Tears formed in her eyes. In hardly more than twenty-four hours, they'd be separated again. It was so

119

easy when they were together, and so hard when they were apart.

"I'm sorry," he said.

"You're being depressing again," she told him as they drew each other's bodies close.

"Stupid me," he whispered to her.

"Stupid this," she whispered back.

Trujillo told himself that he was doing it "old school," the way it was done by detectives he admired when he first joined the police force.

He was going from one restaurant to another, asking if they had served lobster to either of two men in photographs the law officer held in his hand.

He could have done it using the internet, he thought. He could have emailed the restaurants and attached the two photos. But no restaurant manager was going to look at the email tonight.

That manager would have food to serve and a staff to manage. And Trujillo wouldn't be able to rest if he went home without finding out. He knew that he was close to something big.

Neon signs floated past the car window as he proceeded slowly down the street. It was harder to see. It was dark and the snow was starting to collect on the pavement.

He'd exhausted every possibility in Loveland and was now driving down College Avenue in Fort Collins.

He passed a supermarket. He began to shake his head and apply the brakes. Showing his left turn signal, he pulled into the supermarket parking lot. In the window, a sign advertised, "Lobster, $5 a pound."

Trujillo reprimanded himself for failing to think of it sooner. He walked to the back of the supermarket and spoke with the seafood section manager. The detective asked, "When does your shift begin?"

"My shift?" the manager asked. "Depends on who quit without notice."

"Like now?" the detective asked. He voiced sympathy. The night was getting late. Managers don't usually work late at night.

"Like now," the manager smiled, appreciating the recognition.

"How about three weeks ago?" Trujillo asked.

The seafood manager lifted his eyes to the ceiling, thinking back three weeks ago, "I was working dayside, my usual shift."

"Ever see these two guys?" The detective pushed the two photographs across the stainless steel counter. Trujillo noted that it was the second time he'd encountered a stainless steel counter that day. The other was the morgue. It must be good for dead things, he thought.

The seafood manager looked at the photographs. "Funny, but yeah," he told the police officer. "One of the guys. I see a lot of people, but he made an impression on me. Personable. He bought some lobster, about three weeks ago, like you said." The store manager was pointing at the photo of Troy Davis.

"Hey," the manager said. "That looks like a mug shot."

"Does it?" the detective responded and gave it a noncommittal look. "Huh."

18

The music was loud.

"Fuck her! What about my manicure?" The singer screamed the lyrics into the microphone while striking the chords on her guitar. Despite the volume, JC thought the words were clever.

"Be a dear, hand me a beer," the singer chirped from the stage, a band playing behind her.

Most of the audience consisted of women, including Shara. The band was called the Girl Squirrels. Their songs, they told the audience, were for women by women.

They took a break and the lead singer, wearing a tee shirt that said "Boi Toy" in sparkles, approached the table JC and Shara were sitting at. The singer sat down. "You're wrong, you know," she told JC. She had asked the TV reporter to come to the concert that night.

Her stage name was Boi Toy. Her real name was Kat Martinez. "It used to be Kim, my name. But, I'm more of a Kat."

She had pink hair tonight for the show, and a pink tee shirt. She was attractive and wore her tee shirt tight. A lot of the women in the audience were at the club to see her. She had plenty of sex appeal.

"That's what you said on the phone," JC told her, glad that he wasn't shouting over the music. "What am I wrong about?"

"Tell your boyfriend to get his eyes off my tits," Boi Toy told Shara. Her tone was more in jest than any suggestion that she'd been offended.

"I had to read your tee shirt," JC protested. "'Boi Toy,' that means you're a girl who likes girls, but likes girls who are kind of tomboys?"

"Ooo," she looked at Shara. "He's not just pretty, is he? He's smart." Kat gave him her best meow. The two women laughed.

"When I'm not on stage," Boi Toy explained, "I'm a girlie girl. I like to look pretty, and I like a boi. Though I could make an exception." Boi Toy brushed Shara's leg. Shara was amused and made a noise like a kitten purring.

The two women laughed more. So did JC, until he asked, "Am I the third wheel here?"

"Yes!" declared Boi Toy. She was quite the show woman, JC thought. They were all enjoying the banter.

"So, what am I wrong about?" JC repeated.

"Troy," Boi Toy told him, "and call me Kat."

"OK, Kat, go on," JC requested.

"He didn't kill that guy in the canyon. That's not what he does," she said.

"What exactly does he do?" JC asked.

"He's a thief. Ask him," she laughed. "He's proud of it. I remember some guy was standing next to us in line for a movie we were going to see. Troy and the guy strike up a conversation. The guy asks Troy, 'So, what do you do for a living, Troy?' And Troy smiles as he says, 'I'm a thief.'"

Kat looked at JC to see if he understood. "He's proud of it. And he's good at it."

JC asked Kat, "How would you know this?"

"I was his girlfriend," Kat told JC and Shara. "Look, it took me a while to get to know myself, do you know what I mean?"

JC waited for her to explain.

"I wasn't always a lesbian!" Kat enunciated. "I mean, I was, but I didn't know I was, understand?"

JC nodded his head. He got it. Kat told him, "I was Troy's girlfriend. I thought I was in love with him. He was very good to me."

JC rubbed his hands over his eyes. He was trying to keep up. "I know, I know," Kat said with a laugh, "It's a lot. I grant that."

"Anyway," Kat continued, "he was good to me, like I said, and he had a lot of money. He'd come home late at night and fall asleep next to me. The next morning, I'd get up and find his clothing scattered across the floor. I'd pick up his jacket and the sleeves would be stuffed with money! There must have been thousands of dollars tucked into two sleeves!" She laughed as she remembered it.

"Where did the money come from?" JC asked.

"He stole it," she said matter-of-factly. "He's a really good thief! He's smart. I think he started college. But he didn't finish, I know that. But he reads a lot. He's smart."

"Where was he stealing the money from?" JC asked.

Kat waved her hand at him, "Oh, I don't know. He didn't tell me stuff like that. He never told me specifics."

"Well," asked JC, "What did he do with the money?"

"You know," Kat reflected, "that's the funny thing. He didn't seem to care that much about money. He didn't drive a fancy car. He drove a beat-up pickup truck. He didn't dress fancy, he wore blue jeans and a tee shirt. We lived in a basic apartment. It was clean, but it wasn't fancy. I still live there."

JC tried to digest it all. He was peering into the life of a man he knew wasn't as transparent as Kat insisted. He had her fooled, JC thought. Or did he?

"Did you know Scott Miller?" JC asked.

"I knew him," she said. "I didn't know him well. Troy didn't like to mix business with pleasure. Scott, I thought, was a business associate." Then she winked and gave him a broad smile, "I was a pleasure associate." Gotcha, JC thought.

"Do you know where he is?" JC asked. Kat shook her head, no. JC wondered if she was telling the truth.

"You don't think he killed Scott Miller?" JC asked.

"No, he didn't do that," she said. "He also didn't hurt girls. He put girls on a pedestal. He never even got mad at me."

"Well," JC followed, "if it was so apparent that he didn't hurt women, did you see him hurt men?"

"Oh," Kat slowed down, "if a guy was asking for it, Troy would put him in his place. I remember him coming home late, and his jacket had quite a bit of blood on it. I asked him what happened, and he said that some guy was being rude to a girl Troy didn't even know. So, Troy intervened, you know?"

"Beat him up?" JC asked for clarification.

"I guess so," Kat answered. "He respected women."

"The money," JC asked. "Did you ever see him do anything with it?"

"Oh!" Kat raised both her hands. "Now that you mention being nice to women! He loved to take me on vacation. He would take me to Mexico, some five-star resort. He'd let me shop, we'd rent jet skis, we'd eat at the best restaurants. He loved to spend money when he was on vacation!"

"Any guys ever come on these vacations?" JC asked.

"No."

JC knew he had a treasure chest of information sitting in front of him. He was trying to think of anything that might help in his understanding of Troy Davis.

"Jewelry?" JC asked.

Kat laughed, "Oh, he stole jewelry. Look, he gave me this." She pulled a necklace out from under her pink tee shirt. It had diamonds in the shape of a half moon.

"When's the last time you saw him?" JC asked.

"I don't know," Kat offered. "He's kind of a hodophile."

JC gave her a blank stare and started shaking his head. He had no idea what a hodophile was.

Kat frowned a fake frown, "Oh, I thought you were smart. That's someone who loves to travel."

Kat laughed. "When I told him that I was a lesbian, he said, 'I understand, I'm a hodophile.' That's why I know what it is."

"So, you think he's traveling?" JC asked. "How far does he travel, aside from those vacations in Mexico?"

"You know," Kat got a big smile on her face, "I know a guy who moves to different countries depending on who's in charge! If he doesn't like the president of the United States, he moves to Canada if he likes the prime minister there. Then, if someone gets elected in France that he likes, he moves to France!"

"Seriously?" JC asked. He understood why audiences were drawn to Kat. She was funny and talented. But steering a conversation with her, he found, was like trying to steer a child through an amusement park. There were a lot of interesting distractions.

"So, where else would he travel—I'm talking about Troy now—besides Mexico?"

"Troy?" Kat sort of grunted, thinking. "He never wanted to go anywhere where he might know someone, or even where I might know someone. I've got a brother who lives on the Western Slope. He's a brainiac. He works for a museum there. I wanted to go visit him with Troy. But Troy said no. Instead, he took me to Brazil!" Kat started smiling and handled a gold bracelet that Troy had purchased for her there.

"How long ago did you last see Troy?"

"A month ago? Three weeks? We're not an item anymore. You may have gathered that." Kat pointed at her tee shirt saying "Boi Toy."

"Got it," JC told her. "Too bad for me."

Kat looked at Shara as Shara mocked shock, looking at JC.

"Kidding," JC defended himself. "Just kidding."

19

He looked in the mirror and saw Billy Idol looking back at him. John Buford's hair was blond and spiked. He thought that it looked ridiculous on a man who was his age and wasn't a rock star.

To be fair, he told himself, he stayed in shape by doing exercises in his apartment. And he went outside to go skiing and hiking. He'd always looked younger than his 54 years.

It didn't matter if Buford thought he looked ridiculous. It mattered that he didn't look like State Senator John Buford, or like that picture of Senator John Buford in the newspaper. He knew he'd see that picture again. He just didn't know when. He was surprised that it took four years.

He was now going by the name Jose Garcia. He didn't have an ounce of Hispanic blood running through his veins. But he thought that a Hispanic name would put distance between him and what the public knew about Buford.

He learned some Spanish. He had time on his hands. He learned only the basics. After that, he'd just smile and say, "I'm an American. I learned a little bit from my grandma."

He'd picked his new last name, Garcia, out of a list he saw of the fifty most common names in Colorado. Garcia was the second most common of Hispanic heritage. Jose was the second most common first name. There were lots of Jose Garcias in Colorado.

Everything was an effort to minimize calling attention to himself. If he'd chosen the most common Hispanic names, he'd have called himself Angel Martinez. He just didn't think he could call himself an Angel.

He had and hadn't planned to evade capture. He had and hadn't planned to be on the run this long. When "the incident" occurred back in Albany, he didn't really have a plan. He hadn't planned "the incident" at all. It just happened.

He was and wasn't sorry for it. "Something had to be done," he'd told himself hundreds of times. And hundreds of times, he'd forced himself to think about something else. Something more pleasant.

On the night he left their home for the last time … he still thought of it as his and Lucy's home … he'd walked the three miles to his office. It was inside a building across the street from the capitol.

He'd walked on side streets, avoiding the possibility of bumping into someone he knew or even a constituent who wanted to have a conversation.

They wouldn't know what I'd just done, the senator thought. But he just wasn't capable of having a conversation. They might not know what he'd just done, but he couldn't ignore it.

So, he walked down dark side streets toward the capitol. It was snowing lightly, but his footprints would quickly be buried by more snow or compromised by other foot traffic. Police weren't looking for him. Police wouldn't know that his wife was dead until days from now.

He walked on the sidewalk bordering Washington Park. He walked without noticing the picturesque old brownstones he always admired in Center Square. He was in a trance. He arrived at the Legislative Office Building unnoticed. It was late at night.

He knew that he couldn't sleep, but he needed somewhere to wait until his bank opened, down State Street. He'd remove just enough cash to avoid drawing attention to himself. Then, he'd walk down the hill to another of his banks and do the same thing.

He'd do it at other financial institutions, too. Working quickly, by the time regulators saw the red flags triggered by the large withdrawals that were accumulating, he wouldn't be available to answer questions.

"Just moving some money around," he'd say, with that winning smile, to the teller.

No one he met knew that his wife was at home, stuffed into a closet. Her blood had started to coagulate five minutes after she died. The natural process of a body shutting down was finished in about thirty minutes. No one knew.

Back at his office, he made more cash available. There were even greater sums of money at his disposal, as a powerful state senator. But he'd only collect money that belonged to him, not a dime that belonged to taxpayers. He wasn't a thief.

With the capitol open for another business day, he was now greeted by smiles from the secretarial pool and other early arrivals. It occurred to Buford that he was experiencing the last hours of being known as the honorable senator from the Albany District. He thought he'd miss it a little, but what was done was done.

A young intern showed up at the office an hour before the schedule required. His early arrival was such a regular occurrence though, if the boy had shown up on time, he'd be considered late.

His name was Ted Sanderson. Buford's staff talked behind Ted's back. His worship for the senator was apparent. Ted didn't have a father. He was raised by a single, hard-working mother. She believed Ted had grabbed the golden ring on the merry-go-round when he was hired as an intern to the powerful state senator.

She knew Ted would be alright now. A great weight was lifted off her shoulders. She thought Senator Buford, brave and noble, might even become a father figure to Ted. He needed that.

She knew the boy was odd. She blamed the absence of his father. Ted sensed this in his mother. He was glad he finally made her proud.

Senator Buford had noticed Ted. He heard the gossip about the boy who worshipped the ground he walked on. The senator was flattered. Buford would watch Ted sometimes. The young man tried hard to please. He was kind of a nerd but he was smart and very loyal. Buford needed loyal right now.

The senator summoned Ted to his office that morning. Buford told him to close the door behind him. They were alone, just the two of them in Buford's private office. Ted gulped. He could hardly believe the honor bestowed upon him.

"Ted, I need you to do me a favor," the senator stated in a commanding voice. Buford was trying to sound as normal as possible, as though he was going to ask for something usually only asked of grownups at the state capitol.

Ted was in a trance. He thought to himself that at this moment, he was Senator John Buford's confidant, his sole co-conspirator. If only he knew what an accurate choice of words that was.

Ted tried to remain cool. He wanted to come off casual and yet available. He smiled, "Who do you want me to kill?"

Buford suppressed a laugh. It was more ironic than funny, he thought. "That won't be necessary," he smiled at the boy.

"I need you to give me a ride," the senator said. "And you can't tell anyone. Ever."

Ted noted the "ever" part. But he responded with an "OK." He made it sound like a vow.

"Are you a man of your word?" Buford asked him.

"My word is my oath," Ted responded solemnly, reciting a line some medieval knight had sworn to in a movie he saw.

The senator sat back in his chair and looked at Ted. "Horace Greeley once said, 'Fame is a vapor, popularity an accident, and riches take wings. Only one thing endures and that is character.'"

Ted stared at his senator. He thought he should say something, but he was at a loss. "Wow," he uttered quietly, almost choking. He was mesmerized. This was magical, he thought. He had accepted a secret mission from an American patriot and sworn his very character to uphold his vow.

Buford was now looking back at that morning with amazement. As far as Buford knew, Ted had never uttered a word to the police. He had kept his blood oath, even though Buford didn't deserve it.

The blond, spike-haired man in the mirror thought of sending Ted some money, or even a card. The boy might be inspired by an offering from his mystic leader.

But Buford wasn't Senator Buford anymore. He was Jose Garcia. Any communication with his past was too risky. He was saving that venture for one mission, one person. His daughter.

He looked at her picture. She looked back at him, smiling, from a simple frame. No one came into his room, so he had no worries of someone seeing it. Besides, it would come as little surprise if he explained that he had a daughter. Someone his age was bound to have a past. And no one knew what Lucy Buford looked like. Her picture hadn't been in the newspaper.

Buford rented a simple, second-floor room in Nederland, Colorado. Legend had it that the small town in Boulder Canyon had been used as a hideout before, by a famous radical wanted by the FBI in the 1970s.

Nederland was an old mining town with wood-frame homes, some painted in bright colors. Downtown was only one block long, but the singular block was hip. It was lined by restaurants and bars and shops, inside buildings that looked like they had lasted since the days gold was discovered up the canyon.

There was a ski area nearby, loved by the locals and ignored by most of the destination skiers who came to Colorado. It was called Eldora. He remembered when it was called Lake Eldora. He didn't know why the name had been changed.

Nederland and Eldora would sustain Buford. He could ski in a mask, presumably to protect his face from the wind that could whistle across the mountain. Skiing was one of the paltry few pleasures Buford had.

He was Jose Garcia to the people in Nederland who had to know his name. He didn't share events of his past, and they didn't ask. He wasn't the only one in Nederland with secrets. The town motto could have been "We mind our own business."

His secret was probably the biggest, though. So he didn't allow himself to make friends. Some friendly faces couldn't help but take an interest. Maybe a waitress at the pizza place, or a cashier at a store in town. If they asked where he worked, he could say, "You know, here and there."

He didn't need to work yet. When he had and hadn't made a plan to escape capture in Albany, that morning four years ago, he had executed a good master scenario. His instincts had saved him, he thought.

He told himself that he wasn't lonely. He stuck to a formula. He filled his human need for socialization by striking up conversations on chairlifts. He kept his goggles down, mask on. They were ten-minute relationships that expired as soon as the chairlift ride ended with, "Have a good day."

During the summer, he could hike alone in the mountains. Sometimes he'd chat with other hikers who happened to be resting at the same crossroads. He kept his sunglasses on and made sure they saw his spiked blond hair.

When he had to shop for food, he changed stores rather than become known by the checkout cashier. He stayed in his room, most days, looking out his second-floor windows or watching television.

He only came out for Nederland's annual "Frozen Dead Guy Days" festival in March. That, he thought, was a hoot. And it was easy to wear silly sunglasses and a funny mask or makeup that looked like a skull. Everyone else was. No one was going to guess Senator John Buford was inside that masquerade.

There was only one relationship he wanted to sustain. He wanted to see Lucy. But he didn't know how. He assumed she was being watched. Cops never let a case go. They'd work a cold case until the day they died.

He was still a skier. On the chairlift at Eldora, he'd hatch possible plans to surprise Lucy with a visit. He'd have to catch her alone. But every scheme he hatched inside his helmet had its pitfalls.

If he communicated with her and it was intercepted by police, he'd be captured without laying an eye on her. He couldn't bear that. He hadn't come all this way for it to end like that.

It never occurred to him that she might not want to see him, or that memory of her father might be fading. He was certain that she'd ache for her daddy as he ached for his daughter.

Once in a while, Jose Garcia would ski at Snow Hat. It had so many pleasant memories. Despite his own denials, Buford knew that he imagined he might see her one of the days at Snow Hat.

That's why he kept coming back to that ski resort, where he and Lucy had enjoyed better times together. He looked for her each time he was there. But at the end of the day, he'd tell himself that he was a fool for being disappointed. Did she even know that her knight was looking for her?

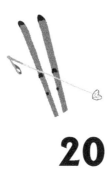

20

Christmas lights illuminated Larimer Square in Downtown Denver as JC and Shara held each other. They shared a lounge chair on the flat roof of the building next to his apartment. His window served as a door to the space and he treated it as his patio. They hid from the cold night beneath a thick blanket.

Overhead, a weathered advertisement was painted on the bricks of the old building rising above them. It was impossible anymore to distinguish what it was trying to sell.

The next morning, he drove Shara to the airport. He was battling the glare of the morning sun as he navigated traffic on I-70. Shara needed to get back to Montana to prepare for the weekend's opening of ski season at Grizzly Mountain and her bar called Shara's Sheep Ranch.

It might be five months before they saw each other again. The holiday spirit did not penetrate the gloom of their predicament. "Maybe I can get up there," JC said. They both knew that was a wish, not an assurance.

"You ever think about kids?" JC asked as he drove.

"Now?" she asked incredulously. "That's a conversation you want to have now?" Silence followed.

Parting at the airport brought expressions of gratitude, tears and embraces. But not happiness. He was in love with her. He let her know that. And she let him know that she loved him. Then she was gone.

JC was hollow as he walked back to his car. He didn't want to feel anything. Nothing good could come of it. He searched for something else to think about. Troy Davis. JC had no doubt that's who killed Scott Miller.

Detective Trujillo had disclosed that they found a ghost gun. It was probably the murder weapon. Ghost guns were one of the newest headaches for law enforcement. They could be ordered online and came unregistered and without serial numbers.

Gang members were the initial market for ghost guns. The order was delivered in a box and required only simple assembly. Instructions and even videos came to help the buyer put a ghost gun together.

They weren't invented for hunting. They were invented to create human ghosts. The guns had surfaced on the streets before there was even a law against them.

JC drove west on Interstate 70 to the TV station. At the same time, Troy Davis was driving east on I-70. He was beating his thumb against the steering wheel of his new car to the rhythm of a song on the radio.

It was actually a used car, a real beater, he thought. But it was new to him. He had to dispose of his pickup truck. It had become an invitation for trouble. Police would be looking for it.

He was traveling I-70 through De Beque Canyon. He'd been told there were wild horses near there. He'd have to come back to see them, he thought to himself.

He was tired but energized. He'd done another good night's work. He'd get some sleep, look for boxes behind the supermarket, buy some newspaper for packing, and ship his newest acquisitions out of the country. There was a brave new world excited to do business with him. His new buyers were overseas and paid top dollar.

Bitsy Stark was heading west on the Denver Airport Rail to Union Station. She was nearly pressing her face against the window of the train to get a glimpse of the mountains.

Her first-ever sighting of the Rocky Mountains had come from the seat of her airplane only an hour before. She thought they looked exotic. They were larger and extended much further above timberline than the mountains in her home state of Vermont.

Even Denver's airport looked exotic to her. From above, she thought it looked like a line of teepees. The architect, she read, hoped the roof resembled teepees or Colorado's snow-capped mountains.

She would be in those famous mountains soon enough, she thought. She'd spend the day exploring Denver and spend the night in the luxury Crawford Hotel inside the historic train station. She was on the adventure of her life, she thought.

Union Station was magnificent, as she rolled her bag off the train in one hand. Her other hand pulled a case carrying her skis on small rollers.

She checked into the Crawford and moved into a room that opened onto a balcony overlooking the large waiting area of the old terminal. It was bright and full of conversations.

Ornamental light bouncing off the white paint illuminated the cavernous space. She looked down on the main floor and saw that the old ticket area, including windows with bars, had now become a bar and restaurant.

She looked down on what had become a popular public living room in Denver. People filled the seats at dark wooden tables with lamps befitting an old library.

There were also people sharing time with each other in comfortable sofas and chairs with big soft cushions. The seats were populated by people of all ages.

Plenty were her age. Many had earbuds plugged into their laptops and they sipped coffee while they stared at their screens. Others drank beer at long tables with friends or slipped in and out of the stores and restaurants that lined the walls of the open space.

Bitsy spent the afternoon investigating the streets of downtown Denver. She adored nearby Larimer Square, its coffee shops and boutique clothing stores with cool names like Cry Baby Ranch.

As the sun began to settle over the mountains in the west, she returned to the Crawford and headed for a bar and restaurant tucked in the corner.

It was called The Coupler. It was railroad lingo for a mechanism that locks railroad cars to a locomotive, though in a bar where men and women met, they could take The Coupler to mean anything they want.

Bitsy slid onto a chair at the bar. She ordered a beer and listened to conversations going on around her. The two women on her left were talking about a relationship. Behind her, a group of friends was talking about a hike somewhere in the mountains. Bitsy was having fun.

"First time here?" an older man interrupted. He had taken a seat to her right. He was alone.

She smiled and said, "Yes." She was being polite. She was thinking that she did not want to be hit on by a man twice her age, and certainly not this particular one.

Bitsy Stark was blonde with blue eyes, a little overweight but pretty, and she had an outgoing personality.

"You know how I knew?" he asked, "that you were new here?"

Bitsy didn't want to have a conversation with this gray-haired, homely man. But she was curious how he knew. "How?" she asked.

"You're wearing your sticky baggage tags around your wrist," he smiled, pointing at them.

"Oh!" she giggled at her surprise. "I didn't know where to put them, so that seemed like a fun place. Very observant."

The man introduced himself, "Milt Lemon."

"Pleased to meet you, Mr. Lemon, Bitsy Stark," she responded. They exchanged small talk for a while and ordered food at the bar. He seemed interested in getting to know the young woman better. She did not return the sentiment.

She made it clear that she was planning on getting a good night's sleep, alone. "I'm heading up to Snow Hat, tomorrow."

"Going to do some skiing?" Milt asked.

141

"Yes!" She couldn't conceal her excitement.

After finishing her meal, Bitsy paid for hers and got up from her bar chair. "Nice to meet you, Mr. Lemon. I hope you enjoy the rest of your night."

Milt was discouraged but seemed to accept defeat. "Goodnight, Miss Stark, enjoy your stay at Snow Hat."

The next morning, Bitsy summoned a car on her ride-sharing app. She was going west on I-70 to the Snow Hat Ski Resort.

She had a plan. She'd get in some skiing and then report for her new job as an au pair for a wealthy family who lived in the mountains.

Bitsy grew up skiing in Vermont. She thought Colorado would be a great fit, a great adventure. She would ski a few days by herself at Snow Hat. That was part of the adventure: having no one to depend on but herself, no one to call the shots but herself.

The wisdom of her decision, to court new exciting surroundings, was confirmed as soon as she stepped off the plane. Yesterday had been wonderful, she thought.

Now, on a bright sunny morning, the road began to climb up the mountains. A sign told her she was passing the grave of Buffalo Bill, the famous cowboy.

She saw real bison grazing beyond a fence along the road. She'd seen bison in Vermont, but not bison living in the Wild West!

She saw a dozen old gold mines cut into the canyon wall on both sides of the highway. They became easy to spot, once her driver told her what to look for.

"And don't get any ideas about hiking up there and looking for samples," the driver told her. "Someone still owns those mines, and they think there may still be some gold in the shafts. They won't take it kindly if they think you're a claim jumper." They both laughed but he added, "It's true!"

Bitsy gasped as they passed Georgetown, the old mining town with brightly colored wood-frame homes. "They call them 'painted ladies,' those old houses," the driver told her.

"They're beautiful," Bitsy exclaimed. Then, she was told to keep her eyes on the steep canyon walls. She might see some bighorn sheep, her driver told her. He said, "You don't always see them, but that's part of the fun driving in Colorado. It pays to keep your eyes peeled. You see some glorious things."

"Are all the ski areas open now?" she asked the driver.

"Most all of them. It was a pretty dry Snowvember, but they got open by Thanksgiving," he said over his shoulder. "And it's been a pretty good Snowcember!"

"There are four extended holidays the ski areas can't live without if they want to have a profitable season," he said to her, looking into his rear-view mirror. "The first is Thanksgiving. If they get a good Thanksgiving, they're ahead of the game. Then there's Christmas, Martin Luther King weekend and Presidents Week. The years that they hit all of those, the snow isn't white, it's green! They're making a ton of money."

"How is Snow Hat doing?" she said in anticipation, still watching the travel show out the window.

"Snow Hat is up pretty high and it's snowed up there," he told her. "They can make snow, too. You've hit it good. The natural stuff started falling a couple of weeks ago."

"If you drive up there," the driver pointed to the exit before the Eisenhower Tunnel, "you can ski in July. They start skiing early and finish late at A-Basin. Their peak is up at thirteen thousand feet."

After the tunnel, they passed Copper Mountain and Vail and Beaver Creek. The young woman was spellbound staring at the iconic ski resorts.

The car passed aspens that had lost most of their golden leaves. And then, Bitsy could see the snow-covered slopes of Snow Hat as they approached her hotel. A dream was coming true, she thought to herself.

The driver carried her baggage, including her skis, into the lobby. He didn't usually do that, but he liked Bitsy. She had that effect on people.

JC was back at his desk at the TV station. His phone rang. It was Peter Post, the Grand Junction TV anchor, who said, "We've got another one."

"Another museum hit?" JC asked with interest. Peter had called him when a museum on the Western Slope had been burglarized about a week ago.

"Yep, near Ouray, about an hour from here. A small mining museum," Post told him.

"Same kind of stuff taken?" JC asked.

"Pretty much," Post responded. "Old mining tools, picks, cowboy stuff, some gold-engraved trays and antiques from the Gold Rush."

"How was security there?" JC asked.

"Same as last time," the journalist stated. "It's a little museum. They have a burglar alarm. There was a camera, but it wasn't connected to anything. They were hoping to bluff anyone casing the joint."

"Smash and grab?" JC asked.

"That's a good description," said Post. "Police say they got there as quickly as they could, and the burglar was long gone."

"Thanks, Peter," JC said into the phone, "I may have to come visit you soon."

"You're always welcome," Post replied. "I'll take you to the Main Street Café."

Bitsy had cleaned up and was taking a look around the resort village at Snow Hat. She smiled at skiers and snowboarders as they walked past. She found a sweater she adored in one shop, and in another, she found Christmas presents for family back in Vermont.

She tucked her new acquisitions back in her hotel room. She posted pictures of her amazing surroundings on social media and then returned outside. It had gotten dark. String lights hung overhead. She would look for a place to toast her new life. She found one and ducked in.

The bar was called the Yardsale, a fun name for falling on the ski hill. A yard sale meant the skier had become disconnected from their skis, poles and possibly a hat during a prodigious fall.

She was taking the room in with her eyes as she sipped her drink. The beers had different names than back home. The faces on the televised newscasts were different. The decorations on the wall were different. It all seemed better.

Her blonde hair captured some of the neon pink and green lighting on the ceiling. Someone slipped onto the barstool next to her. She stole a glance of him in the reflection of the mirror behind the bar.

This was more like it. He was handsome. A little rugged-looking but a nice smile and a full head of brown hair. He was older than she, but not a lot older.

"You skiing?" he asked her.

She turned toward him in her seat, smiling. "I will tomorrow, I just got here."

"Where from?"

"Vermont," she told him, and her smile broadened.

He sort of whistled, "That's a long way. What brings you from Vermont?"

"A job," there was a bit of a song in her voice.

"Don't they have any jobs in Vermont?" he teased.

Bitsy giggled a protest, "Yes." She sipped some more of her drink.

"What part of Vermont?" he asked.

"Bennington," she disclosed, still smiling.

"Troy," he said and reached out his hand to shake hers.

"You're from Troy?" she asked excitedly. The upstate New York city of Troy was less than an hour from her home.

"No, that's my name," he smiled

"Oh." She sounded a bit disappointed, but she took his hand, "Bitsy."

"Seriously?" he said, laughing.

"What's so funny?" she asked, giggling again.

"Bitsy? What's your full name, Itsy Bitsy?"

She was smiling. "No. My real name is Betsy, Elizabeth. My little sister couldn't pronounce Betsy. She'd say 'Bitsy.' It sort of stuck."

"Well, Itsy Bitsy, what's your last name?" Troy asked.

"Stark," she told him.

"Wait a minute," the handsome-enough man said. "Stark? Bennington, Vermont? Like Molly Stark?"

Bitsy's eyes widened. She said excitedly, "That's right! Her husband won the Battle of Bennington! You're a man who knows his history."

"Itsy Bitsy Molly Stark," he said as he took a sip of her drink. "Right here in Colorado."

She gave him a smile of approval. This is going to be the beginning of my great new adventure, she thought to herself.

"Where are you staying?" Troy asked.

"I've got a nice room here, right in the resort," she told him.

"May I see it?" he asked.

She smiled and gave that some thought. She looked at him again. He was good-looking, smart and nice to her. She gave him a look that sealed the deal, "Yes, you may."

The pedestrian walks at Snow Hat were illuminated by fairy lights now. They decorated the trees and stretched over the street from the porches of the stores and bars and eateries.

Families and groups of friends were searching for somewhere to eat. Children had more energy than their parents could keep up with, after a day of skiing.

A large metal globe with snowflake cutouts contained a hot fire inside. The flames licked out the top. Benches surrounded it, to warm those who stopped.

Bitsy and Troy slipped off their barstools and walked out into the night. There was an adventure to be had.

21

S he woke up next to him. She was lying on her stomach, looking at him. Troy was sound asleep. He looks like a child when he's asleep, she thought. Not a worry in the world.

"Oh my gosh!" she cried. She jumped out of bed and dashed to the window. Troy was awakened by the sudden flurry of activity. He heard his companion cry, "Snow!"

Bitsy suddenly realized she was standing stark naked in front of the window overlooking the resort's business district. She laughed and covered herself up with a curtain. Troy laughed with her. He rose out of bed and they watched the large snowflakes fall.

"You're in luck, Itsy Bitsy Molly Stark," he said. "You're going powder skiing today."

Troy dressed and assured her that he'd be back within a half hour. He said that he had to go get his skis from his car. He headed for the drop-off area in the parking lot.

She dressed to ski, teasing herself for sleeping with a man she'd met that same night. But, she thought, he seemed like a nice guy, smart, funny and polite.

He reappeared with his ski gear. "Who's that?" Bitsy asked, pointing to the engraved name on the skis.

"What?" Troy asked. For a moment, Bitsy thought he was truly surprised to see the engraving.

"Oh," Troy told her, "I bought them from a doctor. That's his name. He gets new skis every year, so I buy his old ones."

Bitsy didn't notice that a different name was written in permanent marker on Troy's ski poles. And she didn't observe the calamity at the drop-off area when a vacationer claimed that his skis had been stolen. Someone else claimed they couldn't find their poles.

There was about a foot of fresh powder, with more still coming down. The whole resort rippled with excitement. Happy greetings and declarations were shared by skiers and snowboarders as they pushed toward the lifts.

"Whoo!" That was a frequent war cry from the mouths of bodies hurdling downhill. Their skis and boards were beneath the snow hidden from view.

Troy saw that Bitsy was an accomplished skier. She noticed that Troy was struggling.

"Sorry," he said.

"Don't worry," she told him. "I'm having a good time."

"These children you'll be a baby-sitter for," Troy asked her as they rode up the chairlift, "do they ski?"

"Au pair," she corrected him with a smile. "I hope so! That would be so fun!"

They wore themselves out in about three hours. Troy was deeply appreciative that she was ready to stop for the day. He bought her lunch on a covered patio in the resort village. They ate and watched the snow come down.

"So, tell me what else you know about Bennington, Vermont?" Bitsy asked as they were sharing a plate of cheese-covered nachos.

"Hmmmmm," Troy pondered. "Is Robert Frost buried there? The poet?"

"Oh my gosh," Bitsy exclaimed, "you really are smart. Yes, he is."

Troy patted himself on the back. Then, he stood up and said, "I'll be right back." He moved toward the door inside, probably heading for a restroom, she thought.

Bitsy watched him as he walked away. She laughed when she saw that he had taken off his boots and was walking across the patio in his stocking feet.

She saw him squeeze between tables as he headed for the door, always smiling at anyone nearby who engaged him. His hand brushed one table he passed, and it looked to Bitsy like he'd picked up cash left on a table for a tip.

Was she seeing things? It happened so fast, was she sure it happened? It didn't seem to be the kind of thing Troy would do. He was smart and funny. She decided that her eyes were deceiving her.

She turned her head toward the pedestrian walk where skiers could march to the slopes or drag themselves back to their car. Many were window-shopping.

She gazed across the faces of the crowd. Skiers coming off the slopes looked so weary, she thought. There was snow still packed in odd places on their outfits. Men with face hair now had beards and mustaches made of ice.

One man was just pulling up his goggles as he carried his skis toward the bus lot. He looked familiar to Bitsy. Was it an acquaintance from back East, she wondered?

She gasped when she placed the face. It was Senator John Buford from New York! She had briefly been an au pair for the family when they were on a ski vacation in Vermont.

Bitsy rose and walked over to the man. His back was turned to her. She touched his arm and smiled, "Senator Buford?"

The man turned to see her. There was an expression of surprise on his face. He asked, "What did you say?"

"It is!" Bitsy said with a smile. "You're Senator Buford. I was an au pair for your child when you came to Vermont to ski."

The man tried to walk on. "I'm sorry, you're mistaken. I must be going."

"No," she said as she reached for his arm again. "Don't you remember me? I loved your daughter. How is she?"

"I'm sorry, Ms. Stark is it?" Buford interrupted, polite but firm. "You're mistaking me for someone else."

"I didn't tell you my name," Bitsy exclaimed in a lowered voice. She was confused by his denials.

The man stopped and looked at her. "You must have. Yes, I'm sure you did. How else would I know it?" He pulled off his ski helmet, exposing his blond spiked hair. It really did change his look.

But Bitsy suddenly remembered the news stories about Senator Buford and his family. He was accused of murdering his wife and disappeared. She had completely forgotten, up to that moment. "You ARE Senator Buford!"

The man looked around, a horrified expression on his face. "I'm sorry, I'm not who you think I am," and he turned, rushing toward the bus lot.

Bitsy stood, silently, watching the man disappear in the crowd. She doubted herself a little. Senator Buford didn't have blond hair. Could she be mistaken? How horrible would that be?

"Are you alright?" Bitsy heard a familiar voice behind her. She was startled. She turned to see Troy standing there. "Are you alright? You should see the look on your face," he said.

"The oddest thing just happened," she told her handsome new friend. Bitsy had a look of uncertainty, "I just saw a man accused of murdering his wife."

Her face was nearly white as she told Troy about her assignment as a vacation au pair for the New York state senator. "And he's been a fugitive since then. Police are looking for him."

Troy had his phone out. He was searching Google for Buford's name. "Wow, here it is!" Bitsy observed that Troy was excited by the search engine's discovery.

It was an interesting story, she acknowledged to herself, full of intrigue. "Wow," Troy said again and laughed.

Bitsy had completely forgotten that she thought she'd seen Troy snatching a tip off a table. Her mind was on John Buford, trying to make sense of that. She was drained. "I could use a drink. Do you mind if we go back to the room?"

Troy looked at her. He had just returned from making a phone call regarding the stolen goods inside his room in Glenwood Springs. He needed to get them in boxes and ship them.

"Listen," Troy said. "I should go."

A look of surprise came over Bitsy's face. She knew that he was a one-night stand, only she'd forgotten that a commitment like that only lasted for one night.

"I had a great time," he said with that charming, confident smile on his face.

She was embarrassed. "I mean, thanks. Me too," she said. And he was gone. It was a polished act, she thought, like this wasn't his first time.

She entered her hotel room alone. She felt somewhat stupid, forgetting the adventure she'd bargained for. She wanted a drink.

She began peeling off layers of wet ski clothing. She felt like she needed a shower. Then, she began to remember the prior night, the anonymous passion she had sought. A naughty smile came to her face.

As she climbed out of the shower and exited the bathroom, she turned on the TV. She did it absentmindedly. It was something she did without thinking when she lived in her apartment in Vermont. It was noise, to keep her company.

The noon news was on. She heard a knock on the door. She opened it as she applied a towel to dry her blonde hair. She was wearing a terry cloth robe and nothing else.

Before she could utter a word, her visitor said, "May I come in? I can explain." She backed away from the door, allowing him to enter. She hadn't expected to see him again. She wondered what he could possibly say.

On television, the news was showing the audience a picture provided by police. Bitsy just stared. She recognized the face right away. Her eyes stayed on the TV screen.

"It's you," she said softly without turning around. "That's a picture of you."

The man said, "No. It does look like me, though."

"No," she said quietly. "It's you." She turned around.

"It's not me!" he said, aggravated.

She turned back to the TV screen to take another look. The picture was gone but it was him, she thought. She knew it.

"Let me explain," he said with a bit of impatience. She turned back toward the TV screen.

It was a phone cord, she thought, that suddenly slipped over her head and tightened around her neck. She was choking. She tried to reach between the cord and her throat with her hand. She couldn't do it.

"I don't feel good about this," she heard the man saying.

She tried to look up, show her face to him and he'd see that he was making a mistake. But she couldn't. She couldn't breathe. She was getting dizzy. She needed to loosen the cord around her throat, but she couldn't. She tried to push away, but he held her. He was strong. She couldn't fight any longer.

Bitsy fell to the floor. The weight of her fall pulled the cord out of the killer's hands. His chest was heaving, he was breathing hard. He looked down on her. So pretty, he thought.

He wasn't happy with himself. But he really didn't have a choice, he told himself. Her lifeless eyes stared at the foot of the bed.

He looked around the room. He wiped down the cord draped around her neck. He'd wipe the door handle when he left and hang a "Do Not Disturb" sign.

He really didn't have a choice, he thought, as he pulled the door closed behind him.

22

It was an unmistakable sound. A snow shovel was being scraped along a sidewalk by a store owner in Larimer Square. JC lifted his head from the pillow. He knew he was alone in bed, but he looked at the pillow next to him, hoping to see Shara. He was alone.

It was the weekend, the sun was just rising, and there was nothing to stop him from grabbing his ski gear. If he chose one of the closest ski resorts, he could get there when the lifts opened and ski some fresh tracks in the new snow.

He was happy to find that he felt nothing along the lines of unacceptable pain coming from his ribs. The fog had lifted from his head, too. Effects from his concussion had dissipated.

He grabbed an egg sandwich and coffee from the market down the street, pulled his FJ Cruiser from his rented spot and headed west on I-70.

During the drive, he thought about the stories he'd reported on yesterday. Police had released a photo of the car they believed to be involved in the fatal hit-and-run, killing that woman. It had been more than two weeks and they still didn't know who she was.

Police also hadn't identified the car and were seeking the public's help. There was a partial face seen inside the car. An enlarged photo of that was released too.

The image appeared in the newspapers and on all the TV stations in time for Friday's noon news. Police were hoping someone would recognize the driver.

JC had obtained the images of the car and driver and, hardly looking at them, passed them on to a producer. He already had enough to do. He was also providing updates on the searches for Buford and Troy Davis.

"The rest of us can go home," one reporter joked. "JC has the three top stories in the news today. The rest of us aren't needed."

JC smiled. It was a joke, but it was a joke he could be proud of.

Beating the Saturday morning traffic, he arrived at the Loveland ski area in an hour. It was unique because its slopes cascaded down each side of the Eisenhower Tunnel.

Every year, some out-of-state tourists would pack their ski equipment, look at a map and think they were driving to the Loveland Ski Resort.

But they were to be disappointed. They had assumed that the ski area was near the city of Loveland. Too late, they learned that the ski area and the town were one hundred miles apart.

JC was stoked to arrive at the ski area for the biggest snowfall of the season. It was exactly what ski resorts needed as the Christmas ski vacation season was nearing.

JC changed into his boots, fastened the velcro on a back brace that would help his ribs, and was waiting at the chairlift as operators allowed their first human cargo to board.

The skiing was heaven, JC thought. He was buoyant in the soft Colorado powder. He was skiing "freshies," fresh tracks.

The weight of any worries had been left on the chairlift. He didn't ache for Shara, he didn't think about Troy Davis and he could care less about where John Buford was.

The deep snow confounded some skiers and snowboarders. But that was part of the fun. Skiing powder was an acquired skill.

He saw a boarder do a "melon dance." That's what they called a fall ending as the victim gets airborne and lands directly on their head.

In powder, they pull their face from the snow and there is a big smile on it. Those who fall, rise to fall again. "Whooo!" was a common bird call of exuberance.

There was also much skier hubris. Part of the fun was trying things greater than you had tried before. Some led to said melon dances. Some led to trying jumps.

Landing a jump seemed to require a bellow of success upon its completion. Most of those jumps barely got the skier or boarder more than a foot off the snow, but they felt like they were above the clouds. They have "delusions of grand air," JC chuckled to himself.

Steve Trujillo was not a skier. He sat at his kitchen table procrastinating before having to go out and shovel the sidewalk. He was enjoying his coffee and reading the newspaper. It was Saturday. He looked forward to watching some football on his day off.

His cell phone rang, the one he used for police business. He grumbled. It was the last sound he wanted to hear.

"Steve!" said a cheery voice. Trujillo squinted, trying to place the voice.

"You call to turn yourself in?" the detective asked. He'd placed the voice. It was his snitch, Troy Davis.

"Steve, that wasn't me. I didn't do anything," said the voice.

"Then come on into the station. We'll get your side of the story, and if you're telling the truth, you'll be free to go," Trujillo said.

"Steve, I'm not that dumb. You guys think I did it," Davis said. "I'm going to give you some time to sort it out. You'll see that I'm innocent and everything will be back the way it was."

The detective looked at the screen on his phone for a number. There was none. Davis was probably using a burner phone. "Why'd you call, Troy?"

"I've got a tip for you. See? I'm still on your side," Davis answered.

Trujillo's eyes rolled. "What's your tip?"

"You're looking for John Buford, right?" Davis said. "The senator from New York? Well, I know where he is."

Trujillo took interest. He reached for a pen and prepared to scribble notes on the newspaper. "How would you know where he is?"

"I saw him!" Davis lied.

"Where?"

"The Snow Hat Ski Resort!"

"When?"

"A couple of days ago!"

What was Davis' angle, Trujillo wondered. Did Davis want to create a distraction, allowing for his own escape? "Where are you?" he asked Davis.

"Steeeve, that would just waste both of our time," Davis said. "I'm safe, thanks for asking."

"I didn't," Trujillo told Davis. Trujillo was fed up with Davis' game. Davis had burned him.

Davis continued, "I'm just going to lay low while you sort out the misunderstanding concerning me. In the meantime, I'm doing you a favor. Call it a good-faith measure."

"How did you cross paths with Senator Buford?" Trujillo asked.

Davis laughed. "It's the darndest thing. I was minding my own business, doing some skiing. I'm grabbing a bite to eat, and I recognize Buford. His picture has been in the news, right? He was walking in the company of a beautiful young blonde. She wasn't his daughter, if you know what I mean."

Troy knew he was laying it on thick. Why not sell it? He needed room to work. He needed police to find some real bad guys to go after.

Snow Hat, Trujillo thought. This rat may not be lying. The detective asked Davis where he saw Buford with the young woman.

"I spotted them walking down the pedestrian walk, window-shopping. They were quite amorous, I thought," Davis told the police officer.

Why soil her reputation, Davis asked himself. Eh, why not?

"What did he look like?" the law officer asked. "Was he wearing a disguise, did he color his hair?"

Troy wasn't ready to describe a man he hadn't really seen. "No, he looked just like in the picture in the news. Well, he wasn't wearing a tie," Troy laughed.

Trujillo wasn't laughing, "Do you know who the girl is?"

"Never seen her before in my life," Davis lied.

"You said she was blonde, good-looking. What else can you tell me about her?" the detective inquired.

"Blonde, blue eyes," the snitch responded. He'd keep it vague.

"Great, so I've just got to find a blonde at a ski area. And you're just doing your civic duty." Trujillo barked, "Why didn't you call me a couple of days ago?"

"Steeeve, I'm a busy guy," Davis said. "Anyway, I've gotta go. Good luck! You always get your man!" The phone clicked. Davis was gone.

Trujillo sighed. He was watching his day off evaporate. He called the county sheriff's office near Snow Hat. He told them about the potential sighting of Buford. He said that he got it from a reliable source. He didn't mention Troy Davis' name.

The shift commander said that they'd send a couple of cars over to Snow Hat to take a look around. Trujillo said he'd get there in about two hours.

When he arrived, the detective pulled his car into a spot at Snow Hat's unloading area. Skiers used those short-term parking places to drop their skis off. Then they were expected to find a parking spot in a distant lot and ride a free shuttle back to their ski equipment. Trujillo showed the attendant his badge.

Trujillo heard the snow as it was crushed beneath his boots with Vibram soles. He'd found his police-issue parka in the back of a closet at home. This was the first time he'd needed it since last winter.

He met with the deputies who had arrived upon his request. They'd come up with nothing. No one said that they recognized the man with salt-and-pepper hair and a necktie, the face looking out from the four-year-old official photo of the New York State Senate.

"Great," Trujillo said to the deputies. "Everyone is wearing helmets and goggles. We can't even see their faces. We might as well be looking for someone in costume on Halloween."

After a few hours, Trujillo sent the deputies home. He stayed to eyeball the crowd as the lifts closed. Maybe Buford would be spotted, without a helmet, in the après ski crowd.

He wasn't. "A perfect ending to a perfect day," the detective mumbled to himself, walking back to his car in the dark. He couldn't help thinking that he'd wasted a day off. And he still had to shovel his driveway.

23

"Do you have a description?" Trujillo spoke into the phone at his desk at District Two. He was cradling it between his neck and shoulder and writing some notes.

"You're kidding me," he said, stopping his fidgeting. The detective hung up the phone after a few minutes. He rubbed his eyes with his hand. It was a sign of frustration. He reached for the phone and dialed the county sheriff's office near Snow Hat.

"Thanks for your help on Saturday," Trujillo spoke into the phone.

He listened, and then he said, "Well, it may not have been a waste of time. Maybe we just didn't know what we were looking for."

Trujillo asked for assistance again from the sheriff's office. It was their turf, not his. He'd rather do it by himself, he thought, but that wouldn't be considered playing nice with neighboring jurisdictions.

"A young woman has been reported missing in Garfield County," he said into the phone. "She didn't report for her new job."

Trujillo listened on the phone. Then he said, "We don't have her name yet. We're getting that. She was hired through a placement agency. We're getting in touch with them. They're back East and they're closed because of a big snowstorm."

He listened some more and then said, "Yep, probably the same storm that clobbered us here. But we're tracking them down. It won't be long before we have a name."

He listened and replied, "Blonde, blue eyes, attractive." He was winging it. He hadn't been given a description of the missing woman. That was the description he'd been given by Davis, of the woman seen with Buford.

Trujillo listened on the phone, then he said, "It's a hunch. Someone spotted a woman fitting that description on Wednesday or Thursday."

He listened. "OK," he said. "Thanks, see you soon."

Trujillo pulled into his familiar spot in the unloading area at Snow Hat. He saw that the resort wasn't as crowded as it had been Saturday. Now it was Monday. He figured that most of the skiers and snowboarders had gone home until next weekend.

He walked back to the stretch of stores and restaurants where he'd spent too many hours only two days ago. He looked around. It was sunny. The snow had stopped falling and was melting on the stone walk. That was Colorado sun for you, he thought.

The buildings were all a uniform mix of logs and stone and cedar. They were massive and had wooden porches, supported from the ground by thick tree trunk beams.

The buildings were designed to look small and homey, but the scale of them disclosed they had large operations working within each one.

This spot fit the description of where Davis said he saw the senator. Trujillo looked up the pedestrian walk in each direction. The chairlifts were to his left and the parking lots were to his right. If Buford was seen by someone who could identify his picture, it probably had to be in these two blocks, the detective thought.

He looked up and saw rows of uniform windows. They would be on the second and third floor. It looked to him like a hotel.

The detective looked along the first floor of the buildings now. It was all retail. But he saw a door between a restaurant and a ski shop. There was a shiny brass door handle, but no sign.

Upon closer investigation, the door required a pass key. It was a side door for guests of the hotel upstairs, he guessed. Trujillo suggested that a couple of deputies come with him. He walked up to the corner of the building and peered around it. There, he saw a grand entrance to the hotel, and doors he could enter.

They walked into a plush lobby, lined with storefronts and shiny brass fixtures. There were comfortable sofas and coffee tables in clusters, designed to create multiple living room settings. There was a big two-sided fireplace in the middle of the room.

The detective, followed by the deputies, approached the lobby desk and identified himself. He explained what brought him there, "Have you seen this man?" The detective showed the desk clerk a picture of John Buford.

The clerk shook his head. Trujillo asked him if he had a guest that was blonde with blue eyes. The law officer felt stupid offering only that description.

"We don't have a name," he admitted. "But maybe she was with the man in the picture I showed you?"

The clerk called over a colleague behind the desk. Trujillo guessed that she was a Manager of Desk Clerks. He showed his badge and explained his mission a second time. He showed her a picture of Buford. "No," the manager said, "I cannot say that we have anything like that."

"Do you recall a pretty blonde checking in over the past week?" Trujillo asked. The manager clerk smiled. Of course, Trujillo gathered she was telling him, they have pretty blondes checking in every five minutes.

He just had a feeling. It made him impatient. But Trujillo thought he was going to have to wait until police got her name. If she was with Buford, or even if she spent an hour with Buford, it would be a solid lead. She could be a friend, she could be a hooker, who cares?

There were a dozen hotels at the ski resort. Add that to the number of condos and private rentals. It was overwhelming. He needed the name of the blonde woman.

"What about the maid service?" Trujillo asked.

"I am sorry?" the manager said, disclosing that she didn't understand his meaning.

Phil Bayly

"Does your maid service say they have anyone who isn't answering their door?" he asked. "Maybe there's even been a 'Do Not Disturb' sign on the door for a few days?"

The manager clerk excused herself with a smile. She picked up a phone and dialed an extension, presumably the maid's workroom. She spoke in a hushed tone. It sounded like something other than English. The detective knew that ski resorts had been working hard to bring diversity to their mountains. They were hiring a lot of internationals.

Trujillo strained to hear. If she was speaking Spanish, he'd understand the language a little bit.

Trujillo hadn't grown up in a Spanish-speaking home. His parents spoke Spanish, but they didn't want their children to because they'd be discriminated against. His mother and father had worked hard to become Americans. They wanted their children to be accepted as Americans.

He couldn't hear the manager clerk well, and it didn't sound like Spanish anyway.

She returned to her spot behind the desk, in front of the detective and said, "There is such a room."

"May we see it?" he asked.

The manager opened a drawer in front of her and pulled out a passkey. "Come with me, please."

On the top floor, the manager clerk led them off the elevator and down the hall. She stopped in front of a room with a "Do Not Disturb" sign on the door. The hotel employee knocked. No answer. She knocked again and said, "Excuse me, is anyone in this room?" No answer.

The manager produced the passkey and slid it across the reader on the door handle. It clicked and she pushed the door open.

166

There was a short passageway leading into the room. Only the head of the bed could be seen from the doorway. Trujillo tried to catch the hotel employee by the shoulder, to allow him to enter first, but she advanced before he could grasp her.

She let out a small scream and held her hand over her mouth, as though she was about to vomit. Her eyes shut and she turned away, burrowing her face into Trujillo's chest. He clutched her, trying to offer comfort, as he looked toward the end of the bed. There, Bitsy Stark was lying where she was left, a phone cord still around her neck.

Trujillo's phone rang. He dug it out of his pocket as he handed the sobbing manager clerk off to a deputy. "Yeah," the detective snapped into the phone.

His eyes turned back to the manager as she was trying to compose herself, wiping her eyes.

"Elizabeth Stark?" he said to her as soon as he'd heard it over the phone. The manager clerk, hand again over her mouth, nodded "yes."

"We found her," Trujillo said into the phone. "You'd better get the crime-scene guys here. This was no accident."

Over the next few hours, Detective Trujillo explained to the county sheriff, the Colorado Bureau of Investigation and his boss how he came to know that the victim was going to be blonde, pretty and in that room.

"Anonymous tip," he said. Trujillo didn't want to be identified as the guy who was still using Troy Davis as a snitch. He hadn't asked for that phone call from Davis, he just hadn't ignored it.

Trujillo was pressed to provide details of the tip. He was asked, "Was she seen with anyone?" Trujillo thought that the connection was pretty flimsy, but the tipster did say who Elizabeth Stark was seen in the company of.

"Senator John Buford," Trujillo said to a lineup of shocked faces.

24

"You have a captive audience," JC chided Milt, "so show a little pride in your work."

Their live-shot location was back at South Platte Cemetery. "Thumbsucker," Milt told JC.

"Whatever," JC responded. "You have sixty thousand souls in close proximity, watching you work this evening," JC said as he waved across the rolling hills. There were seventy-seven acres of marble and granite markers.

Each engraved name represented a life. Some of those lives lasted only an instant and some of them lasted a long time. There were soldiers, bankers, gold miners and ministers. There were people Denver's streets were named after and people history would never recall. They'd all lived, JC thought to himself.

JC was wearing a winter jacket with the logo of his TV station. It was colder than the last time he was at the cemetery, and the sunlight was disappearing earlier in the day.

JC told his audience that tips to police from people saying they'd seen Troy Davis hadn't panned out. He had disappeared from his usual haunts. Maybe, JC reported, Davis had left the area. At any rate, there hadn't been a cemetery theft reported in two weeks, maybe more.

After JC tossed back to the anchors, his phone rang. It was the newsroom's executive producer. It was his duty to carry out the whims and worries of the news director, among other things. He asked, "You wanted to talk?"

JC said, "Yeah, I think we ought to pursue the connection between Davis and Miller more. There's something there."

"Did police tell you that?" the executive producer asked.

"Actually, I told them," JC answered.

"You think Davis killed Miller?" the EP asked JC.

"I do," the reporter said. "Miller had lobster in his stomach." There was silence on the other end of the phone line.

"Trujillo told me that Davis bought lobster at a Fort Collins supermarket earlier in the same day that police believe Miller was killed. Davis and Miller ate together," JC explained.

"Well, that's pretty interesting," the executive producer stated, "but does that link Davis to Miller's execution?"

"Miller worked at a scrap yard. He didn't hang out with a bunch of gang members, he had a wife." JC asserted, "When he wasn't with her or at work, he hung out with Davis."

"I get what you're saying," the EP answered, "but it's still a stretch."

"He did it," JC said with authority. "He's smart and sneaky." JC wasn't telling the newsroom's second-in-command everything. He didn't say that there had been two burglaries of museums on the Western Slope. No one had accused Davis of doing them, but JC thought it was his style, something he would do.

"If Davis did kill Miller," the EP determined, "you'd only be right because of a lucky guess. What if you're wrong?"

"You don't pay me to be stupid," the reporter answered.

JC ended the phone call and helped Milt and the live-truck engineer wrap up the gear. His phone rang again.

"I can give you something, but it doesn't go public until the morning, OK?" It was Detective Trujillo's voice. He knew that JC had been in Albany, New York and was way ahead of the other journalists in Colorado on the John Buford story. JC was the conduit chosen by police, this time, to air their suspicions that Buford had just murdered a young woman at the Snow Hat Ski Resort.

"What?" JC responded to the news that Buford was the murder suspect.

"I had a tip over the weekend that he was seen at Snow Hat," Trujillo said over the phone. "There was a young woman with him, blonde and pretty."

JC was listening intently. He was staring at the now-dark cemetery. When the detective paused, JC said, "He is fond of Snow Hat. Even his daughter told me that."

"Well," Trujillo disclosed, "today we found that young blonde woman dead in a Snow Hat hotel room."

"And you think Buford did it?" JC asked.

"It's not a slam dunk," the detective acknowledged, "but there's reason to believe he's here. And the tipster was right about the girl."

"Do you have her ID?" JC asked.

"Again, none of this gets reported until tomorrow," Trujillo repeated. "Her name is Elizabeth Stark. Twenty-four years old. She just arrived here from Bennington, Vermont. She was going to take a job in Garfield County as an au pair."

JC was scribbling notes as quickly as he could. "We can report this tomorrow morning?"

"Yeah, tomorrow morning," the detective confirmed. "Don't use my name. Just say 'a police source.'"

"OK," JC agreed. "Do you really believe Buford did this?"

There was a pause on Trujillo's end of the line. "He's a killer. He murdered his wife four years ago, there's no question about that. Don't they always say, 'The first murder is the hardest?'"

Trujillo hung up the phone on his desk. He began to throw notes and records into manila folders so they'd be out of sight. He'd just toss them on top of everything else in a drawer. They were the first thing he'd pull out of the drawer in the morning. He was bushed. He wanted to go home.

He still had his parka on when his supervisor called him into her office. She probably wanted to know how the conversation with JC Snow went.

"Sit down," said Detective Sergeant Trudy Johnson. She was sitting behind her desk. The paperwork spread out in front of her looked as though she'd had a long day, too.

Trujillo's detective sergeant had dark hair pulled back tight into a bun. She didn't wear much makeup, just some eyeliner. She'd come up through the ranks when there weren't a lot of women to help pull her along. The hairstyle, she thought, helped her look not so much like a woman.

She had a lot of empathy from her force. Her husband had died in the first wave of Coronavirus. He wasn't an official member of the police department, but he was part of the police family. There was a color guard and an impressive send-off at his funeral. Now, perhaps, Detective Sergeant Johnson was married to her job.

"A task force has been formed to find John Buford and solve this woman's murder," Detective Sergeant Johnson told Trujillo. "You've been assigned to it."

"Buford and the girl?" he asked. "We're assuming Buford killed her?"

"We're not assuming anything," his superior said. "We're just helping out. The investigation is crossing a lot of jurisdictions. Two sheriff's offices and the Colorado Bureau of Investigation and New York State Police are on the task force, too. The FBI will also be available, if we need them."

"OK," the detective answered.

"How'd it go with the reporter?" she asked.

"He'll get us some hits," the detective answered.

"You find anyone who can positively identify Senator Buford?" she asked.

Trujillo shook his tired head. "Not one. But we just got started. The news media will plant the seed tomorrow and maybe we'll get someone who saw something."

"How were you led to Buford?" the detective sergeant inquired.

"A tip," Trujillo told her. The detective hoped he wouldn't be asked who the tipster was. He didn't like that this all led back to Davis. The snitch was on his shit list.

Trujillo continued to tell his supervisor most of what he knew. "The tipster said he saw Buford. He said he saw him with a pretty blonde. It sort of clicked when I heard there was a young woman missing."

"You said the tipster was anonymous?" she asked.

"Yep, with a burner phone," he answered.

"What do you think his angle was?" the supervisor asked. "Why wouldn't a tipster want to be known to police. There might even be a reward offered."

"Maybe he was calling from a crack den," Trujillo offered, half joking. There could be a hundred reasons to remain anonymous.

"A crack den, at Snow Hat?" his boss asked with doubt in her eyes.

Damn, she's good, he thought. Trujillo sensed it was time to come clean. It was clear that his immediate superior knew he wasn't telling all that he knew.

"It was Davis," the detective said as he looked for the crease in his pants.

"Troy Davis?" she asked in a raised voice.

"Yeah," Trujillo admitted as he looked up at her face.

"You didn't think it was important to mention that you got a call from a man we're looking for? To arrest?"

"You're right," Trujillo surrendered. "I just didn't like the fact that the creep still thought he could call me. He burned us! I want to throw him in a holding cell, personally!"

The detective sergeant understood Trujillo's misgivings. She lowered her voice quickly. Maybe, Trujillo thought, that was something they taught at the school for police supervisors.

"But you should have told us that it was Davis who led us to the body," she told him.

"He didn't lead us to the body," Trujillo protested, "but he may have led us to Buford."

Johnson stared at Trujillo without speaking. She was judging his guilt. She moved a pencil around on her desk, thinking. Finally, she said, "Alright, let's all get some sleep.

You've told me now. We'll make sense out of it in the morning."

Trujillo stood and headed for the office door. He stopped and turned toward the detective sergeant as she remained seated behind her desk.

"It means," Trujillo noted, "Davis might have left Denver. He was at Snow Hat last week."

25

The stunning news that New York State Senator John Buford was a suspect in a homicide at the Snow Hat Ski Resort broke on the morning news show.

JC had worked at his desk from the moment he got the call from Detective Trujillo, the evening before. Then, the reporter crawled out of bed after a few hours of sleep and met a live truck back at Snow Hat.

They broke the news at 4:30 a.m. and repeated it each half hour on the early morning news.

JC reported that Buford was a "'person of interest" in the murder of Elizabeth Stark. It would set the trajectory of the entire news day. It would still be the lead story on the evening news. JC would still be reporting live from Snow Hat.

"We have the luxury of time," JC said to his photographer after the last morning live shot was wrapped up. "I'll buy you breakfast." The photog's name was Edgar Pabor. He regularly worked for the early morning news show. JC didn't know him very well. He was young, probably in his late twenties, and full of energy.

Pabor proudly declared that he was a descendent of the earliest settler in the Grand Valley—"At least, that's what my grandpa told me." Edgar was from Fruita, Colorado.

The reporter and news photographer sat down at a table inside a restaurant with a glass wall looking out on the pedestrian path leading to the chairlifts.

Fruita's name came from its unlikely location as a fruit-farming area.

"There are three hundred days of sunshine a year," said Pabor. He grew up on his family's fruit farm.

"The Fruit Festival in Fruita is the best fair on the Western Slope," bragged Pabor. But then he said in a hushed tone, "Well, the best festival is in May. But it's in Fruita, too. You know what it is?"

JC was caught by surprise. He'd been half-listening to the young news photographer. "Do you know what the best festival in Fruita really is?" Pabor asked JC again.

"Ummm," JC tried to participate, "It's NOT the Fruit Festival? I've been to the Fruit Festival, it's great!"

"It is," agreed Pabor. "And it makes a lot of money for Fruita's farmers. But just between you and me ..." Pabor looked in both directions, as though his secret might be stolen, "The best festival is the one for Mike the Headless Chicken."

JC wondered if he heard right. "There was a headless chicken?"

"Yeah, Mike!" Pabor explained that the festival for Mike the Headless Chicken paid homage to a real chicken who lived for a year and a half after his head was cut off. The farmer who beheaded Mike kept feeding him, with an eyedropper.

JC looked at Edgar in silence. Then he said, "I don't think that anything we report all day ... can come as a bigger surprise to me as Mike the Headless Chicken." Edgar laughed in glee. JC laughed in wonder.

But JC's mind returned to John Buford, and Elizabeth Stark from Vermont. He'd asked a producer in the newsroom, after Trujillo's call yesterday, to find a picture of the dead woman. The producer could only come up with a high school yearbook photo.

Stark was twenty-four when her life ended, and seventeen when the photo was taken at her high school. But it was the only photo they had to show the audience, and at seventeen, she'd already become an attractive young lady.

Her appearance probably hadn't changed that much, JC thought. It would be close enough for viewers to know if they'd ever seen her. JC told those viewers that police were hoping to hear from anyone who had seen Ms. Stark.

JC wondered if the news audience realized how many times they were looking at high school yearbook photos of victims who lost their lives in tragic circumstances. They were the stopgap in the news business until reporters could ask the family for a favorite picture of their loved one.

For a while, social media had been the news industry's modern miracle provider of photos of victims. Then, legal questions began to arise about those photos from social media sites.

A waitress approached the table JC and Edgar were sitting at, to check on their progress with breakfast. She asked, "Is everything alright?" Both men nodded their approval, as their mouths were full. But JC swallowed, "Can I ask you something?"

The young waitress said, "Sure."

JC pulled out a picture of Elizabeth Stark. "Do you recognize this woman? Has she been in here?"

"Yeah, actually she has," the waitress told the reporter after looking at the photo. "I remember her because she's from Vermont. I'm from New Hampshire. I think she was staying in the hotel." The waitress pointed her pen over her shoulder in the general direction of the hotel. The waitress clearly did not connect the photo with the woman whose body had been found upstairs.

"I think she was here alone, so we chatted a bit," the waitress said. "She asked about places to go and where to ski."

JC pulled another photo out of his pocket, the four-year-old likeness of John Buford. It was the most recent one he had. "Have you seen this man?" JC asked.

The waitress looked at the photo and began shaking her head, "No, I don't recognize him."

"You didn't see him with Elizabeth, the woman from Vermont?"

The waitress shook her head after thinking a moment, "No, I haven't seen him. I'd have remembered if he was with her. She was alone when I waited on her."

The waitress smiled and turned her attention to her other tables.

"I'm going to take a look around," JC told Edgar. "I know where to find you if I need you." JC picked up his bagel to take with him.

"OK," Edgar said and continued to eat.

JC walked around the corner and through the door leading to the hotel lobby. He approached the desk and asked if the clerk was on duty who had shown police to Stark's room. The clerk summoned a woman with dark hair and features.

"May I help you?" the woman asked as she approached JC. She stood before him on the other side of the desk.

"You helped police find this woman?" JC asked as he slipped a picture of Stark across the granite desktop.

"I do not want to talk about this, I am sorry," the manager clerk said.

"But that is her, right?" JC rushed his question before the woman had a chance to turn away.

"Yes, it is," she confirmed.

"What about this guy?" JC hurried as he pushed the picture of Buford across the desk.

To JC's relief, the hotel employee paused to look at the man's picture. She looked up and said, "No, I am sorry, I have not seen this man." Then she walked away and through a door into an office.

The cold morning air hit JC in the face as he pushed out the hotel's revolving door. He walked around the corner back onto the stone path leading to the slopes. He showed the pictures to more employees who worked in stores and restaurants along the pedestrian walk. They were just opening up their shops. Some still had wet hair from their morning shower. None of them could identify either Stark or Buford.

He poked his head into a bar that seemed to serve breakfast, too. It was called the Yardsale.

A middle-aged woman was behind the bar, cleaning glasses. She was attractive but looked like she'd worked long hours for a long time.

JC approached her with a smile. He pulled out Stark's photo and showed it to her.

"Yes, I saw her here. I'm a manager. I was working the floor. It was a few nights ago. She was sitting at the bar with a man," the manager said. "They seemed to be getting along." She said it with a smile and much-intended innuendo.

"This guy?" JC pushed forward the picture of Buford. The manager looked at the photo for a long time. JC thought she had doubt in her eye.

"Yeah, sure," she said as she looked up. "That could be him."

JC asked, "Could I get my photographer and do a quick interview with you?"

"Oh, I don't know," the woman said. JC thought she was mostly camera shy.

"I don't think it would hurt business," he told her. "We start the interview with a wide shot, showing off what a cool place this is. People tend to be drawn to settings they see on the news, if it's not a dark alley or somewhere dangerous. It's like seeing a restaurant in a movie. Viewers kind of want to go there."

The woman agreed. JC dashed to the restaurant where he'd left Edgar. They returned with a camera and interviewed the woman about what she remembered seeing that night, when Elizabeth Stark was in her bar with a man that could be Buford.

The journalists left the bar knowing they'd scored an interview that would be a keystone to their live report on the evening news. "And it's not even eleven in the morning. I wish we'd brought our skis," JC said with delight.

JC and Edgar interviewed the waitress, too, shocked to hear that her customer from Vermont had been murdered. "She was nice," the waitress told the camera, with a sad look.

His phone rang. It was the producer helping JC with the Buford story. Her name was Robin Smith. JC liked her. She was relatively new to the news business. Her job in the newsroom entailed helping anyone with anything they asked for.

JC thought that she was smart and didn't mind getting dirty. He guessed that she was in her thirties. She'd first done something else with her life. Archaeology, he thought he remembered her telling him.

She told JC that she'd just spoken to the placement agency in Vermont. "That's where Bitsy Stark got her jobs," Robin told JC.

"Who?" JC asked.

"Oh," the producer answered, "that's what she goes by, Bitsy. The placement agency says everyone calls her Bitsy."

"Bitsy, it is," JC said. "Thanks."

"Wait," Robin said into the phone, afraid JC was going to hang up. "They're sending her files to us. They all really liked Bitsy. They want to help. I asked if they could send us a list of people she's worked for as an au pair. I'm not sure why, I just thought it might be interesting. They're going to email it to me this morning."

"Wow," JC responded. "Great work. Are you going to send them to me, or are you going to look them over?" he asked. He thought for a moment, "Can you do both?"

The producer said that she would. "Nice work," JC repeated.

JC and Edgar headed for the live truck. They expected to report their breaking story for the noon news also. They had a few new items to include. Otherwise, it would be a repeat of the story they broadcast that morning.

JC did tell the noon audience that he had found employees at Snow Hat who said they recognized Bitsy Stark. He told the audience they could hear what those people had to say when he reported live that evening.

Saying he had an interesting interview without showing the interview, was a deliberate tease to get viewers to watch the evening news for a fresh update. Teasing had become standard fare on television news, even when there wasn't going to be anything new to report. This time there would be.

JC's phone rang. It was Robin Smith in the newsroom again: "I have the list of Bitsy Stark's former jobs. You're not going to believe this."

"Is it in my email?" JC asked.

"It should be," the producer answered.

"Well, you found something, you tell me," JC said.

"It was only a one-week assignment, but Bitsy Stark worked for Senator Buford and his family!"

JC was silent. He'd heard what Robin said, but it wasn't what he expected to hear.

"It was about six years ago," Robin continued. "Just for a week, while the family was on a ski vacation in Vermont. There was a little girl."

Lucy, JC thought. "But she was about twelve then," JC said out loud. He asked, "Why an au pair?"

"It was really more like babysitting," Robin said. "I was told by the person at the placement agency that Bitsy was young, maybe 18. The placement agency says that the Bufords wanted to go out on a couple of nights, and they wanted someone to keep their daughter company at the hotel room."

"So Bitsy knew Buford," JC offered. "Buford shows up here at Snow Hat at the same time Bitsy is here. Was it a rendezvous? Were they having a fling?"

"Maybe," Robin said.

"A manager who says she saw them together at her bar says they looked pretty amorous," JC told the producer. "Maybe they were having an affair and she threatened to give him up to the police?"

"That could get her killed," Robin supposed.

JC said nothing for a minute, thinking about other likely explanations. Robin could hear his breathing. She waited patiently.

"Huh," JC said into the telephone. "Something inside kept telling me that Buford didn't do it. Shows what I know."

26

"**N**o!" she shouted into Beverly Pruyn's face before stomping out of the room. Lucy made sure each of her steps up the stairs was a noisy declaration of her rejection. Her door slammed and there was silence on the first floor.

Beverly Pruyn was still standing by the telephone in the hallway leading to the kitchen. That's where she'd heard Denver Police Detective Steve Trujillo tell her that John Buford was implicated in the murder of Bitsy Stark.

"No," Beverly had quietly said when the detective asked her if she knew where her brother was.

"No," she said when asked if she knew Bitsy Stark.

"No," she'd told the police officer when he asked if Lucy might know where her father was.

"The night of Fiona's ... passing." That was her answer when Trujillo asked when the last time was that she'd seen John Buford.

"Oh dear," she'd said when the detective told her that they had to consider Buford dangerous and it would be better if he turned himself in.

"He may be a two-time killer," Trujillo told her. "Our officers have been told to protect themselves. I wouldn't want your brother to be shot. If you know where he is, he'd be better off if you told us."

Beverly Pruyn told him that she didn't know where her brother was, "Please don't hurt him, this is all a misunderstanding."

"How do you know that, ma'am?" Trujillo asked. He wasn't convinced that Buford hadn't been in touch with his family. Even good families, he'd experienced, often lied for their loved ones.

"That's just not him," Beverly said as she started to cry.

Trujillo could hear Mrs. Pruyn choking up. "I'm sorry, Mrs. Pruyn. This isn't your fault. I'm sorry that you have to go through this."

She said something into the telephone that Trujillo couldn't understand. "Could I speak with Lucy?" he asked.

"Not at this moment," Beverly told him. "She's very upset."

"Of course, she is," the detective said. "I'll try again another day. But could you ask her, again, if she's spoken to her father recently? I don't want this to end badly."

"I will," Beverly answered softly. "Thank you. Goodbye." She hung up the phone and cried.

She had collapsed into a chair next to the phone. She didn't blame Lucy for being mad. She was just upset.

As Beverly cried, she felt a presence next to her. She looked up through moist eyes. It was Lucy. The young woman knelt next to the chair and hugged her Aunt Beverly, the best mom she had ever had. They both sobbed as they held each other.

JC's phone rang. He was in the car heading for home after a long day of live shots at Snow Hat. Milt was driving. He had relieved Edgar at midday, so the younger photographer could get some sleep before his next early morning shift.

"It's not true," said a quiet voice on the other end of the phone line. JC moved the phone away from his ear and looked at the number on the screen.

"Lucy?" he asked.

"It's not true," she repeated.

JC didn't want to lose this call in the mountains. This wasn't going to be an easy conversation, and there wasn't going to be a second chance. He directed Milt to look for a place to pull over his car.

"Hang on a second," JC said into the phone. Milt found an escape ramp for trucks, to be used when they gained too much speed coming down steep portions of the mountain roads.

"How did you hear?" JC asked.

"A police officer called my aunt, my mom," Lucy answered.

"I don't know what happened," JC told the young woman. "There's still a lot of guessing going on. But can I speak with you honestly? There may be some things that aren't easy to hear, but you're an adult. I'll talk to you like an adult, if you can take it."

"OK," the voice said, sounding like she was beginning to cry.

JC had reported during the evening news that one police theory suggested Buford and Bitsy Stark had been having an affair. JC had already shared his producer's discovery with Trujillo, that Stark had briefly worked for Buford in Vermont.

The reporter's live shot at noon had also led police to the same manager of the bar that JC had interviewed. She also told police that Stark and her male companion were getting intimate while they shared drinks. She also told police that, while he didn't look exactly like that picture, she thought the man with Bitsy was Buford.

Perhaps, police hypothesized, they were having an affair and she was going to disclose his whereabouts, so he killed her.

JC tried to choose his words carefully as he prepared to speak with Buford's daughter. Lucy wasn't guilty of anything, he reminded himself. She'd been a victim all her life.

She hadn't seen JC's live shot. She was in Albany. But police had probably suggested the affair with Bitsy to see if Lucy knew anything about it.

"Did your father know Bitsy Stark?"

"A little," Lucy said. "She was my babysitter, years ago."

"Do you remember her?" JC asked.

"I do. She was nice. I thought she was really cool," Lucy recounted. "She was older and she spoke to me like I was a peer. But I only saw her like twice."

"Do you think your father ever saw her again?" JC inquired.

"I know what they're saying, that they were having an affair," Lucy said tersely.

"Is it possible?" JC tried to ask gently.

"I don't see how," Lucy told him. "She was really young. And he ... Fiona ... It only happened two years later."

There was silence, then Lucy said, "If he wanted to do that, there were girls at the Capitol. It's not like things like that don't happen right at the Capitol."

"You haven't talked to him since you and I last spoke?" JC asked her.

He could hear soft sobbing on the other end of the line. "No," Lucy squeaked.

"I'm going to let you go," JC told the young woman. "I'm really sorry that you're being put through this. I'll call you if something comes up. You call me, if you hear anything, K?"

"OK," she said quietly.

JC was physically and emotionally spent. Milt pulled back onto the highway to drive home.

Milt had been quiet ever since he arrived at Snow Hat and sent Edgar home. "Anything on your mind?" JC had asked him.

"No, why?" Milt responded.

"You're quiet. That's not a trait that normally defines you," JC kidded.

"Nope," Milt responded. JC thought to himself, Nope what? But he thought it was clear Milt didn't want to talk about it, so the reporter left him alone. Silence took less energy after a long day, anyway.

Detective Trujillo hung up another phone call. The tactic had worked. Calls had been coming steadily since JC's report that morning. The task force was hearing from people who had been at Snow Hat last week and said they had seen Bitsy. But she was always alone, they said. No one had seen someone matching the description of Buford. Trujillo thought that was odd.

Up Boulder Canyon, John Buford sat motionless on his bed inside his simple second-floor room. He was paralyzed. He was afraid to go outside. He was afraid to stay in Nederland. He was trying to regain his composure since seeing JC's reports. He needed a plan, he thought.

He asked himself how could someone have possibly seen him? Sure, Bitsy saw him. That was shocking. Where did she come from? He was surprised that he even came up with her name when he spoke to her. It was his political training, he surmised. It was important for a politician to remember voters' names.

But this fantasy by police that he was having an affair with the girl? He saw her, what, twice? And she stayed back with Lucy while Buford went out with his wife.

He thought back to the vacation in Vermont. They were skiing, he remembered. He wanted Lucy to have company. He and Fiona needed some "alone time." That's just when things were coming unraveled. He thought that if he and Fiona could share a couple of "date nights" everything might blow over.

Poor Bitsy, he thought. Wrong place, wrong time. Lucy liked her, he recalled.

Bitsy recognized him, he thought, because he had his helmet on and his goggles up. If she'd seen his blond spikes, she wouldn't have given him a second look. He should keep his goggles down, he thought.

It occurred to him that no one on television described him as having blond spikey hair. They kept showing that old "head-and-shoulders" shot from the Capitol. The audience would be looking for a man with graying hair, distinguished.

In Nederland, people already knew him vaguely, and he wasn't John Buford. He was Jose Garcia. He might be OK, he dared to think.

27

He thought he looked like a zombie. But he was only half done shaving his head. All Troy Davis had really done was use a set of clippers to cut his hair as short as possible. It was dreadfully uneven. He made faces in the mirror that he thought zombies would make.

Davis laughed as he looked at his reflection. He whistled some golden oldie while he pulled the razor across his head. He was having fun. He'd shave around portions of his hair to create patterns. A diamond, a circle, a short mohawk, a racing stripe.

His landlady smiled as she walked down the hall past the door of his rented room. She liked happy tenants. She thought that he was such a pleasant man.

He held up the mirror to see the final result. He saw a man with a clean scalp smiling at him. He was growing a goatee, too. It was still a little thin. He thought that he might fill it in with a black sharpie until it grew in more.

He continued to whistle. He'd seen the headlines. They were all about Buford. Davis' name wasn't even in the paper.

Davis was thinking of going for a hike in the Book Cliffs, outside of Grand Junction. He thought he'd enjoy getting some exercise and he might see those wild horses. "It's warmer there," he said.

Maybe, he thought, he'd take his bike. "I could take my new haircut for a test drive," he thought. "I'll be streamlined." He laughed at himself. He felt like he was on vacation, being out of Denver. "Every day is vacation," he thought.

He thought about going to Aspen later that night, hitting a few bars. Maybe he'd meet a girl like Bitsy. It was a shame, he thought, about what happened to Bitsy.

He thought about giving Kim Martinez a call. "Kat," he corrected himself. "She likes to be called Kat, now."

Maybe she'd come to Aspen if he got a room. "She's changed teams," he thought, "but she's still a lot of fun to hang out with. And maybe a few old embers will flare, for old times' sake. We used to have a good time together."

Davis was right. The idea that Senator John Buford had surfaced, and in Colorado, and was the suspect in a murder, had buried the Troy Davis story.

JC sat at his desk in the newsroom and made a routine phone call to Detective Trujillo. It had been two days since Bitsy Stark's body was found.

"Nope, no sign of him," Trujillo told the reporter when asked if they'd found Buford.

After a few follow-up questions that led nowhere, JC was resigned to ending the call without much gained.

"How's your photographer taking the news?" the detective asked.

JC was at a loss. Which news was Trujillo referring to?

"That was his ex-wife, wasn't it?" Trujillo asked.

"Which photog? Are we talking about Bitsy?" the journalist asked, somewhat confused. He could hear the detective snickering a little.

"Lemon. Milt Lemon, right?" the detective finally said.

"What about him?" JC inquired, still lost in the conversation.

"That vic at the auto-ped, the hit-and-run you showed up at," Trujillo offered. "Wasn't that Milt Lemon's ex-wife?"

"The woman killed near the golf course?" sputtered JC. "That was Milt's ... Sandy Lemon?"

"That's the name we have." Trujillo now sounded like he was reading from a form in front of him: "Thirty years old. Daughter: Jayne Lemon. Father of child: Milt Lemon. Divorced."

"This, I didn't know," JC confessed over the phone. "I just saw him yesterday. He didn't say anything."

"Well, maybe I shouldn't have said anything," the law officer replied, "I just figured you'd be one of the people looking out for him."

"When was he notified?" JC asked.

"Well, that photo you guys ran on TV and in the newspapers filled in some blanks," the detective explained. "We only found out who she was over the weekend. She wasn't carrying ID, she wasn't near the address she claimed to reside at, and no one told us she was missing."

"No one reported her missing?" JC repeated. "She lived with her parents. They didn't let her piss without informing them beforehand."

"Oh yes," Trujillo acknowledged, "I hear they are a piece of work. I guess there were a lot of problems in the family. They say they thought she'd run off to live with a friend they didn't approve of. They weren't on speaking terms at the moment."

"Sounds like them," JC muttered.

"Oh yes," Trujillo answered.

"Catch anyone, yet?"

"No," the detective said. "But someone is going to recognize that partial face in the car."

"When did you notify Milt?" JC inquired again.

"That would have been Tuesday morning," Trujillo told him.

JC went through the timeline in his head. Tuesday was the day he reported on the discovery of Bitsy Stark's body. He was reporting from Snow Hat.

Milt joined him in the afternoon to take over Edgar's duties as photographer. So, by the time Milt arrived at Snow Hat, he knew Sandy was dead. He didn't say a word to JC. In fact, the reporter remembered, Milt barely said anything. He was uncommonly quiet.

JC hung up the phone. Sandy Lemon, he thought. For a woman with looks and some brains, she wasn't born with a thimble full of luck.

He surveyed the newsroom from his desk. No sign of Milt.

He saw the anchor for the noon news. JC didn't know him well. He'd been on television in Denver before half the staff in the newsroom was born.

He looked it. He was old. He had a toupee that looked like it was made out of a dead cat. It was a strange hue of orange. His body was atrophied, with a belly sticking out.

But on television, with a good suit on, he looked twenty years younger. He was ageless and television made magic.

He was an institution. The older audience cherished him and the younger audience had grown up watching him. On the business end of things, though, he wasn't trusted by management to anchor the important evening news like he used to.

JC saw Milt. He was across the room, having just returned from a shoot in the field. He was headed for the cafeteria, probably for coffee.

JC followed him but stopped at the door to the small room. It had two refrigerators, some vending machines and a pretty nice coffee maker.

JC didn't know how to start the conversation. Milt turned and just looked at him. The two exchanged silence.

"You heard the good news," Milt finally said sarcastically. There wasn't a cell on the man's face that suggested this was good news. The skin around his eyes was darker than usual. He looked like he hadn't slept for days.

"I'm really sorry, Milt," JC said. He thought that Lemon had never lost hope of winning his bride back, however hopeless that was.

Sometimes, since the divorce, Milt would speak of his ex-wife in vile terms.

But, a lot of venting went on between television reporters and photographers during a long drive to an assignment. It involved people who are smart and possess A-Type personalities.

Venting was an industry standard. Sometimes the subject du jour would be a perceived insult in the newsroom. Sometimes it would be thinly veiled jealousy aimed at a colleague competing for a pet assignment. Sometimes it would be about a relationship falling apart at home.

But the foul terms Milt could sometimes conjure up when discussing Sandy made it a conversation that JC had told him he wasn't comfortable being a part of.

JC also knew that there could be a thin line between love and hate, so thin it could become difficult for the suffering soul to discern the difference.

"They say they're going to fight for custody of Jayne," Milt said soberly.

"Sandy's parents?" JC asked.

"Yeah, the maggots," Milt answered. "They said I'll never see her again." He silently sipped his coffee before adding, "That may add up to the total number of words they've ever spoken to me. So, we're at ten now. They hate me."

"Do you see her much now?" JC asked in a soft tone.

Milt shook his head. "No, Sandy always came up with an excuse. She didn't seem to want Jayne to get to know me, like she was ashamed of me."

Milt was looking at the ground, defeated.

"She wasn't living with her parents anymore?" JC asked.

Milt shook his head, "No. She said she was moving in with a friend, and she was taking Jayne. She wouldn't even tell me where she was moving, who the friend was. The last time I spoke with her on the phone, we had quite a fight about it."

"Do you know who the friend is?" JC asked.

"No," Milt told him. "Some guy. That's my guess."

28

Detective Trujillo allowed his feet to drop down the freshly shoveled concrete steps, leading away from the home of Jacob and Roberta Walker.

They were Sandy Lemon's parents. They lived near Denver's Botanic Gardens. Trujillo felt exhausted after the interview. It was never easy to speak with the loved ones of someone who died tragically. But the Walkers, the detective confided to himself, were exhausting people.

Jacob Walker had a stern face. He had a neatly trimmed mustache and looked like he should put on a little weight. Roberta Walker was unsmiling. Her hair was short and ignored. They both looked like they were dressed to go to church, though they told the detective that they were not.

Trujillo thought he was disturbed by the visit because the Walkers never spoke warmly of their late daughter. Her existence was acknowledged, chronicled, but little more.

On the fireplace mantle, there was a formal photograph of Sandy Lemon. The detective supposed it was a graduation photo. But his eyes searched the home for the kind of silly photos or mementos like the ones he had of his kids growing up. He found none.

The detective had phoned to ask the Walkers if he could come over, because he had some questions for them. Trujillo seemed to be taking on more of the investigation into the hit-and-run. Police still hadn't caught anyone.

He showed the Walkers a security camera photograph of the car they think hit their daughter. Did they recognize it? They did not.

Did they recognize the partial face seen inside the car? They did not.

Did they know why Sandy was in that area when she was hit? They did not.

Did they know where she was going? No.

Did they know where her baby, Jayne, was at the time Sandy was hit?

The older couple shifted uncomfortably in their seats. "A friend was babysitting," Jacob Walker answered.

"Do you have the name of that friend?" the detective asked.

The Walkers appeared uncomfortable again. They looked at each other in silence.

"Mr. Walker?" Detective Trujillo said, looking for an answer to his question.

"No," Jacob responded.

Trujillo drove back to his office in the industrial section of District Two. He listened to Spanish-language radio. He did this, from time to time, thinking it helped him stay in touch with the language.

He thought of his grandfather, Wilfredo. He was the keeper of the family's Mexican culture. Trujillo thought of his grandfather's collection of Mexican records. They were thick 78s. Trujillo remembered that they were heavy, made out of some sort of shellac.

He remembered how elegant his mother looked on Sundays, when they'd go to church. And he remembered the one day each year when his mother would fully acknowledge their Mexican heritage.

It was Three Kings Day, each January sixth. His mother would prepare a Mexican feast and the children would each get a present.

Trujillo pulled into the parking lot of District Two Headquarters. The building wasn't very old. Brick and glass, a lot of glass. Three flags flew outside. They belonged to the United States, Colorado and Denver.

The public lobby was decorated with oversized cards from school children. They said things like "Thank you for keeping us safe" and "Thank you for saving lives."

He pulled his unmarked vehicle around back, where the law officers and staff parked in a fenced-in area.

He turned off his car but he didn't get out. He wanted to sit there and think about the case of the hit-and-run.

A strong wind rocked the car a little. It was always windy at the spot chosen to build their headquarters, he thought.

He felt the warm sun radiating through the windshield. If it wasn't for the wind, he guessed, it would be a nice day.

He wondered if Sandy Lemon had committed suicide. She'd had a lot of bad breaks. Her parents didn't seem to be a lot of laughs. Sandy permitted herself to do perhaps the only wild thing she'd ever done in her life and she got pregnant.

She did what her parents and her religion trained her to do, and momentarily married a man she didn't love. Maybe she just walked in front of that car, the detective thought.

Suicide wasn't uncommon in Colorado. The suicide rate in the state was among the nation's highest. Usually, he thought, they were transplants who came to Colorado to turn around their miserable lives.

They convinced themselves that if they could just get to the promised land, all their wishes would come true. When those wishes still didn't come true, it was all they could endure. And they ended it all.

Trujillo's iPhone rang. "Where are you?" a fellow detective asked.

"I'm in the parking lot," Trujillo answered. He'd try to escape the ridicule that would come if they knew he had been sitting in his car in back of headquarters for twenty minutes.

"We've got a hit on the car. The hit-and-run," the voice told him.

"Where?" Trujillo asked.

"The car was stashed inside a garage off Santa Fe," he was told. "The guy was biding his time," the other detective told him. "Then, he was trying to find a body shop down in Pueblo that would do the repair work. He figured they wouldn't hear about the hit-and-run down there. But they watch the news in Pueblo, too. The shop owner recognized the car from the photo."

"Where are you?" Trujillo asked.

"We're bringing him in," the other detective said. "You gonna be around to help with the questioning?"

"Yeah," Trujillo answered. "I'll be waiting for you."

The detective remained in his car. He wanted to think about Sandy Lemon more. If the driver of the car told them that Sandy just walked in front of his car without warning, the detective had a feeling that he might believe him.

The driver would still be charged with leaving the scene and failing to report, but he might escape a homicide conviction.

Trujillo got out of his car and walked toward the back door of headquarters. The wind grabbed at his jacket and tie.

The Denver Police Department operations manual determined that he could dress business casual. So, he wore nice slacks, a tie and a nice shirt under a sport coat. The sport coat hid a .38 "Detective Special" in a holster on his hip.

It would be some time before any difficult questions would be asked of the driver of the car. Right now, Trujillo thought, the suspect was in the back of a police cruiser on his way here. Then, they'd "sweat him" for a while.

The guy would know that he's in a world of trouble. Presently, he'd be perfecting a rational story that would explain his situation. He'd been working on it for weeks, ever since the hit-and-run.

But he hadn't realized how frightening it would be, telling his fabrication to men wearing badges. The rest of his life was riding on this. He had to make it a good story.

Maybe he'd say his car was stolen and someone else must have hit that poor woman. Maybe he thought he hit a bear and just kept driving.

"Why would you get your car repaired in Pueblo if you thought you hit a bear?" the detectives would ask him. Trujillo was laughing at the situation. The crazy stories they heard. It was one of the perks of being a cop.

The suspect would be at the top of his game when he arrived at headquarters. He'd be alert. He'd have refined his story. He'd be prepared. So, the detectives would drop him into an interrogation room and let him stew.

He'd be left alone in there for quite some time. They'd let him think about the gravity of the situation. They'd let all that emotion and preparation wear him out.

He'd start rethinking his plan. It was probably a good plan, but he'd start rethinking it. He'd get scared. He'd be alone and the stakes were terrifying, if he really thought about it.

They were sweating him.

The suspect's name was Wallace Simmons. His friends knew him as Wally. He was in his mid-forties. He was in between boring jobs and leading a boring life.

He smelled like alcohol. "Do you always have a drink for lunch, Wally?" a detective asked him.

"No," Wally responded. "And I just had one, today. It's Friday."

"That it is," the detective said. Trujillo was a silent partner, sitting in the corner of the interrogation room. They'd never get him for drinking and driving, he thought, even if Wally was drinking and driving when he hit Sandy Lemon with his car.

The collision happened three weeks ago. They could look for a bartender who served him multiple drinks, but they'd have no blood evidence.

Unless, Trujillo thought, Wally got hurt in the collision and went to the hospital. The hospital would have taken a blood sample. It might be tough to obtain, but it was a start.

"Did you get hurt when you thought you hit the bear, Mr. Simmons?" Trujillo interjected. "Did you go to the hospital?"

"No," responded Wally. "Did you say a bear? I didn't say I thought I hit a bear."

"What did you think you hit," Trujillo asked, "requiring you to park your vehicle for three weeks and then contact a body shop in Pueblo?"

"I want a lawyer," Wally responded. Interrogation over.

"Crap," thought Trujillo. The other detectives were giving Trujillo looks. They weren't particularly nice looks.

Steve Trujillo left the interrogation room and settled into his desk. It had been a long day. He wasn't certain what he'd accomplished. He thought that he'd better do some Christmas shopping tomorrow.

Grudgingly, the other detectives agreed that Trujillo hadn't spoiled the interrogation. They had already realized that Wally wasn't going to offer an easy confession. The process had just started. Trujillo had just rung the bell. Class was dismissed for the day.

They were all in agreement that they had their man. The gash on his fender, and blood evidence that police forensics experts would find on the car, were enough to convict him. Eventually, his lawyer would negotiate a plea.

The landline on Trujillo's desk rang and he picked it up.

"Lisa Miller," the voice on the other end said.

Trujillo thought he recognized the voice on the phone. "Mr. Walker?"

"Lisa Miller is the woman who was watching our grandchild," Jacob Walker said on the other end of the phone. "She lives in Loveland. Sandy had just moved into a spare room there. For your information, we're going to court to acquire full custody of Jayne."

The detective scribbled Lisa Miller's name on a piece of paper in front of him. Like I'd forget that, he thought.

"Why didn't you tell me that when I was at your home?" Trujillo asked.

"It's a sensitive subject," Mr. Walker answered. "We didn't approve."

"That doesn't give you permission to lie to a police officer," the detective informed the man. Mr. Walker didn't respond.

"You don't like Mrs. Miller?" Trujillo inquired.

"It's not whether we like her. We don't even know her," Walker spat back. "It's sinful. What they were doing is sinful."

Uh oh, Trujillo thought. He chose his words carefully. "What were they doing, Mr. Walker?" he asked.

Jacob Walker sounded like he was struggling for words on the other end of the phone. Finally, he blurted, "It's sinful. Look it up! I have to go. I'm sorry."

The phone line went dead. Detective Trujillo pulled the receiver from his ear and gave it an incredulous stare.

29

Frozen Dead Guy Days. He thought it was probably the most macabre masquerade in the entire United States. He was looking forward to it.

John Buford was sitting at his window in a second-floor apartment above a restaurant in Nederland. He was looking out on his world. He planned to spend the day in that seat.

There were Christmas lights and Christmas trees decorating the landscape. It would be especially busy outside his window today. The Saturday before Christmas was always the busiest shopping day, wasn't it?

He'd been staring out that window, and one across the room, for the better part of four years. He knew every inch of what there was to see out of both of them.

He'd come to feel fortunate. He had two windows and they faced in opposite directions. He didn't feel fortunate at first, but he'd grown accustomed to his new life. He'd always been able to adapt.

The window he presently planned to stare out of for the day faced northwest. It looked down on First Street. First Street was the main drag in a town with only three drags. First Street was the busy single block that constituted "Downtown Nederland."

He couldn't decide which time of day he liked best. There was morning, when almost no one was stirring and he could envision Nederland as it was when cowboys chased Indians and vice versa.

There were business hours, when First Street was bustling, at least relatively so. That brought customers to a marijuana dispensary, the co-op and the bike and ski shop on Snyder Street

There was also the feed supply store, a boutique clothing shop and a diner to keep an eye on.

Then there was sundown. That was when First Street became Nederland's entertainment center. There were fairy lights strung across the street. And light poured out onto the road from the gourmet pizzeria, the smokehouse and brew pub, and other restaurants.

Sometimes, to his delight, music also poured out of those windows. He called those nights his rock concert. "I've got tickets to the rock concert tonight," he'd say to himself in good humor.

During the day from his northwest window, he could witness the lives of the store owners and their shoppers.

He could also follow the comings and goings of people who owned homes that climbed up the hillside near town. He sometimes considered how he might obtain a telescope without calling attention to himself. His world would nearly double.

On most nights, the restaurants on First Street did well. He wondered where the people came from, to visit the isolated town. It would be called a hamlet in other parts of the country. The population was only about fifteen hundred, including all those homes in the hills and out of sight.

There was a second window, facing southeast. That was also good for a day's fulfillment.

Sunrise was best facing southeast. He looked over Middle Boulder Creek and Barker Reservoir. He'd see the occasional elk grazing alongside the creek. He'd see birds of prey and coyotes.

He'd see one particular coyote repeatedly. Buford knew it was the same coyote because the animal had a dark spot on his left hindquarter. It may have resulted from a fight.

Buford came to adopt him, in a long-distance, no-touching sort of way, as his dog. He named him Spot.

Some of the wildlife was human. Buford had long ago concluded that there were some colorful characters living in Nederland. There were a few who dressed like mountain men.

He'd watch them walk into town along the path following Boulder Creek. He had overheard conversations suggesting that these mountain men tried to live the life.

They trapped and skinned their food whenever they could. They made their own clothing whenever they could. They lived like people lived one hundred and fifty years ago. There was a local name for them, Nedestrians.

Later in the day, from Buford's southeast-facing window, he could watch new arrivals check-in at the Boulder Creek Lodge. Its log cabin construction was a perfect fit for

Nederland. And he could watch guests take a romantic stroll from the Lodge over a covered bridge to First Street.

He could also spy on visitors to the town's shopping center, and the "Carousel of Happiness." A Vietnam veteran hand-carved the animals. The carousel brought happiness to children every summer.

Buford could watch cars roll through town on their way to the Eldora Ski Resort. Frequently, he'd join them. He didn't have a car. It had been impossible to obtain a license as Jose Garcia.

But there was bus service to just about anywhere he needed to go. That would be to ski or hike or to pick up groceries and supplies. He had enough money to obtain a car, but if he blundered, he'd be exposed. Fugitive John Buford would be discovered.

Sometimes, he'd hitchhike to Eldora. A guy with a pair of skis, wearing a helmet and a mask against the cold didn't arouse much suspicion in Nederland.

Nederland was blustery on its best day. Residents of Nederland were used to telling outsiders, "Oh, that's not wind." Visitors didn't know what other name to use for the icy blast of air blowing their hair or the hat off their head.

But residents of Nederland, when they said, "Oh, that's not wind," said so because they knew it got a lot worse than that, and then what would they call it?

Nederland started as an old trading post between the Ute Indians and white settlers. The town boomed when gold was discovered, and later silver and tungsten.

Nearby was the village of Eldora. It was once bustling, too, but now it was nearly a ghost town. There were forty or so log cabins scattered across the old site.

Buford had originally thought he'd rent a room or a cabin in Eldora. But it was too sparsely populated. He'd stand out.

Nederland was small, but it had two highways intersecting in its middle. There was the Peak to Peak Highway, leading north to Estes Park and Rocky Mountain National Park. And there was Route 119, heading down Boulder Canyon to the city of Boulder and the University of Colorado.

Nederland had car traffic passing through all the time. It was normal to see a strange face. It was easy to be ignored, Buford found.

He had a small television set in his room, his world. He rarely watched it, though he had viewed it frequently in the last few days to see the news.

It was unsettling to see his picture on television, after four years of being invisible. And it was the reason he'd be spending more time than ever inside his room, hiding, living life through his windows.

He preferred to look out his windows than watch television anyway. He liked to look at the old buildings. They seemed like they hadn't changed since the days of the Wild West, when they were erected.

Many had wooden porches with a roof overhead. Most had balconies. Some of the wooden railings were broken. They'd be fixed when the weather warmed.

So would the fences, faded by the weather. Some fences surrounded gardens, to keep the elk, the deer and the rabbits out.

Buford thought that it usually seemed to be snowing in Nederland. Even if it wasn't snowing hard, there just seemed to be snowflakes hanging in the air, lazily drifting to the ground.

In a few months, he thought, posters would go up advertising Frozen Dead Guy Days. There wasn't a busier time of year in Nederland than the days of that celebration.

There really is a frozen dead guy. He died in Norway and, on dry ice, was brought to the United States by his grandson.

The grandson soon learned that it was difficult to keep a frozen grandfather among his belongings. The family came to Nederland with plans to build a cryonics facility. But those plans melted away and the grandson was deported.

Ever since then, the grandfather has been "on ice" inside a Tuff Shed. A caretaker now tends to the "cryogenic mausoleum." And tourists flock to town to celebrate the weirdness of the whole thing.

Frozen Dead Guy Days was cause for Buford's greatest celebration of the year. He'd put on face paint, something resembling a skull, and he'd look like everyone else.

It was Frozen Dead Guy Days to everyone else, but to him, it was John Buford's annual Big Day Out.

30

Where had Bitsy Stark come from? And, JC wondered, how could she have crossed paths with John Buford other than by plan?

JC remembered a story about two of his uncles. They both survived the beach landing at Normandy on D-Day. Later, they were marching in columns with their respective fighting units when the two companies passed through the same intersection at the same time. The two soldiers, his uncles, literally bumped into each other.

But how often does that happen? JC knew what was bothering him about the evidence suggesting Buford killed Bitsy, the very evidence he was reporting on television news. What bothered him was that he didn't believe it.

Maybe he was being seduced by the innocence of Lucy Buford, but the reporter didn't envision Senator Buford just rubbing out someone who stumbled into his path. JC needed to be convinced.

Of course, Bitsy Stark wasn't just anyone. There were suggestions that she and the senator had an affair. And whether or not that was true, she could identify the man who had been on the run for four years.

JC told his assignment editor that he wanted to track Bitsy Stark's last movements, since she arrived in Denver from Vermont.

"You might find that she and Buford got together before Snow Hat," Rocky Bauman suggested. "You might even find there was a rendezvous at a hotel in Denver."

"You're a dirty old man," JC told his assignment editor.

"Hey," replied Rocky, "I'm not that old."

JC and Milt Lemon started at Denver International Airport. Bitsy arrived there late in the morning on December ninth. Robin Smith, the redheaded newsroom producer, had provided JC with that. She'd called Bitsy's employers and searched passenger lists.

Walking inside the terminal, the reporter observed the mountains of luggage arriving with skiers. Their bags were overstuffed with warm clothing. And it would only be worse when they returned home, adding a souvenir sweatshirt or sweater, tee shirts, coffee mugs. The travelers also had to lug their skis, packed in a bag to survive the luggage compartment during the flight.

"She wasn't that big a woman," Milt said. "She could have used some help."

"You mean, someone like Buford?" JC asked casually. "Maybe."

"Want to hear my jelly story?" Milt asked.

JC didn't respond. "Do you?" Milt persisted.

"I'm deciding," JC told him.

"I'll take that as a yes," Milt said.

He proceeded with his story. "I was flying out of Denver. At the TSA security checkpoint, they found a jar of jelly in my backpack. A woman I was dating had given it to me just as I was leaving.

"The security guy says, 'I'm sorry sir, you have a container of liquid that's over four ounces. That can't be in your carry-on bag.'

"'It's only jelly,' I tell him, 'how dangerous can jelly be?'

"He says, 'I'm sorry sir, it's over the four-ounce limit.'

"So, I lie a little: 'Look, my friend didn't look that great. She may be dying.'

"The TSA agent says, 'I'm sorry sir. You could step out of line, go to a postal facility and mail it to yourself.'

"I look at the line behind me and it's a mile long. This is DIA, for cripes' sake!"

Milt continued, "I ask, 'How many ounces is this?'

"'It looks like approximately six ounces, sir,' the TSA guy says.

"'And I'm allowed how much?' I ask.

"'Four ounces, sir,' TSA guy tells me.

"So, I hold out my hand and the agent gives me back my jar of jelly. I unscrew the top, right in front of him, and drive two fingers into the jelly.

"I pull out what I'd say was two ounces of jelly, look the agent in the eye, and scoop it into my mouth.

"I chew, smiling because it's really good. I tip the jar toward the security guy, offering him some. He declined. He never smiled, during this whole episode."

By now, JC was laughing. Milt had come up with another ludicrous story that only Milt could tell.

"I look into the jar and then show it to the agent. He goes, without a smile, 'That looks like four ounces, sir. Thank you, you may proceed to your gate.'"

JC and Milt were laughing. They were getting stares from present-moment security agents, as Milt was swearing the whole story was true.

"Of course it's true, Milt," JC giggled. "It's you!"

"Time to get back to business," JC said. "Bitsy didn't have a car at Snow Hat. So how did she get from the airport to the ski resort?"

"Buford or the train and then ride sharing or something," Milt suggested.

"So, Buford may have had a car," JC added. He assumed that police were following up on the same questions, but they weren't going to turn over their notes to a journalist. JC was going to have to figure out things for himself.

"There's no driver's license issued in Buford's name," JC said.

"He's probably using an alias," Milt responded.

"At the moment, we have no idea what that alias would be. So, let's say she took the train to Union Station," JC offered. "If that doesn't work out, we'll try something else."

The airport train was officially called the "University of Colorado A Line." The end of the line was stately Union Station.

"She was a guest here," said the clerk at check-in for the Crawford Hotel. The Crawford offered comfortable rooms on the floors above the terminal. "One night, the ninth," the clerk told JC.

JC scanned the large hall. It was quite a feat, he thought, raising the ancient terminal from the dead and turning it into a home for restaurants and shops and just a cool place to hang out. He remembered that the architects won prestigious awards for their work.

The old station clock towered over the room, accented by gold corbels. Below that, tall gold letters spelled "Terminal."

He looked at the old floors, polished to gleam like new. But there were subtle troughs in the floor, each one parallel to the next.

It had been explained to him that the long wooden benches for passengers awaiting their train used to line up that way.

The troughs were dug during World War Two, when there were eighty trains a day. Soldiers on their way to war packed those trains. The soldier's combat boots harrowed those depressions in the floor. Young men and women, no doubt nervous, fidgeting during their wait.

JC stared at the space where national heroes used to sit. And he noticed a sizable homeless population had taken their place.

The long benches of the 1940s had been replaced by heavy wooden tables. There were also small living rooms shaped in the open space by couches and chairs with overstuffed cushions. And in every direction, there was a smattering of Denver's homeless community. They'd found a place to stay warm.

They weren't loud and they were under strict orders not to panhandle. There was an impressive display of law officers keeping an eye on things. They were a mix of private security, Denver police, railroad Police and federal police.

There were small signs on the tables saying the huge room was only for train passengers and customers of the Crawford Hotel. But tell that to someone who was cold and had nowhere to go.

JC walked outside to Union Station's entrance on Wynkoop Street. There wasn't really a reason, he just liked to get the feel for a place when he was trying to figure it out.

The letters spelling "Union Station" in neon were proudly perched over the main entrance. There was another sign below, also in shining neon. It was a lure—or was it a plea?—saying "Travel by Train."

"You can't get to Snow Hat by train," JC mumbled to himself.

JC walked back inside the terminal hall. He saw that there was a bar tucked into a corner. He'd seen it on prior visits to Union Station. It was called The Coupler. He knew it was busy at night. It was a spot Bitsy Stark would probably choose.

He entered and asked a manager if he could look over credit card receipts for the night of the ninth. It might determine if Bitsy, or Buford, purchased dinner or drinks that night.

The manager refused. "We can't release that information," he said.

JC wasn't surprised by that answer. He drummed his fingers on the bar, thinking. "Security footage? Do you have security cameras?"

JC was prepared for more rejection. But journalists need thick skin. Rejection is a daily diet for journalists. "Not today," the manager said. "Maybe by Wednesday."

"That would be fine," JC answered as though he expected that outcome. He did not. The business was not obligated to share anything with the news media. The reporter tried not to over-display his delight at the good fortune.

"Oh wait," the manager said. JC's heart sank. The manager had decided to refuse after all, he thought.

"Wednesday is Christmas," the manager said as he laughed. "How about Thursday?"

Now JC laughed. He felt like he'd dodged a bullet. "Thursday would be fine." And on Thursday, he thought, he might see exactly who Bitsy Stark was sharing company with.

Milt was quiet on the drive up to Snow Hat.

"How's the custody battle going?" JC asked.

"We've got a court date, to get things rolling," he replied. Silence followed.

"It was ride sharing," a doorman told JC at Bitsy's hotel at Snow Hat. "You know how I know? Because the same ride-sharing driver asked about her a day or two after he dropped her off. He asked if she was still staying here. He brought another fare here and he asked about the girl. He said he liked her. He might have been looking for her."

That was how Bitsy got to the ski resort from Union Station, ride sharing. JC was noting that there was still no sign of Buford in the picture. Were police checking out the ride-sharing guy?

JC walked slowly toward the pedestrian walk. Had he seen John Buford the day of his skiing crash? Concussion or not, the possibility was becoming more likely, he thought.

It was starting to snow at Snow Hat. It was beginning to look a lot like Christmas.

A life-sized likeness of the man who founded the Snow Hat Ski Resort was collecting snow in the town square of the vacation village. The statue had recently been accessorized with a wool scarf and stocking cap.

JC heard the siren of a fire truck. He saw Santa Claus riding on the back of the truck, waving at children. The ladder truck stopped in front of the hotel. Parents dashed after their children who ran to greet Santa. And there was a small present handed to each child.

The day was winding down and a storm was just winding up. Tomorrow would be a powder day for skiers and snowboarders.

"Hey, I know you're trying to get stuff done, but have you seen the updated forecast?" Milt asked JC. "There's a ton of snow coming. If we want to get back to Denver tonight, we'd better head home now."

Milt knew the reporter could be intense when he was hunting for answers. Stubborn was another word that came to mind. JC didn't like to be told No.

The reporter looked at his photographer. He looked at the sky. He looked back at Milt and said, "Mom, do we have to go?"

"I'm afraid so, son," Milt responded. "Daddy doesn't want to die on the highway."

"Coward," was JC's reply.

31

It was a two-tanker. The snow piled so high overnight, it would take two tanks of gas for many Coloradoans to snow-blow their driveways.

Snow Hat was buried under legendary Colorado powder, and it was still coming down. It was light and fluffy. It buried their skis and snowboards and piled on their heads during the ride up the chairlift.

In deep powder like this, celebration and humiliation became interchangeable results. To some extent, and no matter what degree of skill, to powder ski was to fail.

"But that's part of the fun!" a skier said on the gondola to a child visiting from the Midwest. "The worst that can happen is that you get a face full of snow. It beats a face full of knives!" Everyone on the gondola laughed.

JC was in his apartment in Larimer Square. He'd be going into work later, to fill in for an anchor who was snowed-in at Telluride.

JC had just been on the phone with Shara. He was thinking about taking a late flight to Bozeman, Montana, after the show that evening and surprising his girlfriend for Christmas.

Now, that was out of the question. Denver's airport was barely open. Flights were being cancelled. Certainly, the one to Bozeman would be among them. It would be snowing hard there, too.

JC put on a coat, descended the stairs and pushed out into the blowing snow. He'd need to walk past only a few storefronts before ducking into a quaint market with a place to sip cappuccino and get something for breakfast.

It was Christmas eve. He wanted to be with Shara, but he wanted her to be here. He loved his apartment in Larimer Square.

It was old red brick with tall, arched windows. Below his apartment was a pizzeria, an espresso bar, a bookstore and a boutique dress shop where he'd purchased one of Shara's Christmas presents.

His apartment building was constructed in the 1880s. There was a decorative false front on the top, typified in photographs of the Old West.

He was near 15th Street. Some of Denver's first log cabins were built on that spot. It then became Denver's most prominent shopping district, before becoming a skid row and then becoming Denver's favorite shopping district again, all over the course of a century.

JC sat in the market, nursing his cappuccino and listening to neighbors come in from the cold and thanking the staff for remaining open in the adverse elements.

The customers spoke amongst themselves, saying they were lucky to live in Larimer Square. Denver residents were being advised not to drive in the storm. But with Christmas only a day away, many would slip and slide their way to the best shopping district in the city.

JC's thoughts wandered. He wondered, for example, if police officers were any closer to finding Buford. "He is good at hiding," JC thought. "But he's here, somewhere in Snow Country. At least, he was."

"I'll work Christmas, if somebody wants it off," JC had told his news director, Pat Perilla.

If he could work the holiday, he'd get a day off later, maybe more than a day. A few more of those and he could fly to Montana, while he still had a girlfriend there. The news director said that he'd ask around.

Despite the snowstorm raging outside, the newsroom's management had come to work. So had every reporter, producer and photographer, except for the anchor trapped in Telluride who JC would be substituting for.

JC preferred reporting, but on occasion, the change of pace that was anchoring could be a welcome thing. It was especially welcome when there was a blizzard outside. He'd be inside.

During that night's newscast, JC pitched to one reporter and then the next for a live update on the storm. They were all standing out in snow that was blowing sideways.

They would grimace in the cold wind as they stood next to a jackknifed truck on I-25, or a traffic jam approaching Eisenhower Tunnel with cars spinning their wheels on the compacted snowfall.

They would stand outside the airport and explain why airplanes couldn't land or take off. In many cases, they'd tell viewers that the plane couldn't take off because the plane wasn't even in Denver. The airlines saw this storm coming and diverted their planes to Florida or Arizona.

After the newscast, JC walked out from under the bright studio lights and away from the magic of television. He walked down a hallway with an institutional paint job and across worn-out carpet that got worse as you approached the newsroom.

He sat at his desk and picked up a pen. "What's that?" The redheaded producer, Robin Smith, was standing by his desk smiling at him.

"A pen," JC responded in an understated manner.

"That's not just any pen," Robin protested.

JC looked the pen over. She was right. JC typically brought floater pens to work. Any office has its share of pen thieves. Bringing a floater pen, he found, made it easy to track down his pen, and the thief.

"This particular pen," he explained to the lovely 30ish producer, "came from the John Shedd Aquarium in Chicago. Great town."

He showed her the whale in the plastic window of the pen. When he lifted the pen so the ball point was aimed at the ceiling, the whale swam to the other end of the window.

"Do you have one of those pens," Robin asked, "where the woman's clothes fall off when you flip it over?"

JC laughed a little, "Those are collector's items. Much too rich for my tastes." Robin laughed, too.

"And that?" She was pointing at an oversized toothbrush in a dusty coffee cup on his desk.

"That," he began, feigning a bit more historic importance than the toothbrush really deserved, "that is a toothbrush given to me by a presidential candidate in New Hampshire."

"Seriously?"

"Sadly, yes," JC answered. "The New Hampshire Primary is both politics and a statewide hootenanny. And it may be hard to win, but it's not that hard to enter."

"So, a number of people enter the New Hampshire presidential primary to either have fun or get attention for reasons other than wanting to be the leader of the free world," JC explained.

"This toothbrush," JC said as he picked up a radiant green, footlong toothbrush, "came from a candidate who promised to eradicate tooth decay if elected president."

"Was he a dentist?" Robin asked.

"Judging from the upside-down rain boot he wore on his head, I'd say no," JC replied.

"You've had a cool career," Robin told JC.

"I'd have to agree. I've met a man who dreamed of eradicating tooth decay," JC responded with mock pride.

"And this is what brought you to my desk?" JC asked the producer.

"Oh," she laughed. "No. Detective Trujillo called. He asked if you knew that your photographer, I think he means Milt," Robin interjected, "he asked if you knew that Milt was acquainted with the guy who was driving the car that killed Sandy Lemon. Are they related?"

It was a lot for JC to take in. "It was before your time," JC told Robin. "Sandy and Milt had the shortest marriage in the history of Colorado."

Whatever Robin's response was, JC didn't hear it. He was thinking about the connection between Milt and the man who killed his ex-wife.

32

"Fort Bragg," Milt told JC.

"You know what the police are thinking?" JC asked. "They're thinking that your ex-wife wouldn't let you see your daughter and you got angry. They're wondering if you didn't arrange to have Wallace Simmons kill Sandy for you."

Milt looked at the floor of the newsroom cafeteria and quietly said, "Shit."

He looked up at JC. His eyes were tearing. "I hadn't seen Wally in years," Milt said. "We knew each other when we were in the Army, stationed at Fort Bragg."

"When was the very last time you saw him?" JC asked.

"He's had a bad run of luck. He's unemployed," Milt said. "He wondered if I could get him a job here. Anything, the mail room."

"When did you last see him?" JC repeated.

Milt looked at JC like he was signing his own death warrant. "Lunch."

"Lunch? When?"

"That day," Milt nearly choked on the words.

"That day? The day Wallace Simmons killed your ex-wife?" JC asked the question in disbelief. "You're the guy Wallace Simmons had drinks with at lunch and then ran over your ex-wife?"

Milt stared at the floor for a long time. Finally, he said quietly, "It doesn't look good, does it?"

JC began to laugh but stopped. He wasn't intent on making the man suffer. They had a professional relationship and a friendship, albeit a friendship based on Milt's being the strangest man JC had ever dared call a friend.

JC asked him, "Why didn't you tell police, right away?"

"I didn't know Sandy was dead until almost the same time you did," Milt reminded him. "And I didn't know Wally was arrested until after that."

"And then?" JC asked.

"And then, I knew it would look pretty bad," Milt admitted.

"It does," JC told him. "Now, you just have to tell police the truth, and everything you know."

Milt nodded in agreement.

"Unless you did it," JC added. "Then, shut up and get a lawyer."

Christmas wasn't merry. JC had worked the holiday, as requested. A grateful news director and the grateful anchor who got the day off instead of JC both thanked him repeatedly. In return, JC would get two "days in the bank," days he could take off later.

He and Shara had spoken over the phone on Christmas day. She said she would be working at her bar all day, so one of her employees could have the day off to spend with her kids.

"I'm sorry," JC stated.

"We're both sorry," she answered.

The conversation brought no joy to the world. He worried about where her breaking point might be.

The next morning, he was riding north to Loveland. Colorado is the fifth-worst state to drive in, according to a new study. That was the news on the radio as JC and a news photographer advanced up I-25. The pavement was still slick after the big storm, because of wind that kept blowing snow on the surface that D.O.T. plows had just cleared.

The new study that declared Colorado a bad place to drive cited the weather, wind and snow. It also spoke about rush hour and car theft.

JC had told the assignment editor that a news photographer other than Milt should accompany him to Loveland. Milt's appearance, JC said, would be inappropriate.

Instead, Bip Peters was along for the ride. JC didn't know him well. He was young and spiked his dark hair. JC knew he was an avid snowboarder. They spoke about that for a while as Bip drove the news car.

JC's phone rang. It was the manager at The Coupler bar at Union Station. He said that the surveillance video wouldn't be available until tomorrow. JC said, "OK, thanks."

It's all he could say, but he was concerned that a lawyer would get involved and the bar manager would change his mind. JC wouldn't relax until he got to see that video of Bitsy, if she was there that night and if there was anything to see.

Lisa Miller answered the door and invited the news crew in. For a woman still grieving the loss of her husband, she dressed like she was going out on a date. Her hair was perfect, not disheveled but not pinned down. Her clothing was simple but alluring.

JC had visited dozens of homes belonging to those mourning a lost loved one. No two were alike. Everyone grieves differently.

Lisa Miller directed JC and the photographer to the same sun porch where JC had spoken with her on his prior visit inside the house.

That didn't include the visit when he arrived just in time to see police informing her that her husband had been murdered.

JC told Bip that he wanted to speak with the woman, at first, without the camera rolling.

"How did you know Sandy Lemon?" JC asked her.

"It's funny," Lisa Miller told him. "Your name came up. We met at a bar and started talking. Somehow, you came up. Then we realized I had met her ex-husband when he was with you. We sort of hit it off."

"She was staying here with you?" JC asked. "In a spare room?"

The recent widow dropped her eyes and gently stammered a little. Wow, JC thought, she even does that seductively.

"The same room," Lisa whispered.

"I see," JC replied. He could hear Jacob Walker declare, "It was sinful."

"This was a romantic relationship?" JC asked carefully.

She shrugged her shoulders. "Yes, more or less," Lisa responded. "She was just experimenting, I think. She was lost. So was I."

"Please forgive me," JC said. "This was after you learned that your husband ... had passed?"

"Yes," Lisa said. "Thank you for putting that so sensitively. I thought Sandy would eventually settle down with a guy, hopefully a good guy. Me too."

"Milt knew about your relationship with Sandy?" JC asked.

"Yes," the widow replied. "He and Sandy didn't get along very well." Then she whispered, "She didn't like him very much."

JC asked, "Did Sandy say that Milt was particularly angry about their custody situation? With Jayne?"

"Sandy seemed a little embarrassed about Milt," Lisa disclosed. "She really worried about him raising their child. Sandy was pretty classy. She didn't think Milt was, or that he had many important lessons to teach their child."

"Did Sandy worry about Milt hurting her?" JC asked. Bip's eyes widened. JC made a mental note to himself to tell Bip that he isn't to repeat this conversation to a soul, not a soul.

"She didn't ever say she was afraid of him," Lisa told him.

JC asked, "How long had Sandy lived here?"

"Not very long at all," Lisa said in a soft voice. "Listen, she just needed somebody. I needed somebody, too. We found each other. I didn't convince her to do anything, and she didn't convince me to do anything. This was our choice."

"I'm not judging you," JC told her. "Everyone has a right to be loved."

"Thank you," Lisa said to him with warm eyes.

"Where's the child, Jayne?" JC inquired.

"With her grandparents, the Walkers. She's an adorable thing," Lisa said.

"So," JC asked, "what do you do now?"

"Oh," Lisa Miller responded with a coquettish smile. "Looking for love again." Her eyes were on JC.

Bip powered up his camera and JC conducted an interview. It was part reaction and remembrance regarding Scott's death and a little bit about Sandy Lemon.

The interview about Scott Miller, or even about Sandy Lemon, wasn't really the reason JC came to Loveland. The real reason he came was to learn what he could learn about Milt.

33

"Making nonsense out of sense!" Boi Toy screamed her lyrics into the microphone on stage. "Making virtue out of her too .."

She energized the musicians behind her, as well as the crowd in front of her. The crowd erupted in cheers and applause at the end of the song.

Boi Toy had worked up a sweat. She told the audience that the band was going to take a break and they'd be back for another set. She growled into the microphone, "Don't let me catch you with an empty drink. And tip your fucking waitress!"

"Where's your hot lady friend?" Kat asked as she seated herself at JC's table.

"Love can't read a map," he told her.

"Back in Montana?" Kat surmised.

"Until we can figure out a way out of this mess," he answered.

"Why doesn't she buy this place?" Kat said with a smile.

"Because you'd steal her from me," he teased.

"You see right through me," she teased back.

The last time JC had visited Kat Martinez at a club, Shara had been with him. The three of them had a fun night, talking and enjoying Kat's performance as the lead singer of her band, the Girl Squirrels.

Her short spiked hair wasn't pink anymore. It was dark. It looked like her natural color.

In the outfit she was wearing onstage tonight, tattoos of stars reached down her midriff where her top crawled up.

Kat was scribbling something on a napkin. She told JC she was writing a lyric that occurred to her.

"I like that the word 'punk' is inside the word spunk," she told him.

"How do you like this lyric?" she asked as she scribbled something else: "I got in the line for 'stunning' when God was giving out looks."

"Not far off," JC told her.

Kat was an ex-girlfriend of Troy Davis before discovering she was happier sleeping with women than with men.

JC slid a pair of pictures across the small table. "You ever seen these women in one of the clubs where you play?" Kat played a lot of clubs that attracted lesbian audiences.

Kat had short, painted fingernails. She stroked them over the pictures of Lisa Miller and Sandy Lemon.

"No," Kat told him and lifted her eyes to meet his. "They in trouble?"

"One's alive and one's dead," he said. "They were an item for a little while. I wondered if you had crossed paths."

"Because I'm a lesbian and they're lesbians?" she asked sarcastically.

"Hey, my LGBTQ universe is pretty small. Cut me some slack," he said with a smile.

"Oh, I know plenty of boys who would like to enlarge your portfolio," she said to him with a naughty smile.

"I know plenty of boys who would like to enlarge yours," he replied, his smile growing.

"Don't I know it," Kat feigned exhaustion.

"Why do you want to know about them?" Kat inquired.

"I don't know," JC responded with a disappointed look. He pulled the pictures back and put them into a coat pocket. "I hoped you'd tell me something I don't know."

"Double double toil and trouble," Kat said to the dissatisfied look on the journalist's face.

"Oh, we're quoting Shakespeare now?" JC asked, a grin returning to his face.

"Hey," Kat spat back, "I'm not just a great pair of tits."

JC laughed, "You hear from Troy lately?"

Kat took a swig from a cold beer placed in front of her by a passing waitress. "He asked me to meet him in Aspen."

That got the reporter's attention, "Seriously? When?"

"I don't know. I was out of town. I was near Grand Junction visiting my adorable brother. You know, the smarty pants archaeologist museum guy. I didn't see Troy's message until I got back," she said.

JC asked, "Did you tell police?"

Kat gave him a look, "What have they done for me, lately?"

"Did you get his number?" JC asked.

"No," she replied.

"Where's your phone," JC asked her. "There will be a readout."

"My cell phone?" Kat asked. "He didn't call me on my cell phone. He called me on my princess phone." She said it with attitude, like her princess phone was a prized possession.

JC remembered the princess phone. His sister had one. It was a relic from the 1960s. They were often pink and didn't have a readout. It was "so Kat," JC thought.

"Do you have his phone number?" JC asked.

"No," Kat told him. "We just find each other, when we want to."

"And where do I find you," JC asked, "if it's not dark out?"

"During the day?" Kat asked. JC nodded yes.

"I'm a hair stylist. I own a hair salon. I'm a girly girl, remember?" She smiled, "My shop's called Hair Brained." She pushed her hand into a pocket in her tight, micro-blue jean shorts and pulled out a card. She handed it to him.

Then she pushed her beer across the tabletop. "Finish it," she said with a smile.

Kat stood up and turned toward the stage. "My public awaits me," she said, looking over her shoulder. She gave him a wink and walked toward the microphone.

JC stopped by Union Station on the way home. He walked under the granite façade and two-story, arched windows.

He turned into The Coupler Bar. The manager gave JC a nod of his head. After pouring a pair of beers, to help the busy bartenders, he walked toward JC.

"Follow me," he said. He didn't break stride as he pushed through one door and opened another. They were in his office.

"I cued it up to the night of the ninth. That's what you wanted, right?" the manager asked. He showed no intention of leaving JC alone in his office.

"Right, thank you for going to the trouble." JC sat down in a chair positioned in front of a screen. The manager quickly explained how to fast forward, reverse and play the image.

The manager sat on the edge of his desk to look over JC's shoulder. He'd keep an eye on JC and on the video.

It didn't take long. JC touched his finger to the screen. "I think that's her," he said.

"Really?" the manager said. He was taking an interest in the quest and leaned forward for a better look.

The video showed Bitsy taking a seat at the bar. "Yeah, that's her," JC confirmed.

She sat with her back to the camera. Before long, a man seated himself to Bitsy's right. They struck up a conversation.

Was it Buford? JC didn't think it looked like him, at least not like the four-year-old picture.

The security footage was extremely grainy. But JC just didn't think the guy had Buford's build or hair.

Bitsy and the man ate at the bar. Bitsy got up eventually and shook the man's hand and left.

JC pressed "pause" on the machine. He looked at the time code on the screen. Bitsy and the man had spent about fifty minutes together.

JC hit "play" on the machine. Bitsy shook the man's hand and he turned in his seat. JC leaned closer to the screen. He hit "pause."

He looked at the controls and pushed "reverse." Then hitting "play," he watched Bitsy's departure again.

JC watched her extend her arm to shake hands with the man. The man turned, and JC hit "pause." He had a good look at the mystery man's face now.

JC asked the manager, "Do you recognize him?"

The manager leaned toward the screen and squinted. "No," he said. "He doesn't appear to be one of our regulars."

JC stared at the image. Then, he hit stop. The screen went blank and JC promptly stood up.

"Did you recognize him?" the manager asked.

"No," JC lied. "But we'd still like to get a copy of that. Is that possible?"

"I'll have to ask my boss," the manager said. "He was OK with showing it to you. I didn't ask if you could make a copy."

"Thanks," JC said. "We'll be in contact."

JC walked out into the cold air. It was dark out and pedestrians were hopping over snowbanks to get from the street to the sidewalk.

The journalist knew what he just saw on the security tape, he just didn't know what to make of what he saw.

He'd parked his FJ Cruiser in his rented garage space before walking over to Union Station. As he walked toward his apartment, he pulled his phone out of his jacket.

"It's getting a little late, JC," the voice on the other end of the phone told him.

JC apologized, "Sorry, did I catch you at home?"

There was a pause, "No, but I wish you had. I'm sitting at my desk."

"Did you check out the ride-sharing driver?" JC asked.

"Oh, you know about the ride-sharing driver, huh?" answered Detective Trujillo. "I'm glad to see you're keeping busy."

"It pays the bills," JC responded. He still wasn't exactly sure what he was going to tell the police detective.

"Yeah, we checked the ride-sharing driver out," Trujillo told the reporter. "He says he's got an alibi, but it's not working out for him. He's lying."

"Really? Interesting," JC thought out loud.

"Yeah," Trujillo agreed. "And a doorman says the ride-sharing guy was asking about her, showing an interest."

"Was she raped?" JC asked.

"We're not ready to discuss that type of thing," the detective responded.

JC stayed on the phone as he proceeded to walk down a dark sidewalk toward Larimer Street. "And Sandy Lemon's daughter, Jayne, is back with the Walkers?"

"Yes," sighed Trujillo. "So it would seem." The detective was thinking that it would have been nice if the Walkers had told him that when he visited them in their home. They are difficult people to like, he was thinking.

"Now, it is my turn," the police officer said to JC. JC took that to mean Trujillo had shared information, and now it was JC's turn to share something.

"I understand that you've been looking at security footage," Trujillo said.

"Wow, Big Brother really is watching," JC told him.

"Well," Trujillo sounded like it had been a long day, "it's better to have a Big Brother than a drunken father. So, did you see anyone you know?"

JC had seen something, and he wasn't eager to share it just yet. On the other hand, he wasn't eager to fall on the wrong side of a police murder investigation.

He also knew that Trujillo would be in The Coupler first thing in the morning, looking at the same security tape.

"Yeah, I saw someone," JC admitted.

After a moment of silence, Detective Trujillo asked, "Who?"

JC answered, "I've got to talk to someone, first."

When his call with the detective was disconnected, JC called the newsroom. "Is Milt Lemon working a shift tomorrow?" he asked.

34

"Well, I feel like a farmer growing a crop of stupid!" JC was staring at Milt Lemon like he'd caught him stealing his horse.

They were sealed inside an edit bay in the newsroom. The glass doors were shut. It's where anyone in the newsroom went when they wanted privacy.

"Is it even possible, according to the laws of physics," JC scowled, "that you aren't somehow tied to all of this?"

"I didn't know, JC!" Milt was angry, contrite and terrified. "I didn't put it together, that the blonde at the bar was the same woman as the murder victim up at Snow Hat. And I didn't know that Wally was going to leave lunch and go run over my ex-wife!"

"Crap, Milt," JC jeered. "Where else are you going to show up? Did you happen to be on the grassy knoll when Kennedy was shot? Did you happen to have lunch with Jimmy Hoffa the day he disappeared?"

Milt Lemon looked at the floor, sheepishly.

"A crop of stupid," JC muttered. He worked to compose himself.

"The police have got to know, by now," JC told him.

"Oh great," Milt uttered.

"I spoke with them last night. They already knew I was looking at that security tape. I didn't tell them I saw you, which I most certainly did, sitting there with Bitsy Stark. But I told them I saw something. I'm sure they went down and took a look for themselves, this morning," JC admitted.

"Well, what did you do that for?" Milt shouted.

"Because they were going to see you! And I don't want to go down with you!" JC shouted back. "And I'm just waiting for our news director to get out of a meeting and I've got to tell him to prepare for one of his photographers to be questioned by police."

"You're going to tell him?" Milt shouted.

The edit bays provided privacy as long as no one inside them was shouting. In that case, employees would raise their heads from their cubicles to see what the shouting was about. All eyes were now on JC and Milt, visible through the glass sliding doors.

"This is not a small deal," JC said, lowering his voice. "If he read about it in the newspaper or heard it from one of our other reporters before we told him, we'd both be fired."

There was a knock on the glass door. JC opened it and was told the news director was ready to see him.

JC glanced at Milt long enough to see an angry glare being returned.

It was Saturday. JC had planned to be in the mountains by now, at Snow Hat to do some skiing. But his phone call to the newsroom last night had informed him that Milt was working a Saturday shift.

JC decided to stop by and get things out in the open between them.

The news director, Pat Perilla, showed up in the newsroom unexpectedly, wearing blue jeans and a plaid shirt. He said he wanted to catch up on his own paperwork. JC recognized that what had to be said probably shouldn't wait.

When JC emerged from the news director's office, Milt was in the outer office. He pushed past and JC heard him asking his boss, "Do you have a minute?"

Milt later left work for the rest of the day. He'd received a call. Police asked him to stop by District Two headquarters for a talk.

There, he admitted to Detective Steve Trujillo that he knew Bitsy Stark was headed for Snow Hat, though Milt insisted he didn't put together that Bitsy was the young woman later murdered.

"Pretty girl," Trujillo observed as he spoke with Milt Lemon during questioning. "Did you score?"

"Did I score?" Milt asked.

Trujillo gave Lemon an inpatient look, "Did you have sex with the woman? That would be quite a triumph, Milt. Good for you."

"I didn't score, for cripes' sake," Milt responded. He was agitated. "We shared a meal at the bar."

Trujillo felt he had lost an advantage. Lemon knew exactly what police had seen on the surveillance video. JC had told him. Police had looked at the same video that morning, after JC informed Trujillo of it.

"Did you just bump into her at Snow Hat?" the detective asked Milt.

"No!" implored Milt. "I wasn't at Snow Hat! Well, not that day. You know we've been there covering the Buford story."

Trujillo took a walk around the empty office he'd borrowed. He hadn't wanted to put Lemon in an interrogation room. He wasn't going to be arrested that night unless he blurted out a confession. The detective thought a more informal setting might put Lemon at ease, more likely to talk.

"I thought Buford murdered the girl at Snow Hat," Milt whimpered. He looked like he was about to begin sobbing.

And that opened the door for Detective Trujillo to ask questions about other things he really cared about.

It was beyond his capacity to believe that Lemon had actually crossed paths with two homicide cases, in a matter of days, by coincidence.

"What," Trujillo asked, "did you and Wallace Simmons talk about over lunch?"

"Oh fuck," Milt thought to himself.

35

T he smell of burning wood was in the air as JC climbed out of his car. Evening was setting in at the Snow Hat Ski Resort by the time he arrived.

There was an open fire, surrounded by chairs on the packed snow. It was on the patio of the bar called Kitzbuhel. The bar was named after the Austrian village that hosted the most dangerous downhill ski race in the world. To win that race, even once, was to become a legend for life in Austria.

The bar was just down the road from Snow Hat. Inside, the walls were covered by anything that had to do with skiing. That included skis and poles, old magazine covers, old trophies, banners, flags, jackets and racing bibs. There was an antique gondola hanging from the ceiling.

Without saying a word, JC seated himself at a table next to an old friend. Russell Driver looked up, between bites of his chicken wings, and smiled.

"Hey, look at you!" he said.

"You always look like you don't have a care in the world," JC said with a smile.

Driver responded, "What's to worry about? I haven't met a man yet who I can't beat on a pair of skis."

JC leaned over and gave Driver's exquisite wife a kiss on the cheek. "Hello JC," Loni said with a smile.

"I cannot believe you're still coming to races with him," JC said to her.

"Who's going to drive him home from the hospital?" she replied, laughing.

It was before his time, but JC had been told that if life were fair, Russell Driver would have been the first member of the national ski racing team with black skin.

Instead, that honor waited for two more decades and Andre Horton. Horton's sister, Suki, followed Andre onto the team.

"I truly believe," Russell had told JC, "There is a child of color at this very moment, who is going to grow up and win a medal in alpine skiing for the United States." JC agreed.

It was happy hour. A waitress came to the table and JC ordered chicken wings and a local craft beer.

Russell studied his food and said, "I thought you'd be in your condo, cooking up a fine breakfast sandwich in the microwave."

He and Loni started laughing and looked at JC. His cooking disability was not a well-kept secret, perhaps because Russell and Loni had been staying in that hotel the same night.

"Maybe," Russell suggested, "you ought to ask if they need help in the kitchen here." Russell and Loni laughed some more. JC absorbed the beating with humility.

More customers were filling the tables of Kitzbuhel. Their hair was wet from showering after a day of skiing and snowboarding. The noise-level was rising, and the energy was amping up in the ski bar.

Russell had been at Snow Hat for a race earlier in the day. He asked JC, "Where were you?"

"I had work to do," JC told him.

"You got your gear?" Russell inquired between wings.

"Yep."

"Are you going to race tomorrow?" Russell asked.

"Maybe," JC responded.

He felt his ribs were sufficiently healed. It would be his first race since his crash in November.

His beer and wings arrived. He raised his glass for a toast, "Live fast, and die with your mask on!"

"You mean, ski boots. Die with your ski boots on," Russell corrected.

"I like that better," JC agreed. They both drank.

JC turned to Loni, "How is the book selling?"

"I am very pleased," she told him.

Loni Driver, JC thought, was the definition of sophistication. Like Russell, she was aged in her sixties. She was black and beautiful.

She had written a children's book called "Squeaky the Squirrel." It was about a young Squirrel who was afraid of heights. That was a problem, since his family's nest was about fifty feet up a lodgepole pine.

Squeaky just couldn't find the courage to go up there, so he burrowed a hole in the snow at the foot of the tree. He was terrified because he was afraid that a coyote would find him and eat him.

But in the end, Squeaky conquered his fears and climbed up to rescue his family before the tree was cut down to clear land for a new housing development.

JC saw that Russell was monitoring a college football game, on a television set over the bar. "I'm watching the Game of the Weak," he said.

"That's not a nice thing to say about your team," JC told him.

"That is the esteemed establishment from which I graduated," Russell said. "Thank goodness they had better teachers than they had coaches. They are not very good at football. It's like your phone bill. They both show up once a month."

The music grew louder at Kitzbuhel. More ski racers grabbed seats at their table. They greeted JC and congratulated Russell for having a good race that day. Russell was a good deal older than most of the racers, but he could still ski fast and turn at the right time.

Another face joined the table, one that JC had not expected. Milt Lemon sat down across the table from him.

JC wondered to himself why Milt wasn't in jail. JC searched Milt's wrists for any sign that he'd sawed off some handcuffs.

"It's all cleared up," Milt told JC. The reporter had his doubts. He would check with Trujillo later. For the moment, he introduced Milt to the people at the table.

"I thought I'd see how the other half lives," Milt shouted over the music and crowd noise. "The alternative was to sit in my apartment and choose between staring at a chair where my wife wasn't sitting or the chair where my daughter wasn't sitting. Are you racing tomorrow?"

"I think so," JC told him.

The waitress brought a very large order of wings to Milt. He caught JC staring at the oversized plate of food. Milt said, "I don't know what it is, I wanna eat like I have three rectums."

"I'd like to offer a blanket apology," JC said to the table, "for anything Milt has said since sitting down and anything he's likely to say until he gets up." That triggered some laughter.

Someone tried to quickly change the subject and asked Russell and Loni how long they'd been married.

"Forty-five years," Loni told them.

"What's your secret?" someone asked.

"The one-hour rule," Russell said as he finished off another wing.

Asked what the "one-hour rule" was, Russell told their story.

"Loni," he said, "gets out of bed at the ungodly hour of five-thirty a.m. I sleep until seven.

"In that hour and a half, Loni has come up with chores for me that would fill up a week.

"I'll have just woken up and hadn't had my first cup of coffee. I am just not ready to hear that kind of nonsense.

"So, she is not allowed to tell me what household item needs to be repaired, requiring considerable effort, or replaced at considerable expense, for one hour.

"In one hour, I'll have had my coffee and read my newspaper and I'll be much more agreeable."

People at the table nodded in agreement with that wisdom from the eldest members of the group.

Milt, however, was on a roll. He started telling his stories to the table. Some were ludicrous and funny. Others made JC cringe.

Some of Milt's observations to the group were keen but random. "Eighty-five percent of the universe is dark matter, and we don't really know what dark matter is," he said to anyone listening.

Milt rose from the table, saying, "I've got to go to the urine canyon." JC cringed.

Milt headed for the men's room. Someone at the table said, "Well, he's quite a talketypants."

"You're lucky he's in a good mood," JC told them.

They snickered at the thought of hearing the stories Milt must tell when he's in a foul mood.

"He's alright," a few at the table agreed.

"Yeah," JC said. "He's kinda crusty but he doesn't mean any harm." JC was half certain that he was right.

With wings and drinks polished off, people at the table began to depart. They had skis to wax before the morning's race.

Milt leaned across the table toward JC. "Where are you staying tonight?"

JC had worried it would come to this. He had been looking forward to some quiet time in his hotel room. Maybe he'd give Shara a call.

But there was a certain esprit de corps that came with skiing. It was along the same lines as mi casa es su casa. Not to mention being the only person at Snow Hat that Milt knew.

"You can sleep on the sofa in my room," JC offered with some reluctance.

It wasn't so bad, as it turned out. They drank beer while JC waxed his skis and sharpened the edges. A football game blared from the TV set.

When it was time for bed. JC wrote himself a note to call Trujillo on Monday to hear his version of what Milt described as "All cleared up" after an afternoon of police questioning.

JC glanced at Milt and saw a look of frustration. "What?" JC asked.

"You're wondering if I'm going to murder you in your sleep," Milt accused.

"Nope," JC told him.

"Why not?" asked Milt. "You're not sure I'm not the killer."

"Nope," responded JC. "But I can outrun you."

Milt looked down at his bulging stomach. He was feeling the effects of polishing off his supersized order of wings. He laid down on the couch and said to JC, "You have nice friends. You got any colostomy bags?"

"Paper or plastic?" JC responded.

36

There were tracks from mule deer in the fresh snow, as JC and Milt left the condo and searched for some breakfast.

There was already music pumping from speakers hanging from light fixtures in the resort village. They were intended to energize skiers as they began their day with a march to the lifts.

JC and Milt ducked into a bar that also served breakfast and found a table. The wall of the building was mostly glass, with beer signs lit by neon. It was still the gray color of dawn outside their window. But the tables were nearly full.

"Look at all the Gimmie-its," Milt said.

"The what?" JC hadn't a clue of what Milt was talking about.

"The Gimmie-its," Milt repeated. "Look at all these kids who have had everything handed to them. And all their parents taught them to do was say, 'Gimmie it.' They probably all drive BMWs."

JC looked around the room. It was full of skiers and snowboarders, people who were fit and energetic. It was possible that someone in the room was rich and spoiled, but there was no telling who that might be.

"Maybe," JC responded to Milt. "You would have called me a Gimmie-it when I was their age. But I was going to college. I had a job and ate horrible cheap food so I could afford a lift ticket. I didn't ask my parents to gimmie anything."

Milt frowned and turned his attention to the menu.

"Be right back. Order me an egg sandwich, and gimmie it!" JC said, leaving the table.

He went outside and pulled his phone from his pocket.

"Hey, you beautiful slab of man," he heard the sleepy voice on the other end say. He smiled and missed her terribly.

He told Shara that he thought he could get up to Montana for New Year's Eve, and probably stay through the weekend. He was going to cash in those days he was owed for working through the Christmas holidays.

"That would be wonderful, JC," he heard her say.

JC headed back into the breakfast bar and joined Milt at the table. Steam was rising from their hot plates.

Looking up as he chewed his egg sandwich, JC realized he'd been in the bar before. He'd interviewed the bar manager, with photographer Edgar Pabor, about the night before Bitsy Stark was murdered. He looked at the menu. The bar was called the Yardsale.

The bar manager had said the man with Bitsy looked like a picture JC showed her of John Buford. But JC hadn't had another picture with him at the time. He also didn't have Milt, in the flesh.

JC tried to remember what the woman looked like. He conjured up a memory of a middle-aged woman who looked like she had worked long hours for too long a time.

He didn't see her this morning. She had probably closed the bar only a few hours ago. "I'm going to want to come back here before we leave today," JC said.

After wolfing down their food and coffee, the two men headed for race registration.

"I'm going to be your squire," Milt told JC. He was speaking in an English accent.

"My squire?" JC asked, amused.

"Aye," he said. "Like jousting in medieval times. You're the knight, and I'll be your squire."

"But you don't have skis, do you?" JC asked.

"No," Milt responded. "Well then, I'll be your cheerleader. I look great in those short skirts."

"I hope I never find out if that is true," JC retorted.

Signing up for the race required competitors to display their race licenses. "Allow me to show you my license to kill ... myself," JC said. That amused the race officials.

Bright helmets and racing suits dotted the top of the racecourse, on a ski run called Dragonfly. There was a banner flying over the racers at the start, advertising a ski equipment manufacturer. There would be another banner at the bottom, strung to red plastic netting surrounding the finish area.

As the racers gathered at the start, awaiting the beginning of the two-run giant slalom, a racer nicknamed Cannonball asked JC, "What happened to you in the last race?"

He was called Cannonball because he had a black, old-school helmet that looked almost round. In the mind of his fellow racers, it made his head look like a cannonball.

"The race a month ago?" JC asked.

"Yeah," Cannonball said.

"When I crashed?" JC asked.

"Yeah," Cannonball said.

"I was trying to win," JC answered.

That was all the explanation Cannonball needed. Some racers race to enjoy the camaraderie and a fast run down a closed course. Some racers race to finish first. Taking the risks required to finish first don't always work out.

"I have a very nice collection of wooden spoons," Cannonball deferred. "My wife loves them in our kitchen."

The other racers laughed at his joke. A wooden spoon was racing's slang for finishing fourth, and missing out on a gold, silver or bronze medal.

Russell Driver slid into the start gate. He got to go earlier than most racers because he was older than most racers. They didn't think that was entirely fair because he was also faster than most of the racers.

He was this time, too, after the first run. JC was ahead of him, but not by a lot.

"My goodness," JC said to Russell as he looked at the scoreboard after his own run. JC was still breathing hard. He was smiling as he said, "You need to slow down, Russell. You'll hurt yourself."

"I could say the same thing to you," responded Russell as he pulled on a coat offered by Loni.

"I would have caught you," Russell told JC, "if I hadn't hit a mushroom cap."

That was a term that racers sometimes used to describe rocks or some other impediment popping up unexpectedly from the snow.

To JC, it had always struck him as an odd term. "Mushrooms" was a word he'd heard used by gang members to describe innocent victims who popped up when combatants were shooting each other. It's often how innocents got killed in those situations.

There would be an hour before the new racecourse, set for the second run, could be inspected. Normally, JC would eat lunch with the other racers in the cafeteria of the ski lodge.

But JC had other things on his mind. He and his squire headed for a quick bite back at the Yardsale. Maybe the bar manager would be there by now.

JC and Milt walked through the door. Another man was following them so closely, the three nearly got stuck in the door jamb.

"Sorry," they all said, the man quickly walking away into the darkness of the room.

"Did you bring a news camera with you when you drove up here yesterday?" JC asked.

"No, I have the day off," Milt answered.

"Some squire," JC told him.

"I'm sorry, M'Lord," responded Milt with the English accent.

Two weeks ago, the bar manager had complained to JC that she worked long hours. And there she was, behind the bar supervising the lunch rush.

JC took a seat at the bar near her. "Hi, do you remember me?"

The bar manager smiled, as she probably smiled at all her customers, but JC thought that she couldn't place his face.

"I'm a television reporter," JC said. "I interviewed you the morning after the young woman, Bitsy Stark, was found dead in the hotel."

They were alone at the bar, except for a man who sat down a few seats away, his back turned to them.

A smile came to the bar manager's face, "Oh yeah," she said with a gravelly voice. "My friends saw me on TV. That was you?"

"Yep," JC told her.

"Such a shame about that young lady, she was having such a nice time here, that night," the manager said.

JC nodded in agreement. It was a shame. He asked, "Do you recognize that man, at the table I was sitting at?"

The woman looked in Milt's direction. She studied him and then said, "No, I can't say that I do."

JC considered that for a moment. He asked, "Can I show you something else?"

"Sure," the woman answered. She coughed. He thought it sounded like a smoker's cough.

JC reached into his pocket. He pulled two pictures out this time. He placed them on the bar, side by side. It was a shame, he thought, that he didn't have a picture of the ride-sharing driver.

The bar manager just looked at him.

"Can you point out, again," JC requested, "which man you saw with Bitsy that night?"

One of the photographs was John Buford's black-and-white photo from the New York State Senate four years ago, the one she had ID'd last time.

She pulled a pair of glasses out of her bar smock and put them on. She studied the two photos, "No, I'm sure this time," she said. "It was this one. Definitely, this one."

She was pointing at a picture of Troy Davis.

37

The first gunshot turned the tip of a ski into splinters. The ski had been leaning against a metal rack. The sound startled everyone.

The second gunshot hit the ski rack. It sounded like a bell. People outside the ski lodge now understood that they were under attack. They started running in all directions.

JC and Milt were collecting his skis and poles from that rack when the shooting started.

"What the hell?" was JC's response to the first shot. It shattered the tip of an orange ski near his right hand.

It dawned on JC, after the second bullet sent sparks flying off the metal rack, that this was gunfire.

Instinctively, he looked toward the sound. For an instant, he saw a figure behind an open window on the second floor of the timing shack. It was the same building used earlier to officiate the ski race.

He saw the figure of a man, a man with no hair on his head, but maybe some face hair. Then, JC saw the man was aiming in his direction.

JC grabbed the arm of Milt's jacket and pulled him to the ground. They landed behind a stone, bomb-proof trash receptacle. A bullet bounced off the stone container.

Quite a few of these containers were installed after the terror attacks of 9-11. The threat of terrorism would now forever be a part of our daily lives.

The trash can was designed with strong walls and an open top, so the force of a bomb would blow up into the air, rather than out, carrying shrapnel into an unsuspecting crowd. The container, JC and Milt found, also deflected bullets.

The stone receptacle wasn't wide enough to protect two men, so JC lifted himself into an upright sitting position with his back leaning against it.

"Get in here," JC snapped at Milt as he spread his knees and offered a landing zone that the photographer could squeeze into.

Milt quickly backed in. He quipped, "I've seen this on TV. Are we entering the luge doubles?"

"Better than being a target in biathlon," JC responded.

Their own scramble to survive caused JC and Milt to overlook the calamity going on around them.

People were running for cover. There were screams. People inside the bar were slow to react because of the noise inside the establishment. But once they witnessed the mayhem going on outside the window, hundreds of patrons collectively dropped to the floor, flipping tables to hide behind.

Milt shouted, "What the hell is going on?"

"Someone's shooting at us," JC informed him.

Milt was disbelieving. "Someone's shooting at a crowd of skiers?"

"No," JC told him. "Someone's shooting at us."

"Us?" Milt repeated.

"Look around," JC told him. "There are plenty of targets out there. The bullets seem only to have landed near us."

Another shot skipped off the stone container the two men were hiding behind.

"Keep your elbows in," JC said to his companion.

They waited for the sound of the next shot. Milt asked, "Now do you believe I'm innocent?"

"Because you're being shot at?" JC answered.

"Yeah," Milt responded.

"You could have paid the guy to shoot at you, to make you look innocent," JC theorized.

"What's it going to take to convince you," Milt pleaded.

"If you're killed," JC told him, "you'll receive my heartfelt apology."

"Oh, nice," Milt jeered.

"You have nothing to worry about. He isn't going to shoot you," JC told him.

"How do you know that?" asked the nervous news photographer.

"Only the good die young," JC reminded him.

"Oh yeah." That actually appeared to put Milt at ease.

"You are twisted," JC mumbled.

There hadn't been a gunshot in a while. JC saw people starting to pick up their heads. A few rose and ran for their cars in the parking lot.

JC peered around the stone container. The timing shack had exterior stairs facing the ski hill, so they weren't visible from his vantage point. He had no idea if the sniper was still there or had fled.

"What we needed on our side were some flying reptiles that breathe fire," Milt offered.

JC looked at him quizzically, "You watch too much TV."

"How is that possible?" Milt asked. "I lead such an exciting life."

Milt stood and reached out a hand to help JC up. People were walking about in the snow, dazed, disbelieving of what had just transpired. Through the bar windows, they could hear tables being turned upright. They could hear crying.

Looking around, JC realized that no one had been struck by the bullets. Milt began to record news footage on his phone. He tried to keep his shots to about twenty seconds. It would be easier to email short footage.

JC pulled his phone out of his pocket and called the TV station. He alerted them to what had just happened. He dictated what details he could. He reported that an army of county sheriff's deputies were now arriving on the scene, some in SWAT armor.

The weekend assignment editor said she'd locate the closest news crew, whatever assignment they were working on, and reroute them to Snow Hat. If they weren't close enough, she could call in a crew from their day off and get them on the helicopter.

About ten minutes later, as soon as the studio could be set up and an anchor could be seated in front of the studio camera, JC was interviewed live over FaceTime on his phone. He was able to scan the aftermath so that viewers could survey the scene.

By then, he saw county sheriff's deputies were waiting to talk to him.

Before speaking with them, JC backtracked events in his own mind:

He and Milt had exited the bar where they ate lunch. It was right after the manager singled out the picture of Troy Davis rather than John Buford.

Milt didn't have a news camera with him to shoot an interview, because he was at Snow Hat on his day off.

JC had called the cell phone number of his news director. Pat Perilla's wife answered and politely told JC that the news director wouldn't be available for the day.

It was not unusual for wives to protect their busy husbands from distractions they didn't deem necessary. It was the only way their husbands got any rest.

At that point, JC determined that the story wasn't going to be reported until the next day.

That being the case, he could see no reason not to complete the second run of his race. He barely made it to the top of the course before he was called to the start gate.

He finished second for the day, behind Russell Driver.

The racers retired to the bar, for the awards ceremony and a couple of beers. It was after that, JC and Milt left the bar and headed for the metal rack where JC had locked his skis. That's when the shooting began.

His equipment was still there as sheriff's deputies interviewed him about what he saw during the gunfire.

"He was shooting at us," JC told the law officers.

"That's interesting," a deputy said. "Why you?"

"Not sure," JC told him.

"Do you know where he was shooting from?" a deputy asked.

"I think so," JC answered. He pointed at the timing shack, about forty yards from the ski rack where he took fire.

"By the way," another deputy asked. "You keep saying 'he'. Why are you certain that it was a man? Did you get a look at him?"

JC described the glimpse he got of the gunman. Bald, maybe a beard, and definitely a man.

The reporter led deputies to the stairs of the timing shack. JC was told to put on his ski gloves and he was given something to go over his Vibram-soled boots.

The deputies looked at the snow around the foot of the stairs and determined there were too many footprints to single out those of the shooter.

They entered the small room at the top of the stairs. A window facing the ski racks was open. There were no shells, but the room smelled like gunpowder. Deputies told JC that they were sure the forensic evidence would determine this was where the gunman had fired from.

JC did not disclose to the deputies that the bar manager had identified Troy Davis as the man with Bitsy Stark the night before her murder. That was something he'd share with Trujillo, tomorrow.

Having finished with law enforcers and his own television newsroom, JC gathered up his gear with Milt's help. They headed for their cars. It was time to get back to Denver.

JC saw requests on his phone for interviews. They were from newspapers, radio stations and out-of-town TV stations. He'd have to figure out a way to accommodate the other news media without it becoming a distraction to his own work. He'd throw it in his news director's lap, he thought.

He left Milt at his own car, "Bye, squire."

JC climbed into his 4x4. He thought about the shooter. He wondered why anyone would want to shoot at him. He wondered about that fleeting moment he got a look at the gunman.

The faceless man looked familiar, not like someone JC knew but someone he'd seen. JC's FJ Cruiser lunged forward for the trip back to Larimer Square. He'd think about that brief glimpse the entire time.

38

"Well, that was fun," Troy thought to himself. He was driving west back to Glenwood Springs. The radio was cranked up and he was singing along. He was happy. He liked adventures.

He was certain that no one had identified him leaving the small building that had been his sniper's nest. People tend to lower their eyes, bury their head in the ground when they're being shot at.

His Glock 26 went back into its little holster and was tucked under his jacket before he descended the stairs. Then, he'd behaved just like the other victims, terrified of getting shot and trying to get away.

It probably wasn't enough gun, Troy thought of the pistol. His target was past the reliable range of his weapon. "But I didn't have much time to prepare. Desperate times call for desperate measures," he thought.

He still might have to come up with a plan to nullify that TV reporter, JC Whatshisname. It would all depend, he thought, on how the timing unfolded.

Troy had good timing that morning, he supposed. He literally bumped into the TV personality as they were entering the same breakfast place.

Troy had recognized the journalist instantly and dipped his head. But Troy was sporting a new hairdo, a buzz cut, and a goatee. It changed his appearance significantly. He's certain he wasn't recognized.

Then, when he saw the reporter speaking with the woman behind the bar, Troy was able to slip into a seat close enough to eavesdrop.

He knew he'd been identified in that photo. By itself, it would mean nothing. But that would lead to something else, and then something else.

During his stay in Glenwood Springs, Troy had been waiting to perform another job. He'd already scouted the location and had a good plan.

Now, he thought he should move up his timeline. Then, maybe he could head for Mexico and lay low for a while.

He'd take a nap when he reached Glenwood Springs, he thought, and then head toward Utah.

JC realized he'd just missed his exit. It was because he was lost in thought. His mind was still on that glimpse he got of the shooter.

The hairless head was familiar. JC passed Exit 261 as things suddenly fell together. It was the man at the breakfast bar!

JC thought the man in the window of the timing shack looked like the man he and Milt had bumped into as they headed through the door that morning.

The reporter also realized it was the same man sitting nearby when JC was speaking with the bar manager, showing her the photos of Buford and Davis.

The reporter never got a good look at the face of the man with the buzzcut, but what he saw was the same man: The man in the bar and the man in the window of the timing shack, holding a handgun.

A handgun, JC thought. Interesting choice. Then, he realized he'd missed his next exit, "Damn!"

Troy Davis heard his alarm ring. It was dark now. The lights along the road outside his window burned orange. There wasn't much traffic on the road. It was pretty late.

He scratched the stubble on his head as he drove his car west on I-70. He was heading for a spot past Grand Junction but just short of the Utah border.

It would take an hour and a half to get there. Then, he estimated, he'd need under five minutes to collect his belongings. He laughed at that, but the stolen goods were soon to be his belongings.

He'd be on his way back to Glenwood Springs before a sheriff's deputy even arrived on the scene.

Troy had already collected boxes and addressed them. He'd probably mail them to Europe from Las Vegas. From there, he'd drive south of the border. He'd be in Tijuana for

New Year's Eve. That would be fun. He was looking forward to taking a vacation.

It was early morning on the next day when he arrived at the Museum of Archaeology, west of Grand Junction. He was excited to be back. He'd enjoyed the museum when he'd taken a look around, a week ago.

He parked under a tree near the entrance, in case the security camera, by chance, was working. It would be difficult to see his car behind the tree and shaded from the lamps in the parking lot. The lot was empty.

He pulled a ski mask over his face and put on gloves. He looked in all directions and exited his car.

He pulled a rather hefty metal contraption from the trunk of his car, which he left ajar. He approached the window and hit it with the heavy metal cylinder. The glass shattered and he walked in. He put the metal contraption down. He'd pick it up on the way out.

He walked straight to a case with gold trophies and awards. He broke the glass and grabbed the biggest and the best of the lot.

Then, he pulled open a case with old skins stained with drawings by first natives. There were images of horses and buffalo and battles.

He stuffed old garments into his bag, the clothing old archaeologists wore. And cowboy stuff. He was going for the visuals. His buyers in Europe loved the visuals.

He grabbed a few rocks and dinosaur bones. Some of the oldest and most valuable artifacts in the museum, namely the dinosaur bones, probably wouldn't get the highest price, but he'd test the market.

It was time to go. Bells from the alarm had been ringing for less than three minutes. He picked up his heavy metal window breaker on the way out, threw everything into his open car trunk and was off. He was back on I-70 heading East.

At least, that is how it was supposed to go. What really happened is this:

After he pried open the display case holding the cowboy apparel, he heard a door open and saw light spill out of a room in the back.

A man walked out. He was probably Troy's age, with a beard and disrupted long hair. "Who are you? What are you doing here?" the confused man in the lab coat asked.

Troy froze. He wanted not to be seen, but the man was staring right at him.

The man in the lab coat adjusted his glasses and took a good look at Troy. "Hey," the man said, "what are you doing?"

Troy's adrenaline began pumping. He wasn't frightened, he was beguiled by the predicament. He thought it was unfolding like a video game.

He reached to his side and pulled out his handgun. "Most of the time," Troy informed the rattled man, "I'm a really nice guy."

The scientist raised his hands and said, "Take anything you ..." The museum employee's last words were lost in the sound of the Glock firing.

Troy approached the man to check his work. "Problem solved. Much better range," Troy said. The man was dead.

The job wasn't supposed to go like that. But, Troy thought to himself, life doesn't always go as planned.

He headed for his car, picking up the heavy metal window breaker and tossing it in his car trunk with the bag of stolen goods.

Troy glanced at his watch. It had now been four minutes. He pulled away from the museum and saw I-70 approaching. He pulled onto the eastbound ramp and still hadn't heard a police siren.

39

"**D**id you almost get shot yesterday?" Detective Trujillo asked.

"Oh, that?" JC downplayed, "It was probably a hunter, mistook me for an elk."

"Um hum," the detective replied into the phone, "I'm reading the report and it sounds like you were the target. That sound right to you?"

"Shouldn't have worn my elk horn hat," JC said.

Trujillo let out a sigh, "We gotta play 'let's make a deal,' huh?"

"Wanna?" JC replied with false enthusiasm.

"OK," Trujillo said, sounding tired. "Who goes first?"

"Oh, I will!" JC was happy to be steering the conversation. "Is Milt Lemon in the clear for the deaths of Bitsy Stark and his ex-wife?"

"No," the law officer said.

"That's not as glowing an acquittal as Milt had led me to believe," JC told the cop.

"That's the way we like it. And this time, keep your mouth shut," Trujillo advised.

"My, we're grumpy," JC observed.

"It's my turn now." Trujillo stated, "Tell me something."

"You're getting the better of this deal," JC said into the phone.

"I'll be the judge of that," Trujillo told him.

Then, JC told the police detective about his return to the Yardsale, and his visit with the bar manager. JC said that the woman picked out the photo of Troy Davis.

"He's the man Bitsy was with the night before she died, not Buford," JC concluded.

"Well, I'll be," Trujillo remarked. "You sure about this?"

JC knew that Trujillo would conduct his own interview with the bar manager, and JC told him how to find her.

JC was about to hang up the phone.

"Hey!" The detective caught him.

"Yeah?" JC said.

"Who do you think was shooting at you?" the officer asked.

"I'm not sure," JC responded. "But I've been turning that event over in my head quite a bit, as you might imagine. I got only a glimpse of the guy. And the way I see him holding his arms? I think he was using a handgun, not a rifle."

"What do you think that means?" the detective asked.

ning Lucy: A Murder on Skis Mystery*

"I dunno," JC muttered. "But in all the movies I've seen, a hit man would have used a rifle, right?"

"You know what I think?" Trujillo asked.

"What?" JC answered.

"I think if it were the hit man in the movies," Trujillo stated, "you'd be dead."

They ended their call. Trujillo was finding himself agitated. His snitch was becoming a one-man crime wave. And it was a mess that he was going to have to clean up.

JC had called Trujillo from the newsroom. The reporter had been told to report for duty at 9 a.m. He knew what was coming, but he had tried to avoid it.

"Hey movie star, here's your schedule. Thanks for being useless to me today." Assignment editor Rocky Bauman handed JC a paper with a schedule on it. It was a list of interviews the station had agreed to have JC on hand for.

He hadn't overestimated the interest in a story about a sniper at a ski resort. It captured the attention of news operations across the globe. The list of interviews ahead of him had an international flavor.

That means, he thought, he wasn't going to get anything worthwhile done for the day. The schedule of interviews went until 5 p.m.

So, whatever he hoped to accomplish today would have to be done tomorrow, New Year's Eve. He thought about the last plane flying to Shara in Bozeman.

JC was wired to a chair in a small studio. It was off the larger main studio where the big news set was. He had a microphone on his lapel and a cord attached to the IFB in his ear, to hear his interviewer.

None of the studios had windows. That included the smaller studio that JC sat in. If all the lights were turned off, studios were as black as a night without a moon. TV technicians liked to supply, and control, their own light.

The artificial light supplied in TV studios was from perhaps ten lamps coming from all directions. They were brighter than the sun. That's the main reason why people on TV wore makeup. It was an effort to return flesh tones to their skin in the glare of those blinding lights.

Behind JC, inside this small studio, was a large picture of downtown Denver with the mountains behind that. The magic of television might make it appear that the reporter was in front of a window. But really, he was in front of a picture of a window.

His first interview was with the Evening News in Edinburgh, Scotland. They were seven hours ahead of Denver.

Scotland embraced its own enthusiastic ski industry. JC had only visited a ski resort there in the summer. He was told that there were enough rocks and wind during the winter that it sometimes got discouraging. But the Scottish were a game bunch.

JC pointed out during the interview that his ancestors were from Scotland. That's where the conversation turned, after discussing the fact that he'd been shot at yesterday at a ski resort in Colorado.

He was interviewed by the BBC in London and then a television station in Paris. It was kind of fun, he decided. It was like traveling to many of his favorite places without breathing contaminated air on an airplane for hours and catching someone else's virus.

He did a taped interview for Japan's morning news. It was just after midnight there, the next day.

He was interviewed by a Moscow TV station, and one in South Korea. And he was interviewed for tomorrow's most popular morning news show in New York City.

He was asked if he was frightened as bullets were zipping past him. "I was more surprised than frightened," he told them. "I was kind of worried about my skis, too. They were still locked to the ski rack and I didn't want them to get shot."

An overseas reporter asked if there are often shootings at American ski resorts.

Another asked if JC returned fire. "With what?" JC inquired. "I wasn't skiing biathlon."

Another asked, tongue in cheek, what the right ski wax was when your skis might get shot. JC laughed at that quip.

Robin Smith stood in the shadow as JC answered questions from an anchor in California. When the interview was over, she approached with a smile.

"Glad you're OK, JC," she said.

"I'm fine. The snow was bulletproof." He smiled at his joke.

"You asked me to keep an eye on museum robberies on the Western Slope?" she stated.

"Yeah," he said. "Did we have another one?" JC stayed in his seat, wired to a microphone and his IFB. He had an interview with Reykjavik coming up.

"There was one early this morning." She handed him a sheet of paper with the details. "A museum employee was shot and killed."

"Really?" JC told Robin that he'd write something for the evening news, if she could get more information.

"Let Rocky know," JC requested. "Do they have a name of the victim?"

"No," she told him. "I'll call the police, there."

"Thanks, Robin," he said.

Troy Davis woke up at noon and turned on the news. There was a small TV set in his room. The heist at the Archaeology Museum outside Grand Junction was the lead story. And the newscast gave the story twice the amount of coverage and time that lead stories normally received.

There was a picture of the museum employee who was found dead. Troy watched the newscast intently.

When the broadcast tossed to the weather segment, Troy was relieved. There was no picture and no mention of him.

He wore a mask during the entire episode that morning, but he just felt better seeing confirmation on TV. If they had his picture or knew who the robber was, they'd have said so.

Still, he decided to shave his goatee. It would change his appearance again. He never really liked it. He thought the face hair made him look like the Devil.

Troy relaxed with a cup of coffee from the machine provided in his room. He lounged on the bed, head propped up by his bent arm, and watched the rest of the newscast.

Toward the end of the news, they recapped their top story: the robbery and murder inside the Museum of Archaeology.

The anchor said they had an update. They showed a grainy photo said to be taken from a gas station near the highway. It was the image of a car police were interested in.

It was Troy's car, the beater. He thought to himself, what did that prove? He'd make up a story. He'd say he was looking for mountain lions. He'd heard they were nocturnal.

Still, he didn't want to get stopped driving that car. There was a warrant for his arrest for the cemetery thefts.

Loving Lucy: *A Murder on Skis Mystery*

He was going to have to make other plans to get to Mexico. Maybe he'd lay low for a couple of weeks.

The car wasn't in Troy's name. He'd obtained some phony paperwork to acquire the car. It was easier than people thought, if you knew what you were doing.

After bringing his bag up to his room to box the proceeds from that morning, he'd parked the car a couple of blocks away.

It was just a precaution he liked to take. He'd been doing it for a few years. They might find the car, he thought, but it didn't mean they'd find him.

"Zachary Martinez," Robin told JC when she walked back into the small studio. He was waiting for another interview to start.

"That's the name of the museum employee who was killed this morning during the robbery. He was the museum's curator," she said.

"I'll put this on your desk," she said, holding up the paper with the details.

"Thanks, Robin," JC said as he heard the next voice in his IFB. It was an interviewer from Canada.

The interview commenced. JC told the same story he'd told a dozen times already. That was alright, he thought, it was the first time they'd heard it. In fact, it was exactly what the Canadian anchor was looking for.

JC's mind began to wander, while never missing a beat in his tale of being pinned down by a sniper at the Snow Hat Ski Resort.

Who had told me that they knew a museum curator on the Western Slope? he asked himself.

"I would have started crying," the self-effacing interviewer said to JC.

277

It interrupted JC's wandering mind with a jolt. The guy just asked me a question, JC panicked. No, he made a remark.

"Well," JC said, "luckily, the guy was a lousy shot."

Kat Martinez! JC thought to himself.

The Canadian anchor was wrapping up the interview with a "Thank you. We're glad you're well."

"Yeah," JC responded with a chuckle. "Me too."

That was the end of the interview from North of the Border.

"I need a minute," JC told the producer that was in the studio with him.

He got out of his seat, pulled off the microphone and pulled the IFB out of his ear.

"You only have a minute," the producer said nervously as JC walked out of the studio.

As he entered the newsroom, he saw Robin. "Can you get Denver Police Detective Steve Trujillo on the phone for me?"

"I'll try," Robin responded.

JC quickly advanced on his desk and looked for the paper Robin said she'd put there. He found it and skimmed over the report. He was looking for the name of the museum curator.

Robin approached and said, "I've got Detective Trujillo on the line, can I transfer him to your desk?"

"Yeah, thanks," JC responded. He never took his eyes off the report about the museum robbery and the dead curator.

He picked up the phone and heard Trujillo's voice: "To what do I owe the pleasure, JC?"

"Are you following this museum robbery outside of Grand Junction?" JC asked.

"I happen to have a copy of the police report on my desk," the detective responded.

There was a pause. The nervous producer from the small studio gave JC a hand signal indicating she needed him back in the seat and wearing the microphone.

JC held up his index finger, asking her for one minute.

"It was a Baby Glock," the detective told JC over the phone. "Also known as a Glock 26. The curator took one shot to the face."

"Do you have his name?" JC asked.

There was a pause. "Zachary Martinez," the detective confirmed.

"I think I know his sister," the reporter told the detective. "She lives here in Denver.

"Interesting," Trujillo responded.

"There's something more here," JC said.

"Like what?"

"She's Troy Davis' old girlfriend," JC said.

There was silence on the other end of the phone line. Then JC heard the detective ask, "Is there a connection?"

"Why do I think there is?" JC asked out loud.

40

"Merry fucking New Year," she said quietly as she unlocked the chic glass entry to her hair salon and let JC in. The sign saying "Closed" swung back and forth on the door.

Kat Martinez had been crying and she seemed slightly drunk. There was a bottle of vodka and an empty glass on the table with the magazines for her customers.

She was still crying. Her mascara was washing down her cheeks. Her eyes were red. She had a towel in her hand and applied it to her face from time to time.

"I'm so sorry," JC told her. She didn't respond. She didn't need to.

After a while, she said quietly, "Zac wouldn't hurt a fly." She'd lost all the edge of her stage persona. She sounded like a child. A devastated child.

There was more silence, except for the sniffling. Then she said, "He didn't have to shoot him."

"Who, Kat? Do you know who shot him?" JC asked.

She looked at him with her wet eyes and said nothing.

If she knew, he thought, she'd say so.

"I'll check in on you," JC said as he headed for the exit.

JC left the salon feeling awful. Kat had suffered a horrible wound to the heart. There was no telling how long it would take to heal, if it ever did.

JC felt horrible, and he was about to feel worse.

"Are you packing? You won't need as many clothes as you might think," said the happy voice on the other end of the phone.

"Shara," JC said gently, "I can't come. I'm so sorry. I just can't come right now."

The bad news was greeted with nothing, not a sound. JC thought he might have heard something, a sob, but he couldn't be sure. He didn't press it. He wanted to give her time.

"You can't?" she finally said in a quiet voice, barely getting the words out. JC knew she was crying.

"I want this as badly as you do, honey. I just can't, not right at this moment," he heard his hushed tone say.

There was another long silence. He was sitting in his car, still outside Kat's hair salon.

He heard Shara gulp, "Don't bother."

"Honey, I'm so sorry," JC told her.

"No, I mean don't bother coming anymore," she said in a broken voice. "And I won't come see you."

"Shara, I'll get there as soon as I can," he said. "Maybe when this case is over."

He hadn't told her that he was shot at the day before. He hadn't told her because he didn't want her to worry. He'd figured that he'd tell her when he got to Montana. Maybe the shooter would be locked up by then. Now, he knew, she was going to see it on the news.

"JC, I love you, but I can't do this," she said.

"Shara, no," JC pleaded. "Let's not do this again."

"I can't keep breaking my heart, JC," she told him. "It's not that I don't love you. I love you too much."

JC didn't know what to say. He said nothing. He was searching to say the magic thing, the thing that would allow her to hold on. He couldn't think of anything.

"It's never going to work out, JC," he heard her saying. "I have to be here and you have to be there. I love you JC, I really do." And the call ended.

He sat in the car without moving, until it felt like the whole world must be looking out their window at him.

Then, he drove up and down streets of residential Denver. He didn't have the stamina to think about ... anything. He just drove.

He ended up in the parking lot of the Denver Zoo. He pulled his 4x4 into a space and turned it off. He closed his eyes.

He wasn't certain how long he'd been asleep in his car, when his phone rang. It was Detective Trujillo.

"Your boy's in the clear," he said. There was a bit of a bounce in his voice. At the moment, JC found it annoying.

"Who?" JC asked. He was still groggy.

"Your photographer, Milt Lemon," the detective answered. "Wally's an idiot. He says he was fiddling with his phone, in addition to being slightly inebriated, when he hit Sandy Lemon."

"We checked phone records," Trujillo continued. "We checked email, we checked snail mail. We checked for a money trail. We interviewed the server who waited on them before the accident. Waitresses listen in on conversations when they're serving a table, by the way.

"Anyway," the detective said, "she says they were talking about their days in the Army. They were talking about the last ten years of their lives. They were catching up. They hadn't communicated with each other for years. They didn't have any time to plan a deliberate hit-and-run.

"And there's no indication that Milt Lemon knew that his ex-wife was going to be crossing the street at Colorado Boulevard and East Thirty-Fifth. So, case closed," Trujillo said.

"Is Wallace Simmons going to be charged?" JC asked.

"Yeah, negligent homicide, hit-and-run, maybe distracted driving," Detective Trujillo explained. "He pretty much copped to the drinking and driving, but without a blood test, it would probably just get dropped in the plea."

"So, Milt is off the hook for both of them?" JC asked.

"Yeah," the detective said. "He didn't do Bitsy Stark, either. Strange set of circumstances. You can't blame us for wondering, but he's not guilty of anything. I hope there are no hard feelings."

"No," JC admitted. "I had my suspicions, too. Like you say, strange set of circumstances. How about the ride-sharing driver?"

"I don't think so," the detective disclosed. "We were suspicious because we knew he was lying his ass off to us. He said he was driving a fare when Bitsy was murdered. But his ride-sharing company said he didn't have a fare. Their records backed them up on that."

"So, where was he?" JC asked.

"It turns out that he did have a fare," the law officer said, "but it was 'off the books.' He'd picked up a fare but he scooped up the rider without ever officially claiming it. That way, he could keep all the money for himself. He lied because he didn't want to get in trouble with his employer."

"So," JC asked, "he's guilty of nothing?"

"He never really added up as Bitsy's killer," Trujillo said. "We just didn't know why he was lying to us. He's in trouble with his employer, but not with us."

"You shouldn't lie to cops," JC said.

"No. And I've got one for you, since you're being so nice," the detective told JC.

The reporter had awakened sufficiently to grab a notebook and start scribbling all of this down.

"The task force tested the bullet fragments from the ski area where you were shot at," Trujillo said.

"And?" JC asked.

"They found nothing that they compared to," the detective told him. "That is, they compared them to bullet fragments from other shootings, including Scott Miller. They didn't get a match."

JC found it interesting that the bullets were compared to evidence in the Scott Miller murder.

"But they were just compared to the bullet used to kill that Martinez boy, yesterday," Trujillo said. "And they're a match."

JC's eyes widened. "The bullet that killed Zac Martinez was fired from the same gun that was shooting at us at Snow Hat?"

"Yep," Trujillo said. "Interesting, huh?"

JC turned things over in his head. There was silence on the phone. Trujillo was letting him take his time.

"It's Troy, isn't it?" JC asked.

"That is what we believe," Trujillo said. JC could hear the smile plastered on the police officer's face.

Some time passed. Both men took a moment to soak in the triumph. This case was quickly getting solved.

"Bitsy Stark?" JC asked.

"We have a forensics unit returning to that hotel and going over the things we removed from the room," the detective told the reporter. "We're confident that we're going to find Troy Davis' prints or fluids or something. This time, we're not looking for John Buford. It was Troy Davis."

"Scott Miller?"

"Same answer," Trujillo said.

Then he said, "I'm going to give you a call back in about five minutes, OK?"

"OK," JC responded.

JC surveyed his surroundings. For the moment, he'd forgotten how or why his car got to the zoo. Then he remembered. The ache returned.

The phone rang. It was Trujillo. "Sorry," the detective said, "I had to go talk to my detective sergeant."

"No prob," the reporter responded. After re-inflicting himself with the pain of his phone call with Shara, JC had spent the remainder of the five minutes thinking about everything the law officer had told him. He wondered why the law officer had told all of that to a journalist.

Yes, JC had been helpful to the investigation. And Trujillo was smart enough to know that JC wasn't going to allow the passage of information only to go one way.

But the police had also used JC as a conduit to the public. The police had shared information that was to their advantage if it became public.

JC was OK with that, as long as he wasn't lied to. The unspoken agreement was over if the police ever caused him to pass along a lie to the public.

And there were no side deals. If JC got word of a bad cop, he reported it. He owed the police department no favors. And if JC committed a felony, he expected to be arrested.

Was he being used? Of course, JC thought. He was in the business of being used.

Politicians used the news media when they wanted to seek votes. School districts used the news media when they wanted to reach parents. The art museum used the news media when it wanted patrons to know they had a new Van Gogh.

JC had long ago concluded he was in a "user business." His job, though, was being smart enough to know what he was being used for. Good or evil?

Now, Trujillo was back on the phone. He asked, "What do you know about this Martinez woman?"

"She's pretty broken up," JC said. "I spent some time with her this morning. She and her brother were tight."

"I'll bet," the detective mused. "It's always tough."

The following silence gave the reporter time to remember that Detective Trujillo had tried to comfort the loved ones of victims, probably a hundred times.

JC wondered what he was up to.

"Do you think she wants revenge?" the detective asked.

41

"No way!" she shouted. "He did not! You're lying!"
Kat pushed him away. JC thought she might actually strike him. All of her edgy, agitated, combustible DNA was balled into a fury.

He had come back to her salon, called Hair Brained, the day after he saw her there crying. The store was still closed, but she opened the door and looked happy to see him.

She still held a tissue in her hand. It meant that she was still crying over the loss of her brother. She wore a plain gray sweatshirt and blue jeans, a departure from her normal avant-garde attire.

"Thank you for being so kind, yesterday," Kat told him.

"I'm really sorry. I know you loved him," JC said.

It was New Year's Day. She was running on instinct when she asked him the question that everyone asked each other on this day, "Did you do anything last night?"

"No," JC told her honestly. "I went to bed early."

"Me too," Kat said as she sniffled.

Kat didn't know that JC's girlfriend had just broken up with him. Kat and Shara enjoyed each other's company. JC thought they were alike in some ways, like their strength.

There was a bit of silence. Neither of them minded. Then, JC said, "Kat, I have some news for you."

The hair stylist, punk rock singer, looked at him. He could see the injury in her eyes.

"Police say they know who killed your brother," JC told her.

Her eyes grew in intensity. She searched his face but didn't say anything. She was waiting for the news.

"They think it was Troy," JC told her.

Kat didn't say anything. She stood there in silence.

"They want you to help them catch Troy," JC told her. "They think you know how to get in touch with him."

"No way! He did not! You're lying!" she suddenly shouted. "You're working for the cops. They'd do anything to get Troy!" JC took a few steps back.

'They don't want anyone else to get killed, Kat," JC tried to explain. "They don't want to get killed and they don't want Troy to get killed. He's hurt a lot of people, Kat. They just want this thing to be over."

The much smaller woman pushed JC backwards. Her face was contorted with anger.

"Kat," JC tried to say in a measured tone, "I think it's true. There's a lot of evidence."

He tried to tell her about the gun that killed Zac. It was the same gun that shot at JC and Milt. He tried to tell her that Troy had been identified as the man with Bitsy before she was murdered. He tried to tell her that Scott Miller and Troy shared a last supper.

"You're lying! You scumbag!" she hollered, "It wasn't him. Maybe it was you!"

JC didn't know what to say. He stood with his arms at his side as she pushed him again.

"Maybe it was the cops!" she screamed in a voice getting hoarse.

Her rage was still building, he thought.

"Get out of here!" she yelled. "Get out!"

JC backed toward the door.

"I'm sorry," was all he could think to say.

"Get out!" she yelled as she slammed the door behind him and he walked toward his car.

He climbed into his 4x4 and pulled away. Around the corner, he pulled over and pulled out his phone. He dialed Shara's number. She didn't pick up. Again.

Detective Trujillo walked back down the hall toward his desk. Normally, he'd have New Year's Day off. He'd watch some football with his kids.

Not today. Too much was riding on today. Maybe he could slip away in the afternoon.

He'd just informed his detective sergeant that Kat Martinez refused to help them capture Troy Davis.

"Maybe she'll think it over and come around," Detective Sergeant Trudy Johnson told Trujillo.

"You've done good work on this, Steve," she said. Then she assured him, "You're going to get him."

Detective Trujillo walked down the hall of District Two headquarters toward his desk. He thought about how the new police building looked like his high school. It was clean, with wide spaces, but kind of generic.

It wasn't like the old police building when he started on the force. That decaying structure was crusty and cramped. It was a professional space, but it was never going to be scrubbed clean. Maybe it was like his chosen profession, he thought to himself.

Kat's phone rang.

She sniffled, "Hello?"

"Hey gorgeous!" the voice on the other end greeted her. The voice was full of energy, fun and mischief.

"Hi Troy," she said softly. Her voice cracked.

"Hey Kitten," he said. "You sound down."

Kat began to cry. She couldn't bear to say it out loud again, "My brother, Zac, is dead."

"Oh no, Kitten," Troy consoled her. "What happened?"

"He was shot," she whimpered. "Someone murdered him."

"Oh baby, I'm so sorry," Troy cooed. "I always wanted to meet him. Didn't he live out West somewhere? Durango? Ouray?"

"Grand Junction," she said between tears. "Or at least, near there."

"What was he doing out there, again? I'm so sorry, baby. I'm so sorry," Troy said, trying to comfort his old girlfriend.

"He was a curator at a museum." She blew her nose and tried to compose herself. "An archaeology museum."

There was silence on the other end of the phone. Then Troy repeated a distracted, "I'm so sorry, baby."

"Thank you, Troy," Kat said into the phone, sniffling.

There was more silence. Troy was stunned. He cared about Kat. She was a lot of fun. He thought that she'd still be a lot of fun, no matter her gender preference.

He was going to be bored, sitting in his room for a couple of weeks waiting for things to cool off. Maybe he could convince Kat to come stay with him.

That would be a party, he thought. He could give her money to get them a nice room in a nice hotel. Maybe Aspen. Maybe the Hotel Jerome.

He might have to lay low, but they couldn't help but have fun there. Maybe light a few old sparks, he thought.

"Hey baby," Troy cooed. "Maybe you need to get away. You want to come see me?"

"Troy," she said, "I can't."

"Come on, baby," he begged, "I've been working hard. I've got a lot of fun tickets. I've been working hard. Fun tickets aren't free, you know."

Fun tickets, Kat remembered. That's what Troy called money. "Troy, seriously," she said into the phone.

Maybe she could drive me to Mexico, Troy thought to himself. I could give her money for another car, and we'd be on our way, he thought. They wouldn't see my face, he reasoned, they'd see her face, pretty and innocent.

"Troy," Kat sighed. "Don't you ever get tired? Don't you ever want to stop?"

"What are you talking about, babe?" Troy asked. "Do I want to die? Is that what you're asking? Because if you're not living, you're dying."

"Oh, Troy," she said, exhausted. "Your fun tickets cost a lot. People get hurt when you hustle them. You've hurt a lot of people."

"Kat," Troy said, "you don't sound like yourself. Life isn't about obeying every rule. It's about obeying the rules that make sense."

"Oh, Troy," Kat muttered, her voice hoarse from crying.

"Say I'm driving a Ferrari," Troy explained. "The speed limit is thirty, but there's no one around. There are no school children, there are no nuns, there are no puppy dogs. Should I drive that Ferrari thirty miles an hour? Or should I treat that Ferrari the way it was built to be treated?"

"It's not always about you, Troy," Kat said somberly.

"Kat, you're not fun like you used to be," Troy told her. She felt his compassion cooling. He wasn't getting his way.

"Sorry," Kat said quietly.

"I'm sorry, too, Kat," Troy said. "Say, I've gotta go. Sorry about your brother."

"Thanks," Kat said. "He was the love of my ..." But she realized that Troy had already hung up.

JC was looking for something to eat. He was walking up Larimer Street. The string lights hanging over the road and sidewalks were illuminated. Couples walked past him. Many of them were holding hands or were arm in arm.

He'd tried calling Shara again. Again, she didn't answer. It would be busy at her bar. It was a holiday and the Grizzly

Mountain Ski Resort would be packed. But that wasn't why she wasn't picking up her phone, he knew.

Then his phone rang. He stopped in front of an Italian restaurant and pulled the phone out of his pocket. He put it to his ear, hopeful.

"OK," was all she said.

It was Kat's voice.

42

"Hey, Sugar," Troy cooed into the phone.

"Hi Troy," Kat answered solemnly. "I want to see you."

"That's a girl," Troy replied, his spirits lifted. "You going to come to Aspen? We'll have a ball."

"I can't come to Aspen, Troy," Kat told him. "I have to bury my brother."

Trujillo made a face. He was sitting on the other side of the table in the reception area of Kat's hair salon. He worried that Kat might scare off Troy by bringing up her brother's murder.

Kat read the expression on the detective's face and softened her tone. "Let's meet at the lookout. We'll be alone there. We can talk."

"Lost Gulch Lookout?" Troy responded. "Yeah, I can do that."

Troy and Kat used to go to Lost Gulch Lookout together. They'd sit on the rocks on a warm summer night, share a picnic dinner with some wine and take in the view.

It was a remote spot, Troy thought. Romantic. Perfect.

It was a short drive up a mountain towering over the city of Boulder. No one would spy on them, he thought. They'd have some privacy. Maybe, he thought, she wasn't only into girls. Maybe she was still into Troy.

Kat had lied to JC when she said that she didn't have Troy's phone number. She did. She always did.

"I'll need your car," Detective Trujillo told Kat after she hung up the phone. "You don't need to be there," he said. "But your car does."

Kat instinctively looked toward the back door. Her car was parked in a space behind her business.

"Does he know your car?" Trujillo asked.

Kat nodded that Troy did know her car.

"Good," Trujillo said. "He'll need to see it. I scouted out the area. I'll have police backup behind me. He won't escape."

Kat just nodded, tears coming to her eyes.

Kat's compact car clawed its way up the steep winding road. From some of the switchbacks, Detective Trujillo could see below to the city of Boulder. It was a steep ascent.

The detective felt like he barely fit into the small car. He was trying to see through the windshield beyond the swinging pendants and ornaments hanging from the rearview mirror. They annoyed him a little.

There was a skull, a guitar, and a cross. They hung from braided hemp cords. He finally pulled them down.

Near the road's summit, there was a dirt parking area surrounded by trees and sections of jack fence. There were no cars parked there. Perfect, Trujillo thought.

He pulled Kat's compact into a spot and reached toward the passenger seat for his body armor. Then he pried himself out from behind the steering wheel.

Thirty minutes later, a red Ferrari leaped into the parking area. Troy eyed the short dirt path to Lost Gulch Lookout. He saw Kat's car already parked there. He was surprised because he'd arrived early.

It had been a fun ride, Troy thought. That car could corner and accelerate at the same time. He thought that he'd give Kat a ride later that evening.

The sun would set in an hour, Troy estimated as he climbed out of the low sportscar. The wind was still, so the winter air really wasn't cold. But he pulled on a fiberfill coat.

He scanned the woods and rocks in all directions. There was no one in sight.

In the summer, there would be other people, but rarely in the winter. Kat would be up at the lookout.

He started up the trail. Much of it was covered in snow. But Colorado's warm sun would usually melt the snow on the first sunny day after it fell.

The jack fences that guided a walker to the overlook ended. He saw the boulders in front of him. On the other side, rocks would provide natural seating to look out over a sheer drop at the valley below.

He thought that he'd surprise Kat, maybe give her a little scare. He climbed quietly over the big rocks to their favorite place to perch. No doubt, that's where she'd be waiting for him.

But the perch was empty. She wasn't there.

"Kat!" he exclaimed in a raised tone. There was no answer.

"Kat!" he shouted. Still no answer.

Maybe she went to take a pee, he thought. He sat on a rock that was somewhat elevated. Below his seat was a drop of hundreds of feet.

He heard footsteps and casually turned to greet his former girlfriend. Instead, he saw Detective Trujillo. He was alone.

Troy recognized him immediately. He'd been a useful snitch for the police officer for a few years. That had proved useful to Troy, too.

"Girlfriend," Troy said playfully. "You're not as pretty as I remembered you."

"That disappoints me, Troy," the detective responded. "I put on a clean shirt."

Troy continued to look at Trujillo. He said nothing for a moment. Troy was trying to figure out how much the detective really knew. Trujillo looked back at him, trying to figure out how much Troy knew he knew.

"You know," Troy said, "that rock you're standing on is one-point-seven billion years old. It used to be deep beneath the earth's surface."

Trujillo looked at the rock beneath him. Then, he looked at the suspect. He noticed that Troy had a shaved head, now.

Trujillo thought Troy was buying time, trying to assess his chances.

"Nice car," the detective said. "That yours?"

Troy scratched his face and smiled at the law officer. The fugitive asked, "Isn't possession nine-tenths of the law?"

"You're normally more subtle than that," the detective observed.

Trujillo made a note to himself to look for the report of a stolen Ferrari when he got back to the office. He'd have to see to its return.

"Did you know," Troy asked, "that the first car theft was fifteen years after cars were invented?"

"I did not," Trujillo told his former snitch, without a smile.

"It was a 1905 Maxwell," Troy said.

The detective didn't completely disguise his genuine interest. He was reminded that Troy was an engaging guy. It was probably how he fooled so many people, including Trujillo.

"Here's what I can't understand," Troy laughed. "How did it take fifteen years for someone to figure out that you could steal a car?"

Trujillo eyed the layout of Lost Gulch Lookout. The two men were placed on a large outcropping. On three sides of Davis, there were sheer drops. On the fourth side, there was Detective Steve Trujillo.

"I suppose you're hoping to squeeze me into your schedule today," Troy said to the detective.

"We should move along," Trujillo said. "We have a busy evening ahead of us. I've made an appointment for you in fingerprinting. And I've scheduled a photo session. You need to update your mugshot. A judge has been asked to join us after dinner," Trujillo continued with only a faint smile. "And if I may be so bold, I've booked you a room."

Troy looked at the detective who was standing over him and said in a mocking fashion, "I really do appreciate all the trouble you've gone to."

The detective reached behind him for his handcuffs. Troy reached to his side for his gun.

The advantage turned in an instant. Troy was pointing his handgun at the detective. Trujillo was angry with himself. He'd been caught flat-footed. Now, he was staring at a weapon pointed at him by a serial killer.

They were perhaps ten feet away from each other. Troy thought that his target would be impossible to miss. It would have to be a head shot. He could see the bulk under Trujillo's jacket, caused by a bulletproof vest.

The detective's mind raced. He thought that he needed to keep his cool and keep the conversation going. He needed to use his head to gain back the advantage.

"A Glock 26," the detective observed. "I've been looking at some evidence pertaining to a Baby Glock recently."

Troy paused to think about that. He was still holding the gun on the law officer.

"Then, you're probably not alone here," Davis stated.

"Not really," the detective said.

"I should have known that Kat would figure it out," Troy stated. "I got arrogant."

"It was your hamartia," Detective Trujillo told him.

"My what?" Troy asked.

"You're not the only one who went to college," Trujillo quipped. "A hamartia is a fatal flaw that leads to failure."

Troy Davis gave that some thought. He still held the gun on the detective.

But the crackle of a police radio, from the nearby parking lot, caused Davis' eyes to dart and shoulders to slump. He knew that was the sound of Trujillo's reinforcements. He was trapped.

Then, the fugitive saw two hats appear over the boulders. They belonged to sheriff's deputies. Their guns were drawn, pointed at him.

"Bang, bang!" Just the words passing Davis' lips caused the detective to jump a little. Troy smirked at his little joke.

"Tell Kat that I didn't know he was her brother," Troy told the detective.

Trujillo gave that some thought. Just as he moved forward, Troy Davis gave him a smile, leaned toward the open precipice and disappeared.

"Holy shit!" the detective heard himself say. He lunged closer to the edge of the cliff but stopped. The empty void made him uncomfortable.

He dropped to his hands and knees and crawled to the brim of the rock. He looked around him and felt better when he found a hand-sized protrusion from a boulder. He grabbed it and poked his head out above the open air.

Probably one hundred feet below, he saw the body of Troy Davis lying face up. His legs were crossed. He almost looked comfortable. There was a puddle of crimson blood expanding around his head.

Trujillo thought it looked like a halo.

43

He didn't mind, really, being accused of killing Fiona. He'd done it. He would live with that.

But it had troubled John Buford to be accused of strangling Bitsy Stark. He hadn't had anything to do with that. He wasn't that kind of man, he thought to himself. He felt wronged.

Buford sat in his small apartment, not watching out either of his windows, but watching the news on TV.

He saw Denver Police announce that Troy Davis, a small-time career criminal, had murdered Bitsy. The police chief disclosed that Davis was dead. He died, late yesterday, as police were trying to take him into custody. More would be released later, the police chief announced, about the circumstances surrounding Davis' death.

Buford watched live coverage of the police news conference. The police chief also said that more would be released, perhaps later in the day, about Davis. It was indicated that he was responsible for other serious crimes.

The chief wore the same dark navy shirt and pants of his uniformed officers. The chief, though, wore four stars on each collar.

Buford watched as the chief tried to speak without expression. However, the former senator recognized the emotion behind an occasional smile that surfaced. The chief was proud of the work his unit had done.

The first row of men and women surrounding the police chief at the podium were all in uniform. They looked like the top ranks of leadership of the department.

In the second row, behind the police chief and mostly to the side on the crowded platform, was a mix of uniformed and plainclothes law officers. To the far-right side of the television screen, almost nudged off the small stage, stood Detective Steven Trujillo.

Poor child, Buford thought of Bitsy Stark. Lucy liked her, he remembered.

Buford looked out of his southeast window. The sun was hitting the thick blanket of snow on the ground. It caused a reflection that forced Buford to reach for his sunglasses.

The sun's radiation heated up his apartment. He raised the window to let some fresh air into his congested space.

It was a good snowpack, so far, he observed. Buford had learned, since escaping to Colorado four winters ago, that the winter in this state will determine how the summer will go.

The accumulation of snowfall in the mountains during the winter has everything to do with how much water Colorado will have to live on until next winter.

Colorado is an arid state. It won't receive a lot of rainfall during the summer months. Most of the water used by the populated megalopolis to drink, or to water their gardens or wash their cars will come from the runoff of melting snow in the mountains.

Most importantly, the mountain runoff would provide irrigation for farms in the eastern half of the state. Without water, their crops would die. Without water, dairy cows couldn't produce milk.

In a winter with little snowfall, Denver and the other cities on the Front Range were told to stop watering their gardens, stop washing their cars and be selective about when they flushed the toilet.

Coloradoans understood when restrictions were imposed. Water was a precious resource.

JC Snow was eyeing a photograph of him wearing snowshoes, somewhere near Gunnison. It was among many photographs hanging in his cubicle in the newsroom. This one was taken years ago. He was a little skinnier and his hair was a little longer.

He'd trekked over deep snow with a team from the state as they measured the snowpack. They were doing it "old school."

They drove steel cylinders into the snow. After measuring the snow's depth, the snow inside the cylinder would help calculate how much water was in it. From there, the front range would learn how much water it would enjoy, months from then.

The photo had taken his mind off Shara. He'd called again and been sent to voicemail again.

He rose from his desk and grabbed his coat. He and Milt had been asked to drive to Snow Hat to do live shots wrapping up the death of Bitsy Stark's killer, Troy Davis.

By the time his story hit the air, JC would also be able to report new details about Davis' involvement in the deaths of Zac Martinez and Scott Miller.

JC wondered to himself how much Lisa Miller had known all along. Did she know that Troy Davis had killed her husband, even before she called the newsroom the first time and JC was sent to interview her? Was it her way of getting even with Troy? Did she know it would end like this?

JC's story was mostly written before he and Milt departed for the ski resort. He already knew the details. He was just waiting for police to approve the release of that information.

If police headquarters didn't approve the release of the details, JC would report them anyway. And the police knew it. JC had his facts straight and there was no further investigation necessary, no prosecution at risk. Troy Davis was dead.

Kat Martinez had declined JC's request to do an interview on camera. JC had stopped by her hair salon. They spoke in private. She was glad Troy had paid a price for her brother's death. But she wasn't going to do an interview.

With most of his story written and the video shot, JC told Milt to pull off I-70 at the exit for Georgetown. JC said he was taking Milt to lunch.

"You're buying?" Milt asked.

"That is a fact," JC told him.

"What's the occasion?" the photographer asked.

"That you didn't murder anyone, despite suspicions," JC answered.

They devoured good Mexican food at Lucha Cantina, near Rose Street in the old mining town.

"It turns out," JC told Milt Lemon, "you were a MacGuffin."

"What, in the name of my superb chile relleno, is a MacGuffin?" asked Milt as he enjoyed his meal.

"The British made up the term," JC told him. "It describes something in literature that serves as a distraction. The detail seems important as someone reads a piece of fiction, but in the end, it isn't important at all."

"So, I'm not important at all?" Milt asked with a sly grin.

"You will be, to Jayne," JC assured him. Milt smiled. A judge had assured that Milt would have regular visitation rights, even as custody remained to be worked out.

"Police were distracted while they looked for Bitsy Stark's killer, as well as Sandy's," JC told him, "by looking at your suspicious actions."

"Well, thank you," Milt said as he sipped from his glass of water. "I really wish this were a margarita," he said.

Milt's thirst for a party drink intensified when they strolled down the pedestrian walk at Snow Hat. A lot of skiers and snowboarders had abandoned the slopes for a slopeside bar.

It was Friday and it was a sunny day at the ski resort. Music was thumping from the outdoor speakers hung over stores and restaurants. The crowd was festive. This was their beach.

In a couple of months, some skiers would be wearing shorts. The snow would be soft and spectators would line a pit of water for the Slush Cup.

Skiers and snowboarders who entered the Slush Cup tried to get up a good head of steam and cross a body of water on their skis and boards.

The winner was the one who made it. But the crowd pleasers were the ones who didn't. The bigger the splash into snow-lined freezing water, the bigger the roar of approval.

In the crowd, at an outside bar and wearing sunglasses, JC saw a familiar face. She was surrounded by other young women her age. They were laughing and drinking in the joy that can be Colorado.

JC approached the young woman. "So, you made it," he said.

Lucy Buford looked up and pulled her sunglasses down her nose. A smile appeared on her face. "Hi! I did!"

"How long have you been here?" he asked. He was seeking time to decide what he really wanted to ask her.

"We just got here," she said, almost giggling with delight. "Our first day of skiing will be tomorrow."

"These are your friends?" JC asked.

She said that they were and introduced them. She said she had started college. She was attending Skidmore in Saratoga Springs, close to her aunt and uncle.

"Near where I grew up," JC said.

"I know!" Lucy said. He was happy she remembered. It was a connection.

He asked her where she was staying. She pointed to a second-floor window overlooking the table she was sitting at. It was a condo, she said, near the action.

"Hang on a sec," she said happily.

Lucy Buford pulled out a piece of paper and began writing on it.

JC was hoping it had her phone number on it, then he wouldn't have to ask for it. He was thinking about requesting an interview later, seeking reaction now that her father wasn't suspected of murdering Bitsy Stark.

Lucy's friends had begun talking among themselves again. They were ignoring the encounter between their schoolmate and the journalist.

JC looked down the pedestrian walk. He could see the side door to the hotel. It was the door Bitsy and Troy Davis had entered, at some point ending in her murder.

It was a gruesome thought, not one that he had to share with this happy eighteen-year old.

Lucy had stopped writing. She folded the paper and held it, biting her lip, as though she were reconsidering her impulse.

A shy smile returned to her face and she handed JC the paper. He unfolded it and read the words written in neat penmanship. She didn't take her brown eyes off of him.

"You know that I'd have to say something," JC told her.

"I know," she said.

John Buford rose from bed the next morning without an alarm. He'd not used an alarm for four years.

He lowered himself to a seat at the southeast window and watched "Spot" hunt for mice in a field. Spot jumped high when he attacked, coming straight down on his prey. He made it look fun.

Buford had a thick envelope in his hand. It was full of cash. He pulled out enough money for the next two months' rent and placed it on the dresser.

He put on blue jeans and a nice shirt. He couldn't remember the last time he'd put that shirt on.

He put on a jacket and gloves, threw on a backpack and tossed a garment bag over his shoulder. He looked out the southeast window and said, "So long, Spot."

He glanced at the mirror as he grasped the door handle leading to the hallway.

Jose Garcia stared into the mirror. But he saw John Buford staring back. His hair was no longer blond or spiked.

Buford was a little surprised that his hair was entirely gray when he washed out the color the night before. His salt and pepper had lost its pepper.

Still, he looked like a young fifty-four. He was glad for that. He hoped he didn't look much different.

He walked downstairs to the restaurant and headed for the door outside. He was surprised to find his landlord behind the counter.

"Oh my, Jose," she said when she looked up. "You look very distinguished." He smiled at her.

She asked, "Why are you up and out so early?"

He gave her a little smile and told her, "It's time."

44

"I'm working on something," JC said. That's all he'd tell Milt.

He'd convinced the news photographer to stay at Snow Hat overnight. The reporter called the newsroom and told Rocky Bauman that was where they'd be. "I'm working on something." That's all he'd say.

In the morning, JC rose early and searched the lobby of their hotel for some coffee. A blaze was already burning in the stone fireplace in the middle of the lobby.

JC leaned against the warm stone and pulled out his phone. "Did I wake you?" he said when someone picked up.

Once they were dressed, JC and Milt looked for a place to grab breakfast on the pedestrian walk at Snow Hat. The retail shops were opening up and the two men were familiar with the venues that would be offering breakfast.

Milt instinctively headed for the door of the Spilled Cup Coffee Shop. They'd been there before.

"Hey, Milt," JC stopped him, "let's try this place." It was a cafe directly across from the Spilled Cup.

JC parked himself at a table on the outside patio. Milt followed. JC had told Milt to bring his camera. He placed it on the ground beside him and zipped up his jacket.

"It's a little chilly to be having an outdoor picnic," Milt quipped.

"Yeah," JC responded. "But look at the view."

Milt looked in both directions. It was a view he was becoming accustomed to. The chairlifts were in one direction of the corridor with the parking lot in the other. There were stores and bars and restaurants with condos and hotel rooms on the floors above. He noticed that the string lights overhead were turned off.

JC continued to look about. His eyes never strayed from the pedestrian walk.

"What are you up to?" Milt asked him.

"You might want to put your camera on the table," JC told him. "And be ready to power it up."

The two journalists sat that way for a half hour. They made small talk. Mercifully, the sun rose higher in the sky and began to warm them.

A waitress emerged from the café and told them they weren't serving breakfast outside that morning. But she brought each of them some hot coffee.

There were others using the open seats and benches nearby. Some were pulling on their ski boots.

Some sounded like they were making phone calls to work and pretending that they weren't at a ski resort.

JC continued to scan the pedestrian walk. The crowd heading for the chairlifts was growing in number.

Then, he spotted a familiar face. The man didn't look that different from the photo, but his hair was entirely gray now.

"Hey, Milt," JC nudged the arm of his photographer, "get some footage of the guy in the business suit."

Milt scanned the crowd for a business suit while he powered up his camera. Then he said, "Holy crap," and began shooting video.

The suit looked expensive. He also wore a tie and white shirt. His eyes met with JC's for an instant. Buford stopped. They'd never met, but Milt's camera cleared up any uncertainty.

John Buford opened the door and walked into the Spilled Cup.

Through the window, Milt was able to shoot them embracing. Lucy clutched her father and cried into his shoulder. The senator also appeared to be crying.

It was a long embrace. At one point, John Buford looked out the window at the camera. JC and Milt hadn't advanced. They remained at their table across the pedestrian walk.

John and Lucy Buford sat down at a table and talked. They were interrupted by a waitress, who went for coffee.

Sometimes, Lucy would reach across the table and stroke her father's face. Sometimes, he'd reach out and hold her hand.

Buford reached into his coat and pulled out an envelope. He pushed it across the table toward Lucy. She looked like she tried to refuse, but he slipped it across the table.

It was probably money, JC thought. The senator had to have been living off of cash. He wouldn't be needing it now.

The waitress brought coffee to the father and his daughter. Later, the waitress would tell JC that she overheard him say things like, "When you're young, you want to be a superman. When you're old, you just hope you were a good man."

The morning was warming up. From his seat on the café patio, JC saw another familiar face pushing past the crowd. This one wasn't carrying skis or a snowboard.

Detective Trujillo arrived at the table where the journalists were seated. He looked over his shoulder in the direction JC and Milt's eyes were directed.

"Well, I'll be," the detective said.

"He won't give you any trouble," JC told the law officer.

"That would be a nice change of pace," Trujillo muttered.

"Is that Lucy?" the detective asked, looking again through the window.

"Yep," JC told him. "They've been in there for half an hour."

"They see us," Trujillo said.

"Yep," JC agreed. "They're not going anywhere."

Senator Buford and his daughter remained in their seats at their table. Trujillo saw Lucy pick up her hand and stroke her father's hair.

The detective pulled out his phone and spoke to someone on the other end. JC assessed that Trujillo was talking to the law officers who accompanied him to Snow Hat.

Other officers would keep an eye on the rear entrance to the Spilled Cup and any additional avenue of escape. Then, they'd await the detective's orders.

Trujillo watched the scene inside the coffee shop across from him. He took a seat at JC and Milt's table.

"Four years," Trujillo said. "I think I can wait a few more minutes."

The three men sat on the outdoor patio and watched. Trujillo and Milt saw a father and daughter and hoped the bond with their own daughter was as strong.

John Buford looked out the window of the coffee shop and stood. His daughter stood and embraced him. She was crying.

Then, the former senator walked out the door onto the pedestrian walk and waited. His eyes turned toward JC and mouthed the words, "Thank you."

Detective Trujillo walked toward the man as he pulled his handcuffs out. Buford offered no resistance. Trujillo handed him to the uniformed officers who had emerged from the shadows.

Buford seemed to be gone in an instant.

"How did you find him?" Trujillo asked JC as he walked back toward the news crew.

"I got a tip," JC told him. In his pocket, he clutched the slip of paper Lucy had given him. It provided instructions allowing JC to contact Buford. JC wondered if Lucy had known where her father was the entire time.

The reporter believed that Lucy gave him the slip of paper because she thought that police would be watching her. She wanted this done according to terms selected by her father and herself.

JC had telephoned Trujillo first thing in the morning, calculating how long it would take for the detective to get here from Denver and catch his quarry.

JC considered the dangers he himself would face, the moment he saw what Lucy had written on the paper she handed him. If Buford had escaped, JC would have a lot of explaining to do.

But the law, he decided, didn't specify to the minute when he had to inform authorities that he knew the whereabouts of an accused killer. And he'd have cover from the fact that his tip led to an arrest.

When her father was gone, Lucy looked at JC. He knew it had been difficult for the young woman to watch her father taken away in handcuffs. She would probably hold JC partly responsible.

That wasn't the tone in her voice when she spoke. "Where will they take him now?" she asked.

"They'll probably process him and hold him at county jail overnight," JC told her in as gentle a voice as he could muster.

"Then," he said, "they'll extradite him back to New York State."

"Albany?" she asked.

"That would make the most sense," JC agreed. "That's where he faces the most serious charges. I don't think they'll give him a chance at bail. He was on the run for four years."

Lucy was digesting the information. She asked, "Then he'll go to prison?"

JC gave her a look that he hoped conveyed compassion. "Yes."

JC told her, "If he has a good lawyer, he might be able to make a deal to do his time in a more hospitable corrections center. It doesn't appear that he's been on a crime spree. And he was a respected state senator."

"Could he choose one near me?" she asked. "Near my college?"

JC thought, for a man who was heading to prison, the worst might already be behind him. He was going to have the steady presence of a daughter who adored him.

"Anything is possible," JC told her hopeful brown eyes.

45

"You're a rock star," Rocky Bauman told JC in the newsroom.

Long days had followed for JC. He was reporting a wealth of elements in the John Buford story, and the Troy Davis story. There were aspects of those stories that he alone knew, outside police. The news audience was eating it up.

Finally, he scored some time away from work. He said that he was taking a week off.

He found himself in a hallway outside a slopeside bar and restaurant. Families used the wide hallway, lined with benches, to prepare for the day ahead on the mountain. They could put their bags in lockers attached to the wall.

JC heard the squeak of little voices. Some of the children were laughing and some were having a meltdown. Attentive parents were bending down buckling tiny boots or straightening a tiny helmet.

JC smiled as he squeezed through the crowd and entered the bar.

He walked about twenty feet into the room so that he could turn and watch her. She was still the most beautiful woman he had ever seen. That would never change.

He watched her rinse glasses and assist her staff as they tried to keep up with the lunch orders. She was wearing a blue, long-sleeve tee shirt that he had seen before. Across her left breast, it said Shara's Sheep Ranch.

He'd driven there straight from the airport in Bozeman, Montana. He'd caught the earliest flight.

Shara poured a beer and smiled at a customer as he tried to engage her in conversation. She cleared a spot where a skier had just departed after wolfing down a bowl of chili.

She scanned the large room, looking for her next task. Her eyes met his. She looked down, expressionless.

He could see her tears as she washed more glasses. He couldn't hide the hope that he knew was etched on his face.

She backed away from the bar and walked out from behind it. Her pace quickened as she surveyed the room, but she was headed in his direction.

They collided softly and she wrapped her arms around his neck. She burrowed her face into his chest as he pulled her close.

"I love you," he said into her ear, softly.

"I love you," she whispered, crying.

He kissed her red hair. They both murmured things like, "I'm sorry."

"We'll figure it out," he said gently.

"I know we will," she told him.

Lucy Buford closed her textbook and snapped off her desk lamp. She was as prepared as she was going to be for her English Literature test the next day.

She looked over to her roommate's bed and saw her asleep. Lucy looked at her own bed and longed to be in it.

A quiet bell rang in the darkness. It was her cell phone. She picked it up and saw there was a message.

It said, "Knight."

She typed a return message: "Good Knight, Daddy."

Acknowledgements

I need to thank those who help make this possible: My wife, Carolyn, is an amazing believer in my books and a contributor to every facet of their existence; Jen gives me love and life lessons; my editor, Deirdre Stoelzle, guides us through the scary part of the forest, with her experience and nurturing manner; Debbi Wraga, at Shires Press, expertly sees my projects to the book shelves; the Denver Police Department helped sculpt Det. Trujillo's world; Jim Chappel at Union Station in Denver was a great storyteller; Ken Garcia gave me insights into his Mexican-American family and shared the story of his grandfather, Wilfredo; The Matterhorn in Sunday River, Maine, which is possibly the coolest après ski bar in America; Fred Shook, my journalism professor at Colorado State University, still lends support after all these years. He also has great tales to tell. One or two of them are in this book; Boulder Creek Lodge gave me a perch to watch Nederland's unique charm; The Saratoga Automobile Museum educated me regarding the first stolen car in this country's history; and Eric Hoppel is the original "Cannonball" and inventor of the term, "Talketypants."

About the Author

Phil Bayly has lived in Denver, the Front Range, the Eastern Plains and the Western Slope. A graduate of Colorado State University, he is a veteran of television and radio in Colorado, Wyoming, Pennsylvania and New York.

He grew up in Evanston, Illinois and now resides with his wife in Saratoga County, New York.

Visit Phil at murderonskis.com.

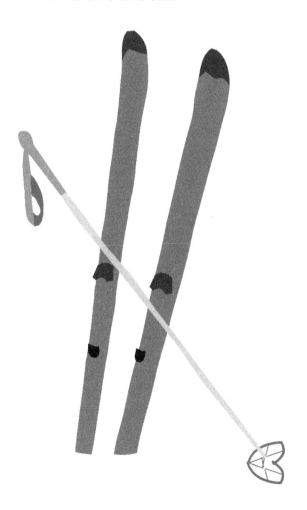